PENGUIN PARALLEL TEXTS

ITALIAN SHORT STORIES II

ITALIAN SHORT STORIES
II

Edited by Dimitri Vittorini

PENGUIN BOOKS

Penguin Books Ltd, Harmondsworth, Middlesex, England
Penguin Books Inc., 7110 Ambassador Road, Baltimore, Maryland 21207, U.S.A.
Penguin Books Australia Ltd, Ringwood, Victoria, Australia

—

First published 1972

—

—

Made and printed in Great Britain by
Hazell Watson & Viney Ltd, Aylesbury, Bucks
Set in Monotype Baskerville

CONTENTS

Introduction 7

THE MOTHER 11
ITALO SVEVO
Translated by Edwina Vittorini

THE MIRACULOUS DRAUGHT OF FISHES 23
GIOVANNI COMISSO
Translated by John Higgitt

WARTIME AUTOBIOGRAPHY. ON BEING A WRITER 39
ELIO VITTORINI
Translated by Edwina Vittorini

NIKOLAYEVKA 26 JANUARY 1943 51
MARIO RIGONI-STERN
Translated by Alexander Mandeville and Patricia Newnham

THE AMBUSH 71
BEPPE FENOGLIO
Translated by Richard Andrews

THE TART 95
PIER PAOLO PASOLINI
Translated by John Higgitt

CONTENTS

OVERTAKING 147
ALBERTO MORAVIA
Translated by Brian Cainen

THE ORIGIN OF THE BIRDS 163
ITALO CALVINO
Translated by Richard Andrews

Biographical Notes on Authors 189

Notes on Italian Texts 199

INTRODUCTION

This choice of texts has been made assuming that the reader of the first Penguin Italian parallel text, Italian Short Stories, has kept up his interest in Italian in these last few years and is now ready and eager for a wider and deeper taste of this complicated, vast and at present probably richest of European literatures. With this in mind I have tried to offer here a picture as varied as possible of different styles together with different aspects of Italian writing before and after the war.

The fossilized classical Tuscan of Svevo is particularly suitable for the Freudian Animal Farm story I have selected. Comisso's story about sea, sunshine and aesthetic sensual pleasure is in a style which is a cross between Gide's and d'Annunzio's, simple and classical. From Vittorini's writings I have chosen two passages of divers styles which he himself had placed next to each other in *Diario in pubblico*, an anthology which he put together to illustrate his literary career. The first is a typical, lyrical piece of Vittorini in the high style, the second a good narrative sequence in his conversational style, which is at present being more and more appreciated as the author's gifts as essayist, historian and philosopher as well as novelist are being recognized.

The passages selected from Rigoni-Stern and Fenoglio show two very different ways of reacting to the war: one by a non-professional writer in plain language, emotional and perhaps sentimental, but wholly unrhetorical; the other, a highly poetic rendering of emotions expressed in action, narrated without comment in the experimental prose of a consciously aristocratic writer who sought stylistic perfection through constant discipline. Rigoni-Stern is an admirer of Turgenev, Tolstoy and Chekhov,

while Fenoglio enthusiastically committed half of English literature to memory.

Pasolini and Moravia, so profoundly different as men and writers, follow each other in this selection as the 'Roman group'. They have in common an unpretentious and generally unpolished style, and they both make good use of the picturesque urban language of Rome. The English reader may at first be puzzled by words like *grana*, *sgamare*, *pischello*, *mignotta*, *pappone*, *pipparolata*, *dritteria*, etc., which are unlikely to be found in official dictionaries and grammars (the new Uthet dictionary, however, includes many of them). Yet any Italian who does not understand this language is a provincial. More than a hundred years ago the progressive north conquered the backward and oppressed south of Italy. In 1870 Rome was made the capital of the new state, but unity still had a long way to go. Now it is the south which is conquering the north, and Rome, an essentially southern city, as different from Milan as Madrid is from Stockholm, is giving its language to the rest of the country, chiefly through the medium of the film industry and television. How important this language is, Pasolini's sub-proletarian characters themselves tell us, as when Mario never misses the opportunity to give Nannina *una lezione di lingua*.

Moravia's characters, a few steps higher on the social ladder than Pasolini's, are superbly manipulated by the author in satirizing the common modern fallacy that sexual potency can be expressed through machinery.

The selection ends with a chapter from the last book published by the greatest and best satirist of them all; Italo Calvino. Of course it is not just accidental that the first story in this book, written about fifty years earlier than Calvino's, is Italo Svevo's own Parliament of Fowls, of mother hens and baby chicks. Calvino has recently revealed a bent towards science fiction. In fact it is just an extension of the main vein running through his work: the satirical spirit which pervades his famous trilogy, combined, this time, with his love for natural history. (Calvino's father was

a distinguished botanist.) His story on the origin of birds might well have been written by that solitary, natural philosopher, *il cavalier avvocato* (cf. Calvino's *Barone rampante*) who understood all languages of men, animals, plants, water and stones, and, locked in his impregnable wisdom, poured scorn on the enlightened despotisms of his age. In his last book Calvino pours rivers of eighteenth-century-like sarcasm on the far less enlightened and much more despotic despotisms of our age.

For obvious reasons this anthology cannot be exhaustive and I am very sorry indeed that so many authors have had to be left out. Merit, of course, has nothing to do with it. The selection is extremely personal and is intended to be merely a very varied foretaste of contemporary Italian literature. I believe that, however varied, it has a certain unity, as linguistic, historical, social and psychological themes run through the book and supply the logical connections between the various authors. I will feel that my labour has been worth while if anybody is stimulated to further reading of this rich and neglected literature, and hope that the bibliographical notes on the authors will prove useful for this purpose. Queries, appreciations, criticism and suggestions will be welcomed.

Acknowledgements are due to the following Italian publishers for permission to reprint passages from their editions: Dall'Oglio for Svevo; Longanesi for Comisso; Bompiani for Vittorini; Einaudi for Rigoni-Stern, Fenoglio and Calvino; Garzanti for Pasolini; and Mondadori for Moravia. My thanks to the translators who worked hard, sometimes at very short notice and put up with the editor's minor inefficiencies.

DIMITRI VITTORINI

Oxford, June 1970

THE MOTHER

ITALO SVEVO

Translated by Edwina Vittorini

LA MADRE

In una valle chiusa da colline boschive, sorridente nei colori della primavera, s'ergevano una accanto all'altra due grandi case disadorne, pietra e calce. Parevano fatte dalla stessa mano, e anche i giardini chiusi da siepi, posti dinanzi a ciascuna di esse, erano della stessa dimensione e forma. Chi vi abitava non aveva però lo stesso destino.

In uno dei giardini, mentre il cane dormiva alla catena e il contadino si dava da fare intorno al frutteto, in un cantuccio, appartati, alcuni pulcini parlavano di loro grandi esperienze. Ce n'erano altri di più anziani nel giardino, ma i piccini il cui corpo conservava tuttavia la forma dell'uovo da cui erano usciti, amavano di esaminare fra di loro la vita in cui erano piombati, perché non vi erano ancora tanto abituati da non vederla. Avevano già sofferto e goduto perché la vita di pochi giorni è più lunga di quanto possa sembrare a chi la subì per anni, e sapevano molto, visto che una parte della grande esperienza l'avevano portata con sé dall'uovo. Infatti appena arrivati alla luce, avevano saputo che le cose bisognava esaminarle bene prima con un occhio eppoi con l'altro per vedere se si dovevano mangiare o guardarsene.

E parlarono del mondo e della sua vastità, con quegli alberi e quelle siepi che lo chiudevano, e quella casa tanto vasta ed alta. Tutte cose che si vedevano già, ma si vedevano meglio parlandone.

Però uno di loro, dalla lanuggine gialla, satollo – perciò disoccupato – non s'accontentò di parlare delle cose che si vedevano, ma trasse dal tepore del sole un ricordo che subito disse:

THE MOTHER

In a valley enclosed by wooded hills and radiant with the colours of spring, there stood side by side two large, roughly finished houses, so much stone and mortar. They looked as if they had both been built by the same hand, and even the hedged gardens in front of them were the same size and shape. But those who lived there did not suffer similar fates.

In one of the gardens, while the chained dog slept, and the farmer was busying himself about the orchard, in a corner on their own some chicks were talking about their great experiences. There were other, older chicks in the garden, but the little ones, whose bodies were still the same shape as the eggs they had hatched from, liked to discuss among themselves the life they had so suddenly been plunged into, because they were not yet so used to it as to cease to notice it. They had already known joy and suffering, for a life lasting only a few days is longer than it looks to someone who has endured it for years, and they knew a lot, having brought part of their great experience with them from the egg. In fact, when they had barely seen the light of day, they knew that it was important to study things carefully, first with one eye and then the other, to see whether they were things to eat or things to be wary of.

And they talked about the world and its vastness, including the trees and hedges which encompassed it, and the house which was so vast and tall. They could see all these things already, but by talking about them they saw them more clearly.

But one of them, whose down was yellow and who, having eaten his fill, had nothing to do, was not satisfied with just talking about the things they could see, but drew from the gentle warmth of the sun a memory which he instantly expressed:

«Certamente noi stiamo bene perché c'è il sole, ma ho saputo che a questo mondo si può stare anche meglio, ciò che molto mi dispiace, e ve ne le dico[1] perché dispiaccia anche a voi. La figliuola del contadino disse che noi siamo tapini perché ci manca la madre. Lo disse con un accento di sì forte compassione ch'io dovetti piangere.»

Un altro più bianco e di qualche ora più giovine del primo, per cui ricordava ancora con gratitudine l'atmosfera dolce da cui era nato, protestò: «Noi una madre l'abbiamo avuta. È quell'armadietto sempre caldo, anche quando fa il freddo più intenso, da cui escono i pulcini belli e fatti.»

Il giallo che da tempo portava incise nell'animo le parole della contadina, e aveva perciò avuto il tempo di gonfiarle sognando di quella madre fino a figurarsela grande come tutto il giardino e buona come il becchime, esclamò, con un disprezzo destinato tanto al suo interlocutore, quanto alla madre di cui costui parlava: «Se si trattasse di una madre morta, tutti l'avrebbero. Ma la madre è viva e corre molto più veloce di noi. Forse ha le ruote come il carro del contadino. Perciò ti può venire appresso senza che tu abbia il bisogno di chiamarla, per scaldarti quando sei in procinto di essere abbattuto dal freddo di questo mondo. Come dev'essere bello di avere accanto, di notte, una madre simile.»

Interloquì un terzo pulcino, fratello degli altri perché uscito dalla stessa macchina che però l'aveva foggiato un po' altrimenti, il becco più largo e le gambucce più brevi. Lo dicevano il pulcino maleducato perché quando mangiava si sentiva battere il suo beccuccio, mentre in realtà era un anitroccolo che al suo paese sarebbe passato per compitissimo. Anche in sua presenza la contadina aveva parlato della madre. Ciò era avvenuto quella volta ch'era morto un pulcino crollato esausto dal freddo nell'erba, circondato dagli altri pulcini che non l'avevano soccorso perché essi non sentono il freddo che tocca agli altri. E l'anitroccolo con l'aria ingenua che

'It is true that we feel fine because it is sunny, but I have found out that it is possible to be even better off in this world; I am very sorry about it, and I am telling you about it so that you will be sorry about it too. The farmer's daughter said that we are poor little things because we haven't got a mother. She sounded so sorry for us when she said it, that I couldn't help crying.'

Another chick, lighter in colour and a few hours younger than the first, so that he could still remember with gratitude the cosy atmosphere which had surrounded him before birth, protested: 'But we did have a mother. It's that sort of box thing which is always warm, even in the coldest weather, that produces real live chicks.'

The yellow chick had had what the girl said impressed on his mind long enough for him to build it up, thinking of the mother she mentioned until he could imagine her large as the whole garden and satisfying as bird seed; and he exclaimed, with a scorn directed both at the chick who had spoken to him, and the mother he spoke of: 'If it was a question of a dead mother, we should all have one. But Mother is a live thing and can run much faster than we can. Perhaps she goes on wheels like the farmer's cart. So she can come over to you without your having to call her, to warm you when you are nearly overcome by the cold of this world. How marvellous it must be to have a mother like that beside you at night.'

A third chick spoke up, who was a brother of the rest since he had come out of the same device, although it had fashioned him a little differently, with a wider beak and shorter legs. They called him the bad-mannered chick because you could hear his beak champing when he ate, while he was in fact a duckling, whose manners would have been considered quite impeccable by his own kind. The girl had talked about the mother in front of him as well. It so happened that on that occasion a chick had died after collapsing with exhaustion from the cold in the grass, in the midst of the other chicks who had not helped him because chicks do not feel cold which affects others. And the gorm-

aveva la sua faccina invasa dalla base larga del beccuccio, asserì addirittura che quando c'era la madre i pulcini non potevano morire.

Il desiderio della madre presto infettò tutto il pollaio e si fece più vivo, più inquietante nella mente dei pulcini più anziani. Tante volte le malattie infantili attaccano gli adulti e si fanno per loro più pericolose, e le idee anche, talvolta. L'immagine della madre quale s'era formata in quelle testine scaldate dalla primavera, si sviluppò smisuratamente, e tutto il bene si chiamò madre, il bel tempo e l'abbondanza, e quando soffrivano pulcini, anitroccoli e tacchinucci divenivano veri fratelli perché sospiravano la stessa madre.

Uno dei più anziani un giorno giurò ch'egli la madre l'avrebbe trovata non volendo più restarne privo. Era il solo che nel pollaio fosse battezzato e si chiamava Curra, perché quando la contadina col becchime nel grembiale chiamava *curra, curra*[2] egli era il primo ad accorrere. Era già vigoroso, un galletto nel cui animo generoso albeggiava[3] la combattività.[4] Sottile e lungo come una lama, esigeva la madre prima di tutto perché lo ammirasse: la madre di cui si diceva che sapesse procurare ogni dolcezza e perciò anche la soddisfazione dell'ambizione e della vanità.

Un giorno, risoluto, Curra con un balzo sgusciò fuori dalla siepe che, fitta, contornava il giardino natio. All'aperto subito sostò intontito. Dove trovare la madre nell'immensità di quella valle su cui un cielo azzurro sovrastava ancora più esteso? A lui, tanto piccolo, non era possibile di frugare in quell'immensità. Perciò non s'allontanò di troppo dal giardino natio, il mondo che conosceva, e, pensieroso, ne fece il giro. Così capitò dinanzi alla siepe dell'altro giardino.

«Se la madre fosse qui dentro» pensò «la troverei subito.» Sottrattosi all'imbarazzo dell'infinito spazio, non ebbe altre esitazioni. Con un balzo attraversò anche quella

less-looking duckling whose tiny face was split across by the broad base of his beak, made the fantastic declaration that when they had a mother, chicks could not die.

The longing for a mother soon infected the whole poultry-yard and became particularly acute and disturbing in the minds of the older chicks. Only too often childhood diseases strike adults, for whom they represent a greater danger, and so it is at times with ideas. The mother-image, which had taken shape in these young heads turned by the spring sunshine, grew beyond all bounds, and everything good was called 'mother', whether it was good weather or ample food, and in suffering, chicks, ducklings and young turkeys became blood-brothers because they pined for the same mother.

One of the oldest swore one day that he would find himself a mother since he did not want to go on being deprived of one. He was the only chick in the poultry-yard who had been christened, and he was called Curra, because when the girl with her apronful of corn called 'curra, curra', he was the first to come rushing up. He was already strong, a young cockerel in whose warm heart fighting instincts were already stirring. Long and slender like the blade of a knife, he required a mother above all to admire him: the mother who, it was said, knew how to bring about every pleasure, and so the reward for ambition and vanity too.

One day, resolute, Curra with a single bound escaped unnoticed through the hedge whose dense growth bounded his home garden. In the open country he stopped short, completely dazed. Where could he find Mother in the vastness of this valley over which hung an even more immense blue sky? Small as he was, he could not possibly search in this vast expanse. So he did not go far from his home garden, the world he knew, and, lost in thought, he walked round its boundaries. Thus he found himself facing the hedge of the other garden.

'If Mother was in there,' he thought, 'I should find her straightaway.' And having overcome the bewilderment caused by infinite space, he had no more qualms. With a

siepe, e si trovò in un giardino molto simile a quello donde veniva.

Anche qui v'era uno sciame di pulcini giovanissimi che si dibattevano nell'erba folta. Ma qui v'era anche un animale che nell'altro giardino mancava. Un pulcino enorme, forse dieci volte più grosso di Curra, troneggiava in mezzo agli animalucci coperti di sola peluria, i quali – lo si vedeva subito – consideravano il grosso, poderoso animale quale loro capo e protettore. Ed esso badava a tutti. Mandava un ammonimento a chi di troppo s'allontanava, con dei suoni molto simili a quelli che la contadina nell'altro giardino usava coi proprii pulcini. Però faceva anche dell'altro. Ad ogni tratto si piegava sui più deboli coprendoli con tutto il suo corpo, certo per comunicar loro il proprio calore.

«Questa è la madre,» pensò Curra con gioia. «L'ho trovata ed ora non la lascio più. Come m'amerà! Io sono più forte e più bello di tutti costoro. Eppoi mi sarà facile di essere obbediente perché già l'amo. Come è bella e maestosa. Io già l'amo e a lei voglio sottomettermi. L'aiuterò anche a proteggere tutti cotesti insensati.»

Senza guardarlo la madre chiamò. Curra s'avvicinò credendo di essere chiamato proprio lui. La vide occupata a smovere la terra con dei colpi rapidi degli artigli poderosi, e sostò curioso di quell'opera cui egli assisteva per la prima volta. Quand'essa si fermò, un piccolo vermicello si torceva dinanzi a lei sul terreno denudato dall'erba. Ora essa chiocciava mentre i piccini a lei d'intorno non comprendevano e la guardavano estatici.

«Sciocchi!» pensò Curra. «Non intendono neppure che essa vuole che mangino quel vermicello.» E, sempre spinto dal suo entusiasmo d'obbedienza, rapido si precipitò sulla preda e l'ingoiò.

E allora – povero Curra – la madre si lanciò su lui furibonda. Non subito egli comprese, perché ebbe anche il dubbio ch'essa, che l'aveva appena trovato, volesse

single bound he rushed through this hedge too, and found himself in a garden much like the one he had come from.

Here too there was a crowd of tiny chicks swarming about in the thick grass. But here there was also a creature not to be found in the other garden. An enormous chick, perhaps ten times as big as Curra, was lording it over the little ones covered with no more than down, who it was obvious, saw the large, powerful creature as their chief and protector. And the creature was looking after them all. It would cluck reprovingly at any chick who wandered too far away, making sounds much like those the girl in the other garden made to her chicks. Yet it did other things too. At frequent intervals it would bend over the weakest chicks covering them with its whole body, no doubt so as to transmit its own warmth to them.

'That is Mother,' thought Curra with delight. 'I have found her, and now I shall never leave her. How she will love me! I am stronger and more handsome than all these chicks. And, what is more, it will be easy for me to obey her because I already love her. How beautiful and majestic she is! I already love her and wish to submit to her. And I will help her, too, to protect all the helpless little ones.'

Without looking at him the mother called. Curra went up to her thinking it was him she was calling. He saw her busily kicking up the earth with rapid movements of her strong claws, and stopped, struck with curiosity at this performance, which he was witnessing for the first time. When she stopped, there was a small worm writhing on the bare soil in front of her. She was clucking now, while the little ones standing round her, understanding nothing, looked on enraptured.

'The stupid idiots!' thought Curra. 'They don't even understand that she wants them to eat that worm.' And driven on as before by his eagerness to obey, he leapt swiftly upon the prey and swallowed it.

And then – poor Curra – the mother flew at him in all her fury. He did not understand straightaway, for he still thought that since she had only just found him, she might

accarezzarlo con grande furia. Egli avrebbe accettato riconoscente tutte le carezze di cui egli non sapeva nulla, e che perciò ammetteva potessero far male. Ma i colpi del duro becco, che piovvero su lui, certo non erano baci e gli tolsero ogni dubbio. Volle fuggire, ma il grosso uccello lo urtò e, ribaltatolo, gli saltò addosso immergendogli gli artigli nel ventre.

Con uno sforzo immane, Curra si rizzò e corse alla siepe. Nella sua pazza corsa ribaltò dei pulcini che stettero lì con le gambucce all'aria pigolando disperatamente. Perciò egli poté salvarsi perché la sua nemica sostò per un istante presso i caduti. Arrivato alla siepe, Curra, con un balzo, ad onta di tanti rami e sterpi, portò il suo piccolo ed agile corpo all'aperto.

La madre, invece, fu arrestata da un intreccio fitto di fronde. E là essa rimase maestosa guardando come da una finestra l'intruso che, esausto, s'era fermato anche lui. Lo guardava coi terribili occhi rotondi, rossi d'ira. «Chi sei tu che ti appropriasti il cibo ch'io con tanta fatica avevo scavato dal suolo?»

«Io sono Curra» disse umilmente il pulcino. «Ma tu chi sei e perché mi facesti tanto male?»

Alle sue domande essa non diede che una sola risposta: «Io sono la madre,» e sdegnosamente gli volse il dorso.

Qualche tempo appresso, Curra, oramai un magnifico gallo di razza, si trovava in tutt'altro pollaio. E un giorno sentì parlare da tutti i suoi nuovi compagni con affetto e rimpianto della madre loro.

Ammirando il proprio, atroce destino, egli disse con tristezza: «La madre mia, invece, fu una bestiaccia orrenda, e sarebbe stato meglio per me ch'io non l'avessi mai conosciuta.»

perhaps want to lavish passionate caresses on him. He would have gratefully accepted all the caresses as yet unknown to him, and was prepared to admit that they might be painful. But the jabs rained on him by the sharp beak were certainly not kisses and removed his last shadow of doubt. He wanted to run away, but the huge bird knocked him over and, having flung him to the ground, leapt on him sinking its claws into his belly.

With a tremendous effort, Curra stood up and ran to the hedge. In his mad flight he knocked over some chicks, who stayed where they were cheeping desperately with their puny legs in the air. Thus he managed to escape, because his enemy stopped for a moment by the fallen chicks. Reaching the hedge Curra, with a single bound and despite the dense branches and thorns, thrust his small agile body into the open air.

The mother, however, was stopped by a thick tangle of foliage. And there she remained, majestically watching the intruder, as if from a window, who, exhausted, had also come to a halt. She looked at him with staring, cruel eyes, red with rage. 'Who are you to take the food I went to such pains to scratch from the earth?'

'I am Curra,' the chick said humbly. 'But who are *you*, and why did you hurt me so much?'

She gave but one reply to his questions: 'I am the mother' and disdainfully turned her back on him.

Shortly afterwards Curra, now a magnificent pure-bred cockerel, found himself in quite a different poultry-yard. And one day he heard all his new companions talking with affection and nostalgia about their mother.

Proud of the dreadful fate which had befallen him, he said sadly: 'My mother, unlike yours, was a revolting creature, and it would have been better if I had never met her.'

THE MIRACULOUS DRAUGHT OF FISHES

GIOVANNI COMISSO

Translated by John Higgitt

PESCA MIRACOLOSA[1]

Eravamo giunti in un piccolo porto dell'isola di Novaglia,[2] arsa e rocciosa. Sulla piazza, vicino al mare, vi era una grande quercia, piccole case basse biancheggiavano sul pendio tutto intersecato da muricciolі che dividevano le proprietà. Tolte a grande fatica le rocce, nei brevi spazi di terra vi attecchiva una pianta buona per uccidere le cimici. La ricchezza del paese consisteva in mandrie di pecore lasciate notte e giorno a pascolare nell'interno dell'isola o confinate su scogli deserti poco distanti. Altri possedevano ancora un buon numero di oscuri porci dal pelo lungo quasi lanoso e una barchetta da pesca. Gli abitanti, pure non essendovi acqua di sorgente, erano belli, agili e svelti sulle scarpe di corda, dimostrando un corpo temperato nei sensi e proporzionato nella forma. Rosei, sereni negli occhi e con denti brillanti, ragazzi e uomini venivano accanto al nostro veliero[3] attraccato alla riva della piazza per vedere la merce che avevamo portata, poi alla sera, seduti su grossi blocchi di pietra disposti in lontani tempi, attorno alla vecchia quercia, si abbandonavano a canti monotoni senza fine: voci tristi d'isolani senza speranza di uscita. E le donne piccole e forti, buone a portare pesanti ceste sul capo, non mancavano di preziose iniziative di lavoro.[4]

Molte erano venute a contrattare l'acquisto di tegole e il capitano doveva armarsi di tutta la sua astuzia per non ridurre al minimo il guadagno. In quel paese, oltre alle pecore, ai porci, agli uomini e alle donne, vi erano anche certi bellissimi asinelli lasciati liberi sulla piazza e per i viottoli. Piccoli asini, dalla testa ricca di ciuffi, fermi come pensosi nelle brevi ombre o allegri a rivoltarsi nella polvere. Si fece qualche buon affare di mattoni e di tegole, perché molti giovini stavano per sposarsi

THE MIRACULOUS DRAUGHT OF FISHES

We had put into a small port on the parched, rock-covered island of Novalja. In the main square on the front stood a great oak, and white houses, small and squat, stood out against the hillside, which was criss-crossed by low walls dividing up the land. The stones had been cleared with great difficulty and an insect-killing plant grew thickly on the small patches of earth. The wealth of the island lay in flocks of sheep left night and day to graze inland or kept near by on the barren rocks. Some people also owned a fair number of dark-coloured pigs covered in long, almost wool-like hair and a small fishing-boat. Although there was no fresh spring water, the islanders were in general good-looking, nimble and quick-footed in their rope-soled shoes; their well-proportioned bodies showed a mastery over the senses. Fair-skinned boys and men with clear eyes and glinting teeth came up to our boat which was moored alongside the square to see our cargo; later, in the evening, they sat on big blocks of stone placed around the old oak long ago and gave themselves up to endless monotonous songs – the sad voices of islanders with no hope of escape. And the short, sturdy women, well suited to carrying heavy baskets on their heads, had plenty of enterprising ideas for work to be done on the island.

Many of these women had come to negotiate the purchase of tiles, and the captain needed all his cunning to keep the profit above the bare minimum. As well as the sheep, pigs, men and women in the village there were some pretty little donkeys left free to wander about the square and up and down the lanes. Small donkeys with thick-tufted manes, still and thoughtful in the short shadows or happily rolling in the dust. We did a few good deals in bricks and tiles as several young couples were about to get married and their

e i loro genitori avevano pensato di costruire per loro una piccola casa. Poi il commercio si arrestò e aspettavamo il buon vento per partire verso altra isola dove si diceva vi sarebbe stata possibilità di vendere grande quantità di tegole, perché un temporale violento vi aveva scoperchiate le case.

In uno di questi giorni di attesa, una mattina, uscito da sottocoperta per fare il bagno, trovai contro al fianco del veliero, proprio dove mi volevo buttare, una barca con due giovini del paese intenti a pescare con una rete certi piccoli pesci che mordicchiavano un'erba cresciuta sotto alla chiglia del nostro veliero. «Ma sono buoni da mangiare quei pesciolini?» chiesi. I due non capivano e dovetti spiegarmi a gesti; sorridevano in uno sforzo d'intelligenza e continuavano a tenere le mani immerse, strette alla rete.

Prima l'uno, poi l'altro mi spiegarono, pure a gesti, che quei pesciolini servivano per la pesca di altri più grossi e continuavano a sorridere in un modo cordiale come per attenuare l'asprezza di non poterci intendere con le parole. Una simpatia affettuosa mi sospingeva e accordai di andare con loro alla pesca. Prima di partire il padre del più giovine si accorse dalla finestra della sua casa del mio proposito e scese dalla scala esterna di pietra, portando un bicchierino e una bottiglia di grappa.[5]

«Beva qua. Io sono stato sempre amico degli italiani, ma lei vuole proprio andare a pescare con quei matti? Guardi che stanno via tutto il giorno. Beva, ché il mare è un poco mosso. Ma come farà a farsi capire da quelli là che non sanno neanche una parola d'italiano?»

Tutte difficoltà che non potevano fermare il mio desiderio di stare insieme a loro che, non potendo parlarci, mi esprimevano con gli occhi tutto un sentimento cordiale raramente intravisto in altri. Il battello ci aspettava sulle onde che si rompevano lungo la spiaggia all'ombra delle vecchie case. Ci imbarcammo ridendo e issata la piccola vela si partì galoppando veloci sulle onde

parents had decided to build them small houses. Then business came to an end and we waited for the right wind to sail to another island where, it was said, we would probably be able to sell a large number of tiles, because the houses had lost their roofs in a violent storm.

One day early in the morning, while we were waiting to set sail, I came out from below deck to bathe and found a small boat alongside ours just where I had intended to dive in. In it there were two young men from the village busy fishing with a net for some small fish which were nibbling the weed growing on the keel of our boat. 'Can you really eat those little fish?' I asked. The young men did not understand and I had to explain with gestures; they smiled, trying hard to understand me, and went on holding the net, gripping it tightly with their hands in the water.

First one, then the other used gestures to explain that these little fish were used to catch bigger fish and they continued smiling in a friendly way as if to soften the pain of being unable to communicate with me verbally. I felt drawn towards them and agreed to go fishing with them. Before we set off the father of the younger man, watching from the window of his house, realized what I was going to do and came out down the outside stone stairs, carrying a small glass and a bottle of grappa.

'Have a drink. I've always liked the Italians, but do you really want to go fishing with those idiots? You realize they stay out all day. Go on, drink it; the sea is a bit rough. But how on earth are you going to get on with those two when they don't speak a word of Italian?'

These difficulties could not dampen my eagerness to join them. Although we could not talk to each other, their eyes showed a warmth of friendship rarely seen in other people. The boat was waiting for us on the waves which were breaking along the beach in the shade of the old houses. We climbed in laughing and, having raised the little sail, set off galloping swiftly across the waves which grew steadily

sempre più ampie e agitate. Vieco, il più giovine, stava al timone. L'altro, Ante, si accovacciò con me al pedale della vela. Il battello era pieno di roba e Ante badava a metterla a posto: due remi molto lunghi, ceste, lenze, funicelle, un cestino di pesciolini per esca, bottiglie di acqua, scalmi, un ancorotto e altre cose indefinite.

Qualche onda avanzava più alta del bordo, ma nel subitaneo sollevarsi dello scafo, solo brevi lembi sfaldati arrivavano a bagnarci il volto, poi il sole li tramutava in salsedine. Più che si avanzava, la terra si appiattiva e si andava così veloci da credere che mai ci si sarebbe potuti fermare. Vieco, tutto preso dal pensiero della rotta, stava curvo come per non sentire il vento. Il suo volto avido e carnoso[6] si profilava contro l'orizzonte e una leggera maglia a righe bianche e azzurre gli fremeva sul petto. L'altro aveva cominciato a parlargli. Alle parole incomprensibili, ma piane, suonò subito una risposta breve. Si parlavano con dolcezza e come se io non vi fossi. Compresi dal continuo indicare il mare che cercavano un punto dove le onde fossero meno mosse. Dopo non molto parve che lo avessero trovato. Allora calarono la vela e tolsero l'albero. Il battello galleggiò sulle acque ondulate come una pasta[7] azzurra e lucente. Rimasero in piedi e si parlarono nel preparare gli arnesi per la pesca. Quando tutto fu pronto, Vieco, che era il più disinvolto, mi disse: «Giovanni», come un'invocazione; prese i lunghi remi, li mise sugli scalmi e me li fece impugnare ordinandomi, come animato da una necessità indiscutibile, di vogare mantenendo costante la direzione del battello.

I remi sugli scalmi assai sporgenti dal bordo, erano di facile manovra e per fare vedere che non ero debole mi diedi subito a vogare con forza. Ma essi che già avevano gettato le lenze mi si rivolsero preoccupati facendomi grandi gesti di andare adagio. Uno da una parte e uno dall'altra si sporsero e lasciarono scorrere la funicella della lenza che il piombo trascinava verso il fondo.

bigger and rougher. Vieco, the younger of the two, was at the helm. The other, Ante, crouched with me under the sail. The boat was full of tackle and Ante busied himself tidying it up – two very long oars, baskets, fishing-lines, twine, a small basket full of little fish for bait, bottles of water, rowlocks, an anchor and various other things.

A few waves rose higher than the side of the boat, but with the sudden rising of the hull only the foam of the breaking tops came in to wet our faces, and then the sun turned it to salt. The further away we got, the more the land seemed to flatten out. We were sailing so fast that it seemed that we would never be able to stop. Vieco, who was concentrating fully on keeping his course, was bending as if to avoid the wind. His strong, keen face was outlined against the horizon; a thin blue and white striped jersey flapped against his chest. The other had started to talk to him. His clearly spoken, but to me incomprehensible, words were answered at once and briefly. They were talking softly as if I were not there. I gathered from the way they continually pointed at the sea that they were looking for somewhere where it would be less rough. A little later they seemed to have found it. Then they lowered the sail and took down the mast. The boat rose and fell on the billowing water, blue and gleaming like wax. They remained standing and talked to each other as they prepared the fishing tackle. When everything was ready, Vieco, who was the more confident of the two, called, 'Giovanni', asking for my help; he picked up the long oars, put them in the rowlocks and made me take them, ordering me, as if driven by an unquestionable necessity, to row and keep the boat in the same direction.

As the oars were in rowlocks sliding out high from the sides of the boat they were easy to use and to show that I was not a weakling I suddenly began to row hard. But having just thrown in their lines they turned to me with concern, vigorously gesticulating to me to row more slowly. They leant out one on either side and paid out their lines as the weights pulled them down to the bottom.

Quando si fermò, la ritrassero appena un poco e rimasero a reggerla con mano leggera.

Lungo tempo passò senza avere potuto pescare qualcosa. Di un tratto dopo avere parlato tra loro, Vieco mi disse: «Giovanni.» E mi fece cenno di vogare più forte e subito ritrassero a grandi bracciate le lenze. Le mani mi si scaldavano sulle impugnature, ma non volevo fare capire che ero stanco, poi mi accennarono di fermare, allora posai i remi, ma Vieco mi venne vicino per insegnarmi a tenerli nell'acqua in modo da mantenerci fermi sull'ondulamento continuo.

Ricalarono le lenze e anche Ante si rivolse a parlarmi, ma meno dolce di Vieco: «Giovanni. Skarda. Skarda . . .» Non comprendevo. «Skarda» e m'indicò un isolotto lontano, mentre l'altro sorridendo aveva preso a spiegarmi di tenere la prua diretta a quell'isolotto che si chiamava Skarda. Annuii e sorrisi, tutto pronto a ubbidirli ed essi si rifecero attenti a ogni minimo vibrare delle lenze. Anche quel punto non era buono, allora ritrassero le lenze e afferrati essi stessi i remi si diedero a vogare ritmici e svelti.

Il sole era forte, ma il vento ne toglieva l'offesa. Mi liberai il più possible dai panni e subito sentii la pelle come rianimarsi al tocco dell'aria.

Trovammo un punto dove il mare era quasi quieto. Mi vennero riaffidati i remi: «Giovanni. Skarda.» E vi rivolsi la prua mentr'essi rapidi come avessero fiutato la preda, si affaccendarono a calare le lunghe lenze. Difatti, dopo un attimo appena, Vieco diede uno strappo e, tirata su la funicella, alzandosi in piedi per fare più presto, con un balzo un bel pesce rosa cadde nella barca per finire estenuato, fermo, sbarrati gli occhi e aperta la bocca da cui gli venne strappato l'amo. Anche Ante diede uno strappo e un altro pesce venne gettato accanto all'altro, rosa anche questo. Subito ricalate le lenze, subito vennero ritratte con pesci della stessa specie e la meraviglia mi fece abbandonare i remi per avvicinarmi

When they had finished, they pulled them back in very slightly, and remained there to steady them gently.

A long time went by without their being able to catch anything. Suddenly, after they had spoken to each other, Vieco said, 'Giovanni!' And he signalled to me to row harder and at once they began to pull in the lines length by length. My hands grew hot on the oars, but I did not want them to think that I was tired. Next they waved to me to stop and I put down the oars, but Vieco came up to me to show me how to hold the oars in the water to steady the boat in the continuous swell.

They dropped the lines back into the water and Ante too turned to talk to me but more urgently than Vieco, 'Giovanni! Skarda. Skarda. . . .' I did not understand. 'Skarda' he said and pointed to a distant island while the other, smiling, had already started to explain to me that I should keep the boat pointing towards that island, which was called Skarda. I nodded and smiled ready to obey, and they again turned their attention to the slightest tremor on the lines. This was not a good spot either; they pulled out the lines, and seizing the oars themselves they began to row fast and rhythmically.

The sun was hot, but the wind made it bearable. I took off as many clothes as possible and at once felt my skin revive at the touch of the breeze.

We found a patch of sea which was almost calm. I was again entrusted with the oars – 'Giovanni! Skarda.' I pointed the bow in that direction, while they got on with lowering the long lines with great speed, as if they had scented the prey. And in fact a moment later Vieco gave the line a tug and pulled it in, standing in order to work faster. With a leap a fine pink-coloured fish fell into the boat and eventually lay still and exhausted with staring eyes and gaping mouth from which the hook was drawn. Ante too yanked in his line and another fish, pink like the first, was thrown down beside it. The lines were immediately lowered again and immediately pulled in with more fish of the same type. I dropped the oars in amazement and moved closer

a guardarli, ma Vieco e Ante mi gridarono quasi arrabbiati: «Giovanni. Giovanni.» Ripresi a vogare. Essi continuarono a pescare senza tregua, ma presto i pesci non furono più rosa, ma grigi con toni lilla e si ammucchiarono con gli altri che ogni tanto davano ancora qualche palpito. Poi riapparvero i rosa. Poi altri argentei e verdastri, ma piccoli e giudicati di qualità immangiabile vennero buttati via. Infine la pesca cessò. Guardarono il mucchio, ma non parvero sodisfatti.[8]

Allora ripresero a vogare e scelto un altro punto tranquillo si fermarono. Ma qui Vieco, invece di dare i remi a me, prese la lenza e mi disse: «Ti, Giovanni.»[9] Calai la lenza fino al fondo e poi la tenni con mano sospesa e leggera per potere avvertire appena l'esca venisse abboccata e subito dare lo strappo. I pesci, con il mare mosso che vi era, riposavano nel fondo. Non fu lunga l'attesa, prima ancora di Ante, sentii la funicella vibrare. Vieco che si era accorto mi gridò nella sua lingua di tirare su presto e con gioia vidi guizzare fuori dall'acqua un pesce roseo e così animato che non riuscivo a prenderlo. Vieco gli strappò l'amo e gridandomi qualcosa che doveva significare di non perdere tempo, gettò il pesce sul mucchio, insieme agli altri già soffocati dal sole. Per lungo tempo fu tutto un continuo calare e tirare su e non potevo indugiare a meravigliarmi della bellezza dei pesci. Poi si esaurirono le esche e allora decisero di fare ritorno. Nel fondo della barca il mucchio inebbriava[10] a guardarlo. Inalberarono la vela. Ante andò al timone. L'altro contò i pesci. Erano novantaquattro. Ne fece tre parti, disponendoli con cura in tre ceste e poi si lavò le mani fuori dal bordo. Aperse una sacca e ne tolse del pane nero che mi offerse: «Ti, Giovanni». Ne passò un pezzo anche ad Ante. Nella sacca vi erano anche due cipolle, una la diede ad Ante e l'altra la divise con me. Doveva essere mezzogiorno, tanto il sole era alto, ma la fame non era forte con tutto quel sole e quell'aria così densa di salso. Vieco impugnò una bottiglia di vino acre che sorseggiammo per turno.

to watch them, but Vieco and Ante shouted almost angrily, 'Giovanni! Giovanni!' I started rowing again. They went on fishing without a pause, but soon the fish were no longer pink but grey with flecks of lilac and they too were thrown onto the heap with the others which now and then still moved. Then the pink fish reappeared. Then another type which were silvery and greenish but little and judged inedible; these were thrown back. At last the fishing stopped. They looked at the catch, but did not seem satisfied.

They then started to row again and stopped when they had chosen another calm spot. But here Vieco did not give me the oars, but picked up the line and said, 'Ti, Giovanni.' I lowered it right to the bottom and then I held it with my hand delicately poised to be able to feel as soon as the bait was taken and jerk up the line immediately. Because of the rough sea the fish were resting at the bottom. I did not have to wait long; even before Ante I felt my line trembling. Vieco noticed and called to me in his language to pull up the line quickly. To my delight I saw a rose-coloured fish dart out of the water. It wriggled so much that I was unable to catch it. Vieco pulled the hook from its mouth and, shouting something to me which must have meant that I should not waste time, he threw the fish onto the heap with the others, which had already suffocated in the sun. For a long time I was constantly dropping the line in and pulling it out and could not stop and marvel at the beauty of the fish. Then we ran out of bait and they decided to sail back home. The heap of fish in the bottom of the boat was glorious to behold. They raised the sail. Ante took the helm. The other counted the fish. There were ninety-four. He divided them into three parts and packed them carefully into three baskets and then washed his hands over the side. He opened a bag and took out some black bread which he offered to me: 'Ti, Giovanni.' He also passed a bit to Ante. He had two onions in the bag as well, one of which he gave to Ante, the other he shared with me. It must have been midday judging from the height of the sun, but with all that sun and with the air thick with salt we were not very

Si mangiava adagio perché si aveva tempo, il porto era lontano e il vento contrario, così si doveva bordeggiare. Finita la cipolla rimanemmo con il desiderio di parlare. Stavo seduto vicino a Vieco, vedevo i suoi occhi sorridere celesti, pieni di simpatia e riuscì a dirmi: «Bravo, Giovanni, bravo.» E continuò a parlarmi in slavo[11] sicuro lo potessi comprendere, ma non era possibile. Allora con tutte e due le mani modellò attorno al suo corpo la forma di una donna e con gesti espressivi mi fece capire che voleva sapere se ero ammogliato. L'altro rideva nel suo volto asciutto e bruno. Dissi di no e anch'egli mi disse che non aveva moglie, aggiunse smorfie di disprezzo e segni che ci volevano denari. Ancora mi fece capire che si divertiva lo stesso, accennò a movenze di ballo e mi disse il nome di un'altra isola vicina, dove sapevo vi erano belle ragazze.

Anche Ante non aveva intenzione di sposarsi e con cenno di partire mi disse: «America.»[12] I loro occhi chiari sorridevano nell'ombra dei berretti consunti. I bordi del battello erano arsi dal sole, i pesci si appiattivano nelle ceste. Tutto nel fondo era asciutto. L'acqua era calda nelle bottiglie, ma l'aria serpeggiava deliziosa. Avanzavamo, puntando verso Skarda o verso il porto che si delineava con il piano della piazza, con la grande quercia e con i tetti delle poche case. Si continuò a parlare. Le parole accompagnate sempre dall'ardore dei nostri volti, oramai erano comprensibili sull'orlo delle nostre pupille. Ogni pensiero era subito inteso come tra amici stretti da tempo.

Quante cose di più ci siamo dette così. «Ante. Vieco. Giovanni»: i nostri nomi s'incrociavano da poppa a prua con il tono di saluti d'addio. E se chiudevo gli occhi vedevo, indimenticabile oramai, il celeste chiaro dei loro occhi: piccoli e fermi in Ante, istintivi e chiamanti in Vieco, giovanili e appena affaticati dal salso in ognuno.

hungry. Vieco picked up a bottle of sharp wine which we sipped in turn. We ate slowly because we had plenty of time; the harbour was a long way off and the wind against us, so we had to tack. When we had finished the onion we felt like talking. I was sitting next to Vieco and I could see his smiling blue eyes full of friendship; he managed to say, 'Bravo, Giovanni, bravo.' He continued speaking to me in his own language, sure that I would be able to understand him, but it was impossible. Then with both hands he traced around his own body the shape of a woman and with eloquent gestures indicated that he wanted to know whether I was married. The lean and swarthy face of the other grinned at this. I said not and he told me that he was not either, grimacing scornfully and indicating that you need money to keep a wife. He also told me in signs that he enjoyed himself anyway. He sketched out dance movements and told me the name of a neighbouring island where I already knew there were beautiful girls.

Neither did Ante intend to get married and with a gesture which implied departure he said, 'America.' Their bright smiling eyes were shaded by their worn-out caps. The sides of the boat were blistered by the sun, the fish were flattening out in the baskets. Everything in the bottom of the boat had dried out. The water in the bottles was warm, but the air played deliciously about us. We sailed on, pointing now towards Skarda and now towards the port which showed clearly with the flat space of its square, its great oak and the roofs of its few houses. We went on talking. Our words had always been accompanied by the warmth of our expressions, but now they could be read clearly in our eyes. Our every thought was immediately understood, as if we had long been friends.

How much else we said to each other in this way! 'Ante. Vieco. Giovanni.' From stern to bow our names played back and forth in the affectionate tones of friends parting. If I closed my eyes I could see the by now unforgettable bright blue of their eyes, those of Ante small and steady, those of Vieco instinctive and appealing. The eyes of both, youthful

Il molo era vicino. Con un'ultima bordeggiata fummo alla scaletta di approdo sulla piazza da dove alcuni ragazzi nudi si buttavano a nuotare. Scesi e mi parve che il terreno mi si rovesciasse addosso, sentivo ancora le onde sotto ai miei piedi. I ragazzi volevano toccare i pesci. Ante li fece scappare e quelli si ributtarono a capofitto nell'acqua. Salutai e ringraziai gli amici, ma Vieco mi fermò per darmi una delle ceste colma di pesci. «Ti, Giovanni.» Non volevo, cercai di spiegare che ero andato con loro solo per divertirmi. «No, ti lavorato.» E cercò di arrabbiarsi nello sguardo.

Con la cesta sulle spalle ritornai a bordo del veliero. Il capitano mi attendeva sotto alla tenda seduto accanto al boccaporto di poppa. Si alzò in piedi e giudicò quel pesce ottimo per condire il risotto. Angelo lo preparò per la cena. Nel fresco della sera si mangiò avidi, i marinai godettero di quel piatto inaspettato, ma non mi rivolsero alcun segno di riconoscenza. Essi non consideravano quel pesce come un dono offerto da me, tutt'altro, ma come cosa che avendo ricevuto ero bene obbligato di cedere, perché a bordo si viveva in regime di comunione.

and slightly tired by the salt. The jetty was close. On the next tack we reached the landing steps leading to the square and from which some naked boys were diving. I got out and the land seemed to rise up ready to crash down on top of me; I could still feel the sea under my feet. The boys wanted to touch the fish. Ante chased them away and they plunged in again head first. I said good-bye and thanked my friends but Vieco stopped me and gave me one of the baskets full of fish. 'Ti, Giovanni.' I did not want it, I tried to explain that I had gone out with them merely for enjoyment. 'No, ti lavorato.' And he tried to look angry.

With the basket on my shoulders I went back on board our boat. The captain was waiting for me, sitting under the awning by the aft-hatch. He got up and said that the fish would go very well with the risotto. Angelo cooked them for supper. In the cool of the evening we ate greedily. The sailors enjoyed the unexpected dish but did not show me any sign of gratitude. They did not consider the fish a gift from me; on the contrary, they looked on it as something which I had been given and was therefore obliged to hand over to them, for on board we lived with all things in common.

WARTIME AUTOBIOGRAPHY. ON BEING A WRITER

ELIO VITTORINI

Translated by Edwina Vittorini

AUTOBIOGRAFIA IN TEMPO DI GUERRA. ESSERE SCRITTORE

Io penso che sia molta umiltà essere scrittore.

Lo vedo come fu in mio padre, ch'era maniscalco e scriveva tragedie,[1] e non considerava il suo scrivere tragedie di piú del suo ferrare cavalli. Anzi, quando era a ferrare cavalli, mai accettava che gli dicessero: «Non cosí, ma cosí. Tu hai sbagliato.» Guardava coi suoi occhi azzurri, e sorrideva o rideva; scuoteva il capo. Ma quando scriveva dava ragione ad ognuno per qualunque cosa.

Ascoltava quello che chiunque gli diceva, e non scuoteva il capo, dava ragione. Era molto umile nel suo scrivere; diceva di prenderlo da tutti; e cercava, per amore del suo scrivere, di essere umile in ogni cosa: prendere da tutti in ogni cosa.

Mia nonna rideva di quello che lui scriveva.

«Che sciocchezze!» diceva.

E mia madre lo stesso. Rideva di lui per quello che scriveva.

Solo io e i miei fratelli non ridevamo. Io lo vedevo che arrossiva; come chinava umilmente il capo; e cosí imparavo. Una volta, per imparare, scappai di casa con lui.

Ogni tanto mio padre faceva questo: scappava di casa a scrivere nelle solitudini. Io lo seguii una volta: camminammo otto giorni nelle campagne di capperi, tra i fiori bianchi delle solitudini, e ci fermavamo sotto un sasso per un po' d'ombra, lui con gli occhi azzurri che scriveva, io che imparavo, e al ritorno mia madre mi bastonò per me e per lui.

WARTIME AUTOBIOGRAPHY. ON BEING A WRITER

I think that one needs a great deal of humility to be a writer.

So it was with my father, who was a blacksmith and wrote tragedies, and did not value his writing of tragedies more highly than his shoeing of horses. Rather the contrary: when he was shoeing horses, he would never let anyone say to him, 'No, not like that . . . like this. You've done it all wrong.' He would look up with his blue eyes and smile or laugh; and he would shake his head. But when he was writing he would give in to anyone on any point whatsoever.

He listened to what anyone said to him, and did not shake his head but agreed with them. He was very humble about his writing; he said that everyone had a hand in it; he tried, for love of his writing, to be humble and to learn from others in every field.

My grandmother used to laugh at what he wrote.

'What nonsense!' she would say.

And my mother was the same. She laughed at him because of the things he wrote.

My brothers and I were the only ones who did not laugh. I would see him blush and humbly bend his head and that was how I learned. Once, so as to learn, I left home with him.

Every now and then this is what my father would do: he left home so as to write in some lonely place. I followed him once. We walked for a week through the countryside where caper bushes grew, through the white flowers of the lonely places, and we often stopped beneath a rock to get a bit of shade, he, with his blue eyes, writing, I learning; and on our return my mother beat me to punish both me and him.

Mio padre, allora, mi domandò perdono per le busse avute a causa sua.

Ricordo come fu. Io non gli risposi.

Potevo dirgli che lo perdonavo?

E lui mi disse con terribile voce: «Rispondi! Mi perdoni?» Pareva lo spettro del padre di Amleto quando vuole vendetta. Non che volesse perdono.

Ma io ho imparato, in tal modo, quello che è scrivere (. . .).

Dal già citato n. 3 di *Pesci rossi*, anno 1949, ritengo torni contro riportare qui alcune notizie su avventure e peripezie che ho avute in connessione col mio lavoro di scrittore:

«Nel 1927 partecipavo alla costruzione di un ponte che ha fatto epoca in me come nella mia prima infanzia la lettura del *Robinson*. Costruire un ponte non è lo stesso di costruire un tavolo o di costruire una casa. Se si comincia non si può piú sospenderne i lavori fino a completamento, almeno per quanto riguarda i piloni. Vi sono dei cassoni di cemento che bisogna far penetrare nel letto del fiume a poco a poco, scavandogli sotto la fossa e pompandone fuori l'acqua dall'interno. Se viene a piovere bisogna fare piú svelti della pioggia sia a scavare che a pompare. E allora si lavora di giorno e di notte senza darsi piú il cambio, senza pensare piú che si lavora per guadagnarsi il pane, e pensando invece a vincere, a spuntarla. Questo fece epoca in me (. . .). Ma avevo anche cominciato a scrivere. Prose varie, racconti. Era il 1927, dico. Mandai un raccontino a un giornale che me lo pubblicò. Direttore del giornale era lo scrittore Malaparte[2] col quale entrai in corrispondenza e che mi incoraggiò a continuare (. . .). Divenni collaboratore di una piccola rivista fiorentina, *Solaria*[3] (. . .). Su di essa pubblicai la maggior parte dei racconti che, nel 1931, raccolsi in volume, come mio primo libro, sotto il titolo di *Piccola borghesia*. Fui cosí un solariano, e solariano era

And then my father asked my forgiveness for the thrashing I had got on his account.

I remember what it was like. I didn't answer.

How could I tell him I forgave him?

And he said in a dreadful voice, 'Answer me! Do you forgive me?' He was like the ghost of Hamlet's father seeking vengeance. He did not seem to be asking forgiveness.

But I learned in this fashion what it is to be a writer . . .

I think it might be worth quoting some information here, taken from the above-mentioned third issue of *Pesci Rossi*, 1949, on adventures and events which befell me in connection with my work as a writer:

'In 1927 I was involved in the building of a bridge which marked a turning point in my life just as the reading of *Robinson Crusoe* in my early childhood had done. Building a bridge is not the same as making a table or building a house. If you once start, you cannot then stop work on it until it is completed, at least as far as the piers are concerned. There are great caissons of cement which have to be driven gradually into the river-bed, digging out holes under them and pumping water out from inside. If it rains you have to dig and pump faster than the rain falls. And then you work day and night without a break, no longer thinking that you are working to make a living, but thinking instead of winning, of succeeding. This marked a turning point for me (. . .). But I had also started writing. Various prose writings and short stories. It was 1927, as I said. I sent a short story to a newspaper which published it. The editor of the paper was the writer Malaparte with whom I entered into correspondence and who encouraged me to go on writing (. . .). I joined the team producing a little Florentine review, *Solaria* (. . .). In this I published most of the stories which, in 1931, I collected in one volume, as my first book, under the title of *Piccola Borghesia*. Thus I became a 'solarian', and 'solarian' was a word which, in the literary

parola che, negli ambienti letterari di allora, significava antifascista, europeista, universalista, antitradizionalista. ... Giovanni Papini[4] ci ingiuriava da un lato, e Farinacci[5] da un altro. Ci chiamavano anche sporchi giudei per l'ospitalità che si dava a scrittori di religione ebraica e per il bene che si diceva di Kafka o di Joyce. E ci chiamavano sciacalli. Ci chiamavano iene. Ci chiamavano affossatori (...). Io ero diventato anche fiorentino oltre che solariano, dal 1930. Avevo lasciato il mio impiego di assistente lavori, avevo lasciato la Venezia Giulia, e mi guadagnavo da vivere correggendo bozze di stampa presso la tipografia del quotidiano di Firenze chiamato *La Nazione*. Sbrigavo il mio lavoro in una gabbia di vetro posta al centro della sala dei linotiposti, e questo era piuttosto male per la mia salute: facevo turno di notte, dalle 21,30 alle 5,30 del mattino, e questo era pure male per la mia salute, ma ebbi la fortuna di stringere amicizia con un vecchio operaio che era stato all'estero e conosceva l'inglese.

«Io non avevo dimenticato il *Robinson Crusoe* letto a sette anni in una riduzione per bambini. Ogni volta che ne avevo potuto avere una traduzione meno incompleta non avevo mancato di rileggerlo. E avrei voluto leggerlo nel testo originale. Avrei voluto leggere tutto quello che Defoe ha scritto. Nella tipografia della *Nazione* si aveva mezzora di tempo libero tra il momento in cui terminava il lavoro effettivo e il momento in cui, messa la firma all'orologio di controllo, si poteva rincasare. Alcuni operai occupavano quella mezzora risolvendo parole incrociate, altri discutendo di calcio, altri leggendo e persino studiando. Il mio amico che conosceva l'inglese accondiscese a insegnarmi l'inglese. E fu in un modo molto speciale che cominciammo. Fu sul testo del *Robinson Crusoe*, leggendolo e traducendolo parola per parola, scrivendo sopra ogni parola inglese la corrispondente parola italiana. ... Poi continuai da solo, un po' come un sordomuto, su testi ancora di Defoe, e su autori del Settecento, su autori dell'Ottocento, su autori

circles of those days, meant anti-Fascist, European, internationalist, anti-traditionalist. . . . Giovanni Papini reviled us from one side, and Farinacci from the other. We were called filthy Jews because of the hospitality we showed to writers of the Jewish faith and because of the favourable comments we made about Kafka and Joyce. And we were called jackals. We were called hyenas. We were called saboteurs (. . .). I had become not only a 'solarian' but a Florentine since 1930. I had left my work as foreman, I had left the province of Venezia Giulia and was earning my living proof-reading at the printing works of the Florentine daily paper, *La Nazione*. I did my work in a glass cage in the middle of the linotype room, and this was rather bad for my health – I worked on the night-shift, from 9.30 at night until 5.30 in the morning, and this was bad for my health too, but I had the good fortune to make friends with an old worker who had been abroad and knew English.

'I had not forgotten *Robinson Crusoe*, which I had read at the age of seven in an abridged edition for children. Every time I had managed to get hold of a fuller translation, I had without fail read it again. And I would have liked to read it in the original. I would have liked to read everything Defoe wrote. In the printing works of *La Nazione* there was half an hour's spare time between the moment when the real work stopped and the moment when we could clock out and go home. Some workers spent this half hour doing crossword puzzles, others talking about football, others reading and even studying. My friend who knew English agreed to teach me the language. And we began in a rather unusual way. We worked on the text of *Robinson Crusoe*, reading it and translating word by word, writing over each English word its Italian equivalent. . . . Afterwards I went on alone, rather like a deaf-mute, using other texts by Defoe and by eighteenth- and nineteenth-century writers, contemporary writers and American ones, too, until at last I felt capable of translating correctly.

contemporanei anche americani fino al giorno in cui mi trovai in grado di poter tradurre correttamente.

«Nel 1934 fu pubblicata dall'editore Mondadori la mia prima traduzione: una di un romanzo di D. H. Lawrence (. . .). Una malattia per intossicazione da piombo, seguita da complicazioni polmonari, mi costringeva intanto a lasciare la tipografia, ma io avevo nelle mani un nuovo mestiere, e vissi di traduzioni fino al 1941 (. . .). Nell'autunno del 36 avevo avuto, piú per ingenuità che per altro, un piccolo infortunio politico. La polizia si limitò a minacciarmi di confino[6] per un'altra volta (. . .). Però il partito fascista decise di espellermi. Io vi ero stato iscritto nel 1925, mentre frequentavo ancora la scuola, come accadeva ad ogni studente. Solo che non avevo piú rinnovato la tessera, e non piú pagato le quote relative. Sono sempre stato piuttosto stordito con le tessere (. . .). Ma i fascisti fiorentini mi fecero pagare anni e anni di quote pur di prendersi il piacere di potermi espellere. Fortunatamente gli editori per i quali traducevo non si lasciarono impressionare e continuarono a darmi lavoro (. . .).

«Nell'autunno del 1937 avevo cominciato a scrivere *Conversazione in Sicilia* e l'andavo pubblicando a puntate su una nuova rivista fiorentina, *Letteratura*,[7] con la quale si cercava di sostituire, un numero ogni tre mesi, la scomparsa *Solaria*. Scrivevo il libro a mano che la rivista lo pubblicava, alternandone il lavoro a quello per le traduzioni. Lo terminai nell'inverno del 1939, poco tempo dopo di essermi trasferito dalla faziosa Firenze, dove i fascisti mi assillavano ormai di continue angherie, alla piú tranquilla Milano. La prima edizione di *Conversazione in Sicilia* fu di trecento esemplari. Fu lasciata passare dalla censura per un cumulo di circostanze che qui sarebbe troppo lungo spiegare. Non vi erano, del resto, che trecento esemplari. Ma il libro incontrò il favore della critica, e Bompiani volle arrischiarsi a stampare, nel 1942, un'edizione di 5.000 esemplari che poteva dirsi la prima vera e propria per il mercato

'In 1934 Mondadori published my first translation, a novel by D. H. Lawrence (. . .). An illness resulting from lead-poisoning, followed by pulmonary complications, forced me meanwhile to give up printing, but I had a new career in my hands and I made a living with my translations until 1941 (. . .). In the autumn of 1936, more on account of my naïvety than anything else, I had had a slight political mishap. The police did no more than threaten to imprison me the next time (. . .). However, the Fascist party decided to expel me. I had joined it in 1925, while I was still at school, just as every other pupil had to. Except that I had never renewed my membership and never paid the necessary subscriptions. I have always been rather absent-minded about membership cards (. . .). But the Florentine Fascists made me catch up on years of subscriptions just to have the pleasure of expelling me. Luckily the editors for whom I did translations did not take any notice and went on giving me work (. . .).

'In the autumn of 1937 I had started writing *Conversazione in Sicilia* and was publishing it in serial form in a new Florentine review, *Letteratura*, which was an attempt to replace with one edition every three months the now defunct *Solaria*. I was writing the book as the review published it, bit by bit, alternating work on that with my translating. I finished it in the winter of 1939, shortly after moving from the turbulence of Florence, where by now the Fascists never stopped harassing me, to the relative tranquillity of Milan. The first edition of *Conversazione in Sicilia* was of three hundred copies. It was passed by the censors because of a combination of circumstances which it would take too long to explain. And anyway there were only three hundred copies. But the book was greeted favourably by the critics and in 1942 Bompiani were willing to take the risk of printing an edition of five thousand copies, which might be called the first real edition for the book market.

librario. Un mese dopo l'edizione era esaurita. Seguí una seconda tiratura pure di 5.000 esemplari. Allora la stessa stampa che aveva lodato il libro in terza pagina (cioè sulla pagina letteraria) cominciò ad attaccarlo come antinazionale, immorale, ecc. sulla prima. Un giorno dell'autunno 1942 mi arrivò un telegramma. Era un ordine di presentarmi alla federazione fascista di Milano per comunicazioni urgenti (...). Ricevuto dal segretario federale mi sentii chiamare canaglia per tre quarti d'ora. Era per il libro. Mi fu detto che sarei stato espulso dal fascio[8] come punizione per aver scritto un libro simile. Arrivato il mio turno di parlare, risposi che non mi si poteva espellere dal partito per il semplice fatto che non vi ero iscritto. Il federale cadde dalle nuvole. Ma non ero impiegato da qualche parte? Non riusciva a credere che qualcuno in Italia non fosse iscritto al partito. Riuscii a convincerlo che non ero iscritto, pur senza dirgli di essere stato espulso già nel 1936. E lui cambiò completamente modo di comportarsi. Disse che, stando cosí le cose, non sapeva che farmi. Si scusò anzi, proprio cosí, si scusò, e potei tornarmene a casa (...).»

A month after its publication it had sold out. There followed a second impression also of five thousand copies. Then the same papers that had praised the book on the third page – the review page – started attacking it as anti-national, immoral, etc. on the front page. One day, in the autumn of 1942, I received a telegram. It was an order to appear before the Milanese branch of the Fascist party on urgent business (. . .). Having been received by the branch secretary I spent three quarters of an hour hearing him call me a villain. It was because of the book. I was told that I would be expelled from the *fascio* as a punishment for having written such a book. When it was my turn to speak, I replied that they could not expel me from the party for the simple reason that I was not a member. The branch secretary was stunned. But wasn't I employed somewhere? He just could not believe that there was anyone in Italy who was not a member of the party. I managed to convince him that I was not a member, and without even telling him that I had already been expelled from the party in 1936. And his attitude changed completely. He said that, as this was how things stood, he did not know what to do with me. More than that, he apologized, yes, he apologized and I was allowed to go home again (. . .).'

NIKOLAYEVKA
26 JANUARY 1943

MARIO RIGONI-STERN

Translated by Alexander Mandeville and Patricia Newnham

NIKOLAJEVKA
26 GENNAIO 1943

In una delle prime isbe[1] lascio i feriti. Vi è una donna russa e la prego di averne cura. Inoltre lascio con loro, ad assisterli, Dotti della squadra di Moreschi. Con Antonelli e la pesante entro in un'altra isba. Mi sembra un posto ottimo per piazzarvi l'arma. Un soldato del mio plotone mi segue con una cassetta di munizioni. Sfondo una finestra con il calcio del fucile e trascino lí il tavolo coperto da una tovaglia ricamata. Sopra il tavolo postiamo l'arma e spariamo dalla finestra. I russi sono a un centinaio di metri, di schiena. Li cogliamo di sorpresa, ma dobbiamo fare economia di munizioni. Mentre spariamo i ragazzini dell'isba si stringono piangendo alle gonne della mamma. La donna, invece, è calma e seria. Ci guarda silenziosa.

Durante una pausa vedo spuntare di sotto a un letto gli stivali di un uomo. Sollevo la coperta e lo faccio venir fuori. È un vecchio alto e magro che si guarda attorno spaurito come una volpe nella tagliola. Antonelli ride e poi fa il gesto di dargli un calcio nel sedere e lo manda dov'è la donna coi bambini.

Spariamo qualche raffica a un gruppo di russi che stanno trascinando un cannone anticarro. Non ci restano piú che tre caricatori.

Usciamo dall'isba e incontriamo Menegolo che veniva in cerca di noi con una cassetta di munizioni. Mi irrito perché non vedo comparire Moreschi con le altre cassette. Antonelli e Menegolo postano l'arma all'angolo di un'isba; io un po' piú avanti, alla loro destra, indico dove devono sparare e sparo con il moschetto attraverso le fessure di uno steccato. Siamo sempre quasi alle

NIKOLAYEVKA
26 JANUARY 1943

I leave the wounded in one of the first izbas. There is a Russian woman there and I ask her to look after them. I also leave Dotti of Moreschi's detachment with them to help them. Antonelli and I go into another of the izbas with the heavy machine gun. It seems to me just the right place to set up the weapon. One of the soldiers from my platoon follows with a box of ammunition. I smash in a window with the butt-end of my rifle and drag the table over, over which is an embroidered cloth. We set the gun up on the table and fire through the window. The Russians are about a hundred yards off, with their backs to us. We take them by surprise, but have to be sparing with our ammunition. While we fire, the kids of the house hang on to their mother's skirts, bawling their heads off. But the woman is calm and grave. She watches us silently.

During the lull I spot a pair of men's boots sticking out from under a bed. I lift up the bedcover and pull him out. He is an old man, tall and skinny, looking about him terror-stricken, like a fox in a trap. Antonelli laughs and pretends to kick him up the arse and then sends him over to where the woman is standing with the kids.

We let off a few bursts of fire at a group of Russians dragging up an anti-tank gun. There are only three magazines left.

We leave the izba and bump into Menegolo coming to look for us with a box of ammunition. It worries me that Moreschi hasn't shown up with the other boxes. Antonelli and Menegolo set up the gun at the corner of an izba. Standing a bit in front and to their right, I show them where to shoot and fire my rifle through the gaps in a log fence. We are still almost on top of the Russians and causing

spalle dei russi e rechiamo loro molto fastidio. Spero intanto che la colonna si decida a scendere da dove l'abbiamo lasciata ferma. Dopo un po' che spariamo i russi riescono a individuarci e un colpo d'anticarro porta via l'angolo dell'isba pochi centimetri sopra alla testa di Antonelli. «Spostiamoci,» gli grido. Ma Antonelli si mette a cavallo del treppiede e dice: «Adesso li ho proprio di mira.» E spara ancora.

Il tenente Danda con qualche soldato della cinquantaquattro (credo) vuole attraversare la strada e venire dove siamo noi, ma da una casa vicina partono dei colpi e rimane ferito a un braccio.

La nostra artiglieria non spara piú da un pezzo. Avevano pochi colpi, li avranno sparati tutti. Ma perché non scende il grosso della colonna? Che cosa aspettano? Da soli non possiamo andare avanti e siamo già arrivati a metà del paese. Potrebbero scendere quasi indisturbati ora che abbiamo fatto ripiegare i russi e li stiamo tenendo a bada. Invece c'è uno strano silenzio. Non sappiamo piú niente nemmeno degli altri plotoni venuti all'attacco con noi.

Compresi gli uomini del tenente Danda saremo in tutto una ventina. Che facciamo qui da soli? Non abbiamo quasi piú munizioni. Abbiamo perso il collegamento con il capitano. Non abbiamo ordini. Se avessimo almeno munizioni! Ma sento anche che ho fame, e il sole sta per tramontare. Attraverso lo steccato e una pallottola mi sibila vicino. I russi ci tengono d'occhio. Corro e busso alla porta di un'isba. Entro.

Vi sono dei soldati russi, là. Dei prigionieri? No. Sono armati. Con la stella rossa sul berretto! Io ho in mano il fucile. Li guardo impietrito. Essi stanno mangiando attorno alla tavola. Prendono il cibo con il cucchiaio di legno da una zuppiera comune. E mi guardano con i cucchiai sospesi a mezz'aria. «Mnié khocetsia iestj,»[2] dico. Vi sono anche delle donne. Una prende un piatto,

them a lot of trouble. I do wish that our support column would come down from where we left them. After we've been firing for a bit the Russians manage to spot us and a shot from their anti-tank gun carries off the corner of the izba a few inches above Antonelli's head. 'Let's get the hell out of here,' I shout. But Antonelli straddles the machine gun and says: 'I've got 'em in my sights now.' And shoots again.

Lieutenant Danda with some soldiers from the 54th Regiment, I think, tries to cross the road and join us, but there are some shots from a near-by house and he is wounded in the arm.

No more fire from our artillery for a bit. They hadn't had much ammunition and they must have fired it all. Why isn't the main column coming down? What are they waiting for? We can't go forward on our own and we've already got to the centre of the village. They could come down almost undisturbed now that we've driven the Russians back and are holding them at bay. Instead there is a strange silence. We don't know anything, not even what has happened to the other platoons who went into the attack with us.

Including Lieutenant Danda's men there must be about twenty of us. What are we doing here all by ourselves? We're almost out of ammunition. We've lost contact with the Captain. We've got no orders. If only we'd at least got some ammunition left! But then I also realize that I'm starving, and the sun is starting to set. I go over the fence and a bullet whines past me. The Russians have got their eye on us. I rush over to another izba, knock at the door and go in.

There are some Russian soldiers there. Prisoners? No. They're armed. And there are red stars on their caps! I've got my rifle in my hand. Petrified, I look at them. They are sitting round a table eating, spooning out food from a communal tureen with wooden spoons. And they watch me, their spoons suspended in mid-air. 'I want to eat,' I say in Russian. There are women there too. One of them takes a

lo riempie di latte e miglio, con un mestolo, dalla zuppiera di tutti, e me lo porge. Io faccio un passo avanti, mi metto il fucile in spalla e mangio. Il tempo non esiste piú. I soldati russi mi guardano. Le donne mi guardano. I bambini mi guardano. Nessuno fiata. C'è solo il rumore del mio cucchiaio nel piatto. E d'ogni mia boccata. «Spaziba,» dico quando ho finito. E la donna prende dalle mie mani il piatto vuoto. «Pasausta,» mi risponde con semplicità. I soldati russi mi guardano uscire senza che si siano mossi. Nel vano dell'ingresso vi sono delle arnie. La donna che mi ha dato la minestra, è venuta con me come per aprirmi la porta e io le chiedo a gesti di darmi un favo di miele per i miei compagni. La donna mi dà il favo e io esco.

Cosí è successo questo fatto. Ora non lo trovo affatto strano, a pensarvi, ma naturale di quella naturalezza che una volta dev'esserci stata tra gli uomini. Dopo la prima sorpresa tutti i miei gesti furono naturali, non sentivo nessun timore, né alcun desiderio di difendermi o di offendere. Era una cosa molto semplice. Anche i russi erano come me, lo sentivo. In quell'isba si era creata tra me e i soldati russi, e le donne e i bambini un'armonia che non era un armistizio. Era qualcosa di molto piú del rispetto che gli animali della foresta hanno l'uno per l'altro. Una volta tanto le circostanze avevano portato degli uomini a saper restare uomini. Chissà dove saranno ora quei soldati, quelle donne, quei bambini. Io spero che la guerra li abbia risparmiati tutti. Finché saremo vivi ci ricorderemo, tutti quanti eravamo, come ci siamo comportati. I bambini specialmente. Se questo è successo una volta potrà tornare a succedere. Potrà succedere, voglio dire, a innumerevoli altri uomini e diventare un costume, un modo di vivere.

Tornato tra i miei compagni appendiamo il favo di miele al ramo di un albero e un pezzo per uno ce lo mangiamo tutto. Io poi mi guardo attorno come risvegliandomi da un sogno. Il sole scompare all'orizzonte. Guardo l'arma e i due caricatori che ci sono rimasti.

plate, ladles out a portion of milk and porridge from the communal tureen and pushes it towards me. I take a step forward, sling my rifle and begin to eat. Time stands still. The Russian soldiers watch me. The women watch me. The children watch me. No one breathes. There's only the noise of my spoon on the plate and the sound of my swallowing. 'Thank you,' I say in Russian when I have finished, and the woman takes the empty plate from my hands. 'Don't mention it,' she replies simply. Without moving, the Russian soldiers watch me leave. There are some beehives in the doorway. The woman who gave me the soup has come forward as if to open the door for me, and in sign language I ask her for a honeycomb for my comrades. She gives me the honeycomb and I go out.

That's how it happened. Thinking back on it now, I don't find it at all strange, but natural, with that naturalness that must once have existed between men. After the first surprise all my gestures were natural. I felt no fear, nor any wish to defend myself or to strike out at anyone. It was such a simple thing. And the Russians felt as I did, I knew. In that izba, between the Russian soldiers and the women and the children and me, there was a harmony that was no mere truce. It was something much more than the respect animals in the forest feel for one another. For once events had allowed a few men to know what it was to behave like human beings. Who knows where they all are today, those soldiers, those women, those children? I hope the war has spared them all. For as long as we live all of us will remember how we behaved that day. The children especially. And what happened once can happen again. It can happen, I mean, to millions of other people, and become a habit, a way of life.

Back with my men, we hang the honeycomb from the branch of a tree, share it out equally and eat the lot. Then I begin to look around me, as if waking from a dream. The sun is disappearing below the horizon. I look at the gun and the two magazines that are left. I look down the empty

Guardo per le strade deserte del paese, e mi accorgo che da una di esse avanza verso di noi un gruppo di armati. Sono vestiti di bianco[3] e procedono con sicurezza. Sono nostri? Sono tedeschi? Sono russi? Giunti a qualche decina di metri da noi si fermano e ci guardano. Sono incerti anche loro. Poi sentiamo che parlano. Sono russi. Ordino in fretta di seguirmi e mi butto tra le isbe e gli orti. Antonelli e Menegolo mi vengono dietro con l'arma. Tutti mi guardano perplessi come se aspettassero di vedermi compiere un miracolo. Mi rendo conto che la situazione è disperata. Ma non ci passa per la testa di darci prigionieri. Un alpino,[4] di non so quale compagnia, ha un fucile mitragliatore ma non munizioni; un altro mi si avvicina e dice: «Ho piú di cento colpi.» Sporgendomi di sopra a uno steccato sparo un paio di caricatori con il mitragliatore a un gruppo di russi poco lontani e poi passo l'arma a un alpino: «Spara,» gli dico. Da sopra lo steccato l'alpino spara ma poi mi cade rantolando ai piedi, colpito alla testa. Riprendo a sparare con il mitragliatore e i russi si diradano. I cento colpi sono già finiti. Anche Antonelli ha finito le munizioni e ora smonta la pesante e ne disperde i pezzi nella neve. La nostra compagnia perde cosí la sua ultima arma.

Siamo meno di una ventina di uomini. «Animo,» dico, «preparate tutte le bombe a mano che avete, gridate, fate baccano e poi seguitemi.» Sbuchiamo fuori dallo steccato. Siamo in quattro gatti[5] ma facciamo baccano per tre volte tanto[6] e le bombe fanno il resto. Non so se siamo stati noi ad aprirci la strada o se i russi ci abbiano lasciato passare; il fatto è che ci siamo messi in salvo. Raggiungiamo di corsa la scarpata della ferrovia, e ci infiliamo in un condotto che l'attraversa, ma come metto fuori la testa dall'altra parte vedo che lí davanti la neve è coperta di cadaveri. Una raffica mi passa rasente al muso.[7] «Indietro,» grido, «indietro!» Ritorniamo fuori l'uno dopo l'altro da dove siamo entrati. Mi getto in una piccola balca e sempre correndo ne risalgo il fondo.

streets of the village, and realize that along one of them a group of armed men is advancing towards us. They are wearing white and they advance confidently. Are they ours? Are they Germans? Are they Russians? About ten yards away they halt and look us over. They are uncertain too. And then we hear them talking. They are Russians. I hurriedly give the order to follow me and tear away between the izbas and the vegetable patches. Antonelli and Menegolo are behind me with the machine gun. They are all looking at me in bewilderment, as if waiting to see me perform a miracle. I realize the situation is desperate, but it doesn't enter our heads to give ourselves up. An alpino from some company or other has an automatic rifle but no ammunition. Another comes up to me and says, 'I've got over a hundred rounds.' I lean on the log paling of a fence and fire a couple of shots from the automatic at a group of near-by Russians. Then I pass the gun to an alpino. 'Fire,' I tell him. He fires over the fence, but then, shot through the head, falls at my feet, his breath choking in his throat. I start firing the gun again and the Russians spread out. The hundred rounds are already finished. Antonelli has used all his ammunition too and is now dismantling the heavy machine gun and scattering the pieces in the snow. And so our company loses its last weapon.

Now there are less than twenty of us. 'Chin up!' I say. 'Get all the hand grenades you've got ready, yell and scream then follow me.' We rush out from behind the stockade. There are only a handful of us, but our shouts are loud enough for three times as many, and the bursting grenades do the rest. I don't know if we burst through the Russians or if they let us pass; the fact is, we get out of danger. We reach the railway embankment on the run and follow one another through a culvert underneath it. But when I stick my head out on the other side I see that the snow in front of us is covered with dead bodies. A burst of fire nearly parts my hair for me. 'Get back!' I cry. 'Get back!' and back we go, one after the other, out the way we came in. I jump down into a little gully and, still running, leap up

I miei compagni mi seguono. Costeggio una siepe e sento arrivare dei colpi alle nostre spalle. Giungiamo alle isbe di dove, al mattino, tiravano su di noi con gli anticarro. Ci fermiamo un attimo a riprender fiato e a guardarci. Ci siamo ancora tutti. Dall'isba piú vicina vedo uscire il tenente Pendoli. «Rigoni,» mi chiama, «Rigoni, venite qui a prendere il nostro capitano che è ferito.» «Ma gli altri,» chiedo, «dove sono?» «Non c'è piú nessuno,» risponde il tenente Pendoli. «Andiamo a prendere il capitano,» dico ai miei compagni. Ma dalle isbe attorno, e dalle siepi, dagli orti, vengono fuori sparando decine e decine di soldati russi. Molti dei miei compagni cadono, altri corrono verso la breve scarpata della ferrovia, raggiungono le rotaie e lí ricevono un'altra raffica come una grandinata. Ne cadono ancora due o tre. Io mi precipito per unirmi ai rimasti. Le pallottole battono sulle rotaie con rumore di tempesta e mandano scintille, ma riesco a rotolare dall'altra parte. Sono ultimo dietro agli scampati che si arrampicano nella neve. La scarpata della ferrovia ci divide dai russi. Passo vicino a un cannone anticarro e mi fermo per cercare di toglierne l'otturatore e renderlo inservibile. Ma intanto, i russi riappaiono sulla scarpata e mi sparano contro. Allora riprendo a correre in su come posso, sprofondando di continuo nella neve sino al ginocchio. Sono allo scoperto sotto il fuoco dei russi e a ogni passo che faccio arriva un colpo. «Adesso e nell'ora della nostra morte»,[8] dico tra di me, come un disco che giri a vuoto. «Adesso e nell'ora della nostra morte. Adesso e nell'ora della nostra morte.»

Sento qualcuno che geme e invoca aiuto. Mi avvicino. È un alpino che era al mio caposaldo sul Don. È ferito alle gambe e al ventre da schegge d'anticarro. Lo circondo con le braccia sotto le ascelle e lo trascino. Ma faccio troppa fatica e me lo carico sulle spalle. I russi ci sparano contro con l'anticarro. Sprofondo nella neve, avanzo, cado, e l'alpino geme. Non ho proprio la forza di continuare a portarlo. Riesco tuttavia a portarlo dove i colpi non arrivano. Del resto i russi smettono di sparare. Dico

from the bottom, my men behind me. I follow the line of a hedge and hear shots reaching us at shoulder-level. We reach the izbas from which we were fired on in the morning by the anti-tank gun. We stop there for a moment for a breather and to take stock of ourselves. All present! I catch sight of Lieutenant Pendoli coming out of the nearest izba. 'Rigoni,' he shouts at me, 'Rigoni, come and get the Captain. He's been wounded.' 'But the others,' I ask, 'where are they?' 'There's no one else left,' says Lieutenant Pendoli. 'Let's go and get the Captain,' I tell the boys. But from the surrounding izbas, and from the hedges and the vegetable patches hordes of Russian soldiers come rushing out, firing. Many of my men are killed, others run towards the low railway embankment, reach the lines, and meet another hail of bullets, which kills two or three more. I rush to join those who are left. Bullets strike the rails like thunder claps, sending sparks flying, but I manage to roll over to the other side of the track. I am last behind the survivors trudging through the snow. The railway embankment divides us from the Russians. Passing near an anti-tank gun, I stop to try and remove the firing mechanism to put it out of action. But in the meantime some Russians reappear on the top of the embankment and open fire on me. So I start running up again as fast as I can, but I keep sinking up to my knees in the snow. I am now in the open under fire from the Russians, and every step I take brings a shot. 'Now and in the hour of our death', I say to myself, like a record stuck in a groove. 'Now and in the hour of our death. Now and in the hour of our death.'

I hear someone moaning and calling for help. I come closer. It's one of the alpini who was at my strong-point on the River Don. He is wounded in the legs and stomach by anti-tank splinters. I put my arms under his armpits and start dragging him along, but this is so exhausting that I hoist him up on my shoulders. The Russians are firing at us with the anti-tank gun. I flounder in the snow, stagger forward, then fall again, and the alpino moans. I've hardly got the strength to go on carrying him, but nevertheless I

all'alpino di provarsi a camminare. Egli tenta inutilmente, e ci fermiamo dietro a un mucchio di letame. «Resta qui,» gli dico. «Ti mando a prendere con la slitta. E fatti coraggio perché non sei grave.»

Io poi, non mi sono ricordato di mandare giú la slitta, ma i portaferiti della nostra compagnia sono giusto passati di là e lo hanno raccolto. Ho saputo in Italia ch'egli si era salvato, e un gran peso mi è caduto dal cuore. Lo ritrovai un giorno, finito tutto, a Brescia. Non lo riconobbi, ma lui mi vide da lontano, mi corse incontro, mi abbracciò. «Non ricordi, sergentmagiú?» Io non lo riconoscevo e lo guardavo. «Non ricordi?» ripeteva, e si batteva con la mano sulla gamba di legno. «Va tutto bene ora.» E rideva. «Non ricordi il 26 gennaio?» Allora mi ricordai e tornammo ad abbracciarci con tanta gente attorno che ci osservava senza capire.

Ora, mentre continuavo da solo il mio cammino nella neve, sento d'un tratto un trambusto e vedo la massa nera della colonna precipitarsi giú per il pendío. Che diavolo fanno? Penso che il fuoco dei russi li sterminerà. Perché non sono venuti giú prima. Ma vi sono di nuovo degli aeroplani. Mitragliano e lanciano spezzoni. È di nuovo come stamattina. In piú dal paese sparano con gli anticarro e i mortai. Alcuni panzer tedeschi scendono lentamente, guardinghi. Uno è colpito e si ferma, ma continua a sparare con il cannone. Gli altri mi passano vicino. Gruppi di soldati tedeschi li seguono e io mi unisco a loro. Cosí arrivo ancora una volta alle prime case. Spariamo coi fucili di dietro ai carri. Spiegandomi a cenni cerco di far avanzare un panzer fin dove si trova il capitano ferito. Do loro a intendere che si tratta di un ufficiale superiore. Dopo molte esitazioni i tedeschi cedono alle mie insistenze. Facciamo pochi metri nella direzione che indico loro, e un colpo di anticarro frantuma il periscopio. Il panzer è costretto a fermarsi e

manage to get him out of the range of fire. Anyway, the Russians stop firing. I tell the alpino to try to walk. He tries, but it's useless, and we come to a halt behind a pile of dung. 'Stay here,' I tell him. 'I'll send someone with a sledge to fetch you. And cheer up, you're not badly hurt.'

I never did remember to send down a sledge, but the stretcher-bearers from our company passed by that very spot and picked him up. Back in Italy I learnt that he had been rescued, and a heavy weight fell from my mind. After it was all over, I met him in Brescia one day. I didn't recognize him, but he saw me from a long way off and ran up to meet me and threw his arms round me. 'Don't you remember me, Sergeant-Major?' I looked at him without recognition. 'Don't you remember?' he repeated, and he hit his wooden leg with his hand. 'It's all right now.' And he laughed. 'Don't you remember January 26th?' And then I remembered and we fell to embracing each other with a host of people around us watching without understanding.

Now as I take up my solitary plod in the snow again, I suddenly hear a commotion and I see the black mass of the column hurling itself down the slopes. What the devil are they doing? They'll be wiped out by the Russians' guns. Why didn't they come down earlier? But there are planes there again, machine-gunning and dropping off anti-personnel bombs. It's like the morning all over again. And from the village anti-tank guns and mortars open up as well. Some German panzers move downhill slowly, warily. One of them is hit and stops, but it keeps firing its gun. The others pass close to me. Groups of German infantry follow them and I join them. Like this I reach the first houses again. From behind the tanks we open fire with our rifles. In sign language I try to get one of the tanks to go forward to where the wounded Captain is lying. I make them believe that it's a question of a high-ranking officer. After a lot of hesitation the Germans give in to my insistence. We advance a few yards in the direction I indicate and a shot from an anti-tank gun shatters the periscope. The tank is

dobbiamo rinunciare. Non siamo in numero sufficiente per addentrarci nel paese senza l'appoggio del carro.

Intanto è cominciata la sera. Mi metto dietro alle macerie di una casa sparando contro i russi che passano per gli orti. Sono rimasto solo. Venti metri piú a destra vi è un soldato tedesco che si avvicina, strisciando cauto sulla neve, a due russi appostati dietro un muricciolo. Egli poi lancia due granate su di loro. Io allora corro fino a una casa piú avanti. Dal marciapiede in faccia un soldato russo mi vede e svolta la cantonata per poi prendermi di mira. Io dal mio riparo e lui dal suo ci scambiamo dei colpi di fucile. Un capitano dell'artiglieria alpina che mi viene incontro cade colpito al petto mentre sta per rivolgermi la parola. Ha uno sbocco di sangue che mi chiazza le scarpe e i calzettoni. Arriva il suo attendente. Arriva un altro ufficiale. Piangono su di lui che rantola. Appena poi è morto l'attendente gli toglie dalla tasca il portafogli e dal polso l'orologio.[9] Io non ne posso piú dalla stanchezza e vado a sedermi dietro un piccolo argine. Un sottotenente mi si avvicina gridando: «Vigliacco, che fai lí? Vieni fuori.» Io non lo guardo nemmeno, e lui finisce che si mette a sedere lí vicino e se ne resta lí anche dopo che io me ne vado.

Vengo a sapere che il tenente colonnello Calbo dell'artiglieria alpina è stato colpito. Lo cerco. Il suo attendente gli sorregge il capo e piange. Il colonnello ha gli occhi velati e già forse non vede piú nulla. Mi parla credendomi il maggiore Bracchi. Non ricordo le parole che mi disse; ricordo solo il suono della sua voce, l'affanno cagionato dalla ferita e lui sulla neve. Qualcosa di grande era nel suo aspetto e io mi sentivo timido e stupito. Intanto i carri dei tedeschi sono tornati ad avanzare. Alpini e tedeschi si mettono dietro. Le pallottole battono sulla corazza dei panzer e schizzano attorno a noi. Su un carro è accovacciato il generale Reverberi

forced to stop and we have to give up our rescue attempt. There aren't enough of us to push on to the village without tank support.

Meanwhile dusk has fallen. I take cover behind the ruins of a house, firing on the Russians passing through the vegetable plots. I am alone. Twenty yards away on my right a German soldier crawls cautiously forward across the snow towards two Russians lying in wait behind a low wall. He lobs a grenade at them. Then I run forward to a house further up. A Russian soldier on the pavement opposite spots me and dodges round the corner and takes aim. We exchange shots, I from behind my shelter, he from behind his. A captain of the Mountain Artillery coming forward to join me falls dead, shot through the chest as he is about to address me. A spurt of his blood splashes over my boots and stockings. His orderly appears. Another officer appears. They weep over the dying man. The moment he's dead, the orderly removes the captain's wallet from his pocket and his watch from his wrist. I am ready to drop with tiredness and go and sit down in the shelter of a low bank. A second-lieutenant comes over to me. 'You coward! What are you doing there?' he shouts. 'Get out!' I don't even look at him, and he ends up sitting down beside me, and stays there even after I leave.

Someone tells me that Lieutenant-Colonel Calbo of the Mountain Artillery has been shot and I go to look for him. His orderly, who is in tears, is supporting the officer's head. The Colonel's eyes are veiled over, and already probably sightless. He speaks to me, thinking I am Major Bracchi. I can't remember what he said to me. I remember only the sound of his voice, his breath coming short because of the wound, and him lying in the snow. There was something awe-inspiring in the dying man's features, and I felt stunned and shy. German tanks have by now returned to the attack, their men and some alpini following behind them. The shots hit the tanks' armour-plating and ricochet about our heads. Crouched on top of one tank, General Reverberi shouts

che ci incita con la voce. Poi egli scende e cammina da solo davanti ai carri impugnando la pistola.

Da una casa sparano con insistenza. Da quella sola casa. «Ci sono ufficiali?» grida il generale verso di noi. Ufficiali forse ve ne sono, ma nessuno esce. «Ci sono alpini?» grida ancora. E allora esce un gruppetto di dietro ai carri. «Andate in quella casa e fatela finita,» ci dice. Noi andiamo e i russi se ne vanno.

È notte fatta, la colonna si è riversata nel paese e tutti cercano un posto per passare la notte al caldo, e, se è possibile, mangiare qualcosa. Che confusione ora! Sembra una fiera. Incontro alcuni genieri e chiedo loro di Rino. Lo hanno visto ferito leggermente ad una spalla durante il primo assalto, da allora non sanno piú nulla. Lo chiamo e lo cerco senza trovarlo. Incontro il capitano Marcolini e il tenente Zanotelli del mio battaglione. Con questi mi metto vicino alla chiesa e chiamiamo: «Vestone! Vestone![10] Adunata Vestone!» Ma potrebbero rispondere i morti? «Si ricorda Rigoni, il primo di settembre?» mi dice piangendo il tenente. «È come allora.» «È peggio,» dico.

Ai nostri richiami risponde Baroni dei mortai e viene con un gruppetto del suo plotone. Hanno ancora un tubo di mortaio, nessuna bomba, nient'altro. Di tutto il Vestone riusciamo a radunarci in circa una trentina. Le isbe sono tutte occupate e prendiamo posto nelle scuole. Ma qui i vetri sono rotti, non c'è paglia e l'impiantito è di cemento. Ci sdraiamo ma non è possibile dormire. Ci congeleremmo. «La Ecia», alpino della mia compagnia, ha trovato chissà dove delle gallette e me ne dà una. Rosicchiamo assieme. Bodei, che mi è vicino, trema dal freddo. Ci alziamo e usciamo. Busso a un'isba; viene alla porta un soldato tedesco con la pistola spianata e me la punta al petto. «Voglio entrare,» dico. Gentilmente, con la mano, gli sposto la pistola e gli rido in faccia. Sconcertato la rimette nel fodero e mi chiude la porta sul viso. Entriamo in una stalla e accendiamo un piccolo fuoco con degli sterpi. Ci riscaldiamo, ma la parte che

encouragement to us. Then he leaps down and, pistol in hand, walks alone in front of the panzers.

From one house there is persistent firing. From just that one. 'Are there any officers here?' the General shouts at us. Perhaps there are, but no one steps forward. 'Are there any alpini?' he shouts again. And a handful of us leave the protection of the tanks. 'Go to that house and put an end to that,' he says. We go, and the Russians push off.

It is night now and the column returns to the village, with everyone looking for somewhere warm to spend the night, and something to eat if possible. Everything is in a shambles. It's like a fair-ground. I run into some sappers and ask them if they have any news of Rino. Nothing, they say, since they saw him slightly wounded in the shoulder during the first assault. I call out his name and search for him, but can't find him. I run into Captain Marcolini and Lieutenant Zanotelli of my battalion. I station myself with them by the church and we call out, 'All Vestone here! Fall in any lads from Vestone!' But can dead men reply? 'Do you remember September 1st, Rigoni?' the Lieutenant asks me, tears in his eyes. 'It's like it was then.' 'It's worse,' I say.

Baroni, of the mortar section, hears our call and comes over with a few of his platoon. They have one mortar, no bombs, nothing else. Of all the Vestone Battalion we manage to round up about thirty. All the izbas are occupied so we quarter ourselves in the school. But here the windows are broken, there is no straw and the floor is concrete. We stretch ourselves out but it's impossible to sleep. We would have frozen. 'La Ecia', an alpino in my company, has found some biscuits somewhere and he gives me one. We munch them together. Bodei, who is next to me, is trembling with cold. We get up and go out. I knock at an izba. A German soldier comes to the door with pistol levelled and sticks it in my chest. 'Let us in,' I say, gently pushing away the weapon with my hand and laughing in his face. Disconcerted, he replaces his revolver in its holster and slams the door in my face. We go into a stable and light a small fire with some twigs. We warm up, but the side away from

non guarda il fuoco è gelata. I muli ci guardano con le orecchie basse. La testa ci ciondola di qua e di là. Lentamente mi addormento con la schiena appoggiata a un palo.

Questo è stato il 26 gennaio 1943. I miei piú cari amici mi hanno lasciato in quel giorno.

the fire is frozen. The mules contemplate us with lowered ears. Our heads are swaying from side to side. Slowly, my back against a wooden upright, I fall asleep.

That was January 26th, 1943. I parted with my dearest friends that day.

THE AMBUSH

BEPPE FENOGLIO

Translated by Richard Andrews

L'IMBOSCATA

Il giorno della liberazione di Roma, i fascisti operarono una forte puntata nel cuore del sistema badogliano.[1] Fu presto accertato che si trattava dei soldati della guarnigione di Asti, audaci ed accaniti reparti, ben dissimili dalla goffa, amletica guarnigione di Alba, che invariabilmente faceva meschine figure contro le incursioni notturne partigiane.

Le prime scariche esplosero nella pianura di Castagnole, affogata in vapori di caldo, con un che di festoso, di ridestante, un che di domenicali campane. Gli uccelli, disturbati e spaventati, al piano, stavano guadagnando le alture, remigavano, già placati, sulle teste intente di Pierre e di Johnny. Il presidio[2] di Castagnole oppose una breve formale resistenza di primo contatto, poi diede via libera ai fascisti verso l'adiacente presidio di Coazzolo, del quale, aveva saputo Johnny, faceva parte Ettore, il suo concittadino e amico ed ex collega nell'U.N.P.A.[3] Coazzolo resisté un po' piú a lungo, favorita dallo scoscendersi delle prime colline, i fascisti poi persero tempo ad incendiare una casa e a godersi quel non straordinario spettacolo. Da Mango il fuoco, benché vicino, era scarsamente visibile, perché il cielo vapido di calore smasiva[4] la colonna di fumo in feerica insostanzialità. Cosí, soltanto alle dieci, l'avanzante colonna fascista fronteggiò Mango.

Pierre voleva postarsi davanti al paese e combattere e morire per la sua verginità. Ma Johnny osservò che era molto meglio il mammellone[5] a destra del paese, coronato di fitta ed utile vegetazione e col pendio apprezzabilmente ripido. Ma Pierre osservò a sua volta che quel piano lasciava via libera ai fascisti per penetrare

THE AMBUSH

On the day Rome was liberated, the Fascists staged a heavy thrust into the heart of the legitimist territory. It was soon ascertained that these were soldiers from the Asti garrison, bold and fanatical squads, quite different from the awkward, indecisive Alba garrison who invariably cut a poor figure against night raids of the partisans.

The first shots exploded in the plain of Castagnole, drowned in its heat-haze, with a certain festive, bracing note, like church bells on Sunday morning. The birds, disturbed and frightened on the plain, were moving to higher ground and were beating their wings, already reassured, above the intent heads of Pierre and Johnny. The partisan detachment at Castagnole opposed a brief formal resistance at first contact, then gave the Fascists a free passage towards the neighbouring detachment of Coazzolo, which Johnny had learned included Ettore, his fellow-townsman and friend, and ex-companion from the U.N.P.A. Coazzolo resisted for a little longer, helped by the sharp slope of the first hills, and the Fascists then wasted time setting fire to a house and enjoying that not unusual spectacle. From Mango the fire, although not far away, was hardly visible, because the heat-soaked sky diluted the column of smoke into an elfin insubstantiality. So it was only at ten o'clock that the advancing Fascist column drew up before Mango.

Pierre wanted to make a stand in front of the village and fight to the death for its virginity. But Johnny pointed out that the round hill to the right of the village would be much better, since it was crowned with thick, protective vegetation and the slope was particularly steep. Pierre pointed out in his turn that the plain would allow the Fascists free

nel paese con le prevedibili conseguenze di ferro e fuoco. . . . «Bruceranno,» disse Johnny, «se noi combatteremo da dentro il paese e non lo terremo. Che non lo terremo è un fatto perché, almeno oggi come oggi, non siamo in grado di controbattere i fascisti campalmente. Se ti consultassi con la gente del paese, vedresti che la pensa come me.» Ma Pierre smaniava cavallerescamente all'idea del paese violentato e Johnny prese a smaniare a quell'abissale differenza. «Pierre, se noi gli uccidiamo un uomo ed essi spazzano via Mango ed un altro paese ancora, la giornata è nostra. Non ci compete tener posizioni, quel che ci compete è ammazzare fascisti. E se la cosa riuscisse meglio in ritirata, io sono pronto a ritirarmi di qua al mare.»

I borghesi delle prime colline salivano in fuga, visibili nelle forre come conigli in torme.

Finalmente Pierre spedí gli uomini al mammellone, spensierati e dilettanti, indugianti al bello scoperto, con scarse armi e munizioni scarsissime. Si attestarono sulla cervice del mammellone, facendo fronte alla sinuosa strada di Valdivilla, il sergente avanti e indietro per sistemare e mantenere. Poi si stese al centro, dietro il mitragliatore Breda.[6] Johnny sbirciava le poche lastre di alimentazione e si infuriava di quelle teorie per le quali esse dovevano inutilmente, platonicamente[7] fondersi.

Nell'attesa giaceva pigramente, con una punta di voluttà intossicata dalla prossima exertion, nell'erba morbida e caldissima, col suo moschetto accanto, vicino e lontano dalla sua mano rilassata, somigliante nell'erba a un serpe raddrizzato e legnificato da un prodigioso taxidermist.[8] Da tutta la linea uscivano ondine e frastagli di ristretta e vasta conversazione, personale e generale, fantasiosa e isterica, finché Pierre dal centro ordinò silenzio e Michele riecheggiò l'ordine con la sua voce catarrosa in piena estate. Allora si poté cogliere i moti minimi, allarmati degli uccelli sul loro provvisorio

entry into the village, with inevitable consequences of fire and slaughter. . . . 'They will burn it,' said Johnny, 'if we fight from inside the village and then don't hold it. And it's a fact that we won't hold it, because we aren't capable, at least not yet, of throwing back the Fascists in the field. If you consulted the people in the village you'd see that they agree with me.' But Pierre was full of chivalrous agitation at the thought of the village being raped, and Johnny grew agitated in his turn at the gulf between their ideas. 'Pierre, if we kill one of their men, and they flatten Mango and another village too, we shall still have won. It's not our business to hold on to positions; our business is to kill Fascists. And if we can do that better by retreating, I'm prepared to retreat from here to the sea.'

The inhabitants of the first range of hills were fleeing upwards, visible like swarms of rabbits in the ravines.

Finally Pierre sent his men on to the round hill, amateurish and scatter-brained as they were, lingering to look at the view, with few weapons and less ammunition. They made a bridgehead up on the crest of the hill, facing the winding road to Valdivilla, with the sergeant chasing up and down to sort them out and keep them in order. He then stationed himself in the centre of the line behind the Breda machine gun. Johnny glared sideways at its small supply of magazines, and was seized with resentment at the mathematical laws which dictated that they would be pointlessly and inevitably used up.

During the wait he lay lazily on the soft, hot grass, with a hint of intoxicated pleasure in the exertion to come, his rifle beside him, near and yet far from his inert hand, looking in the grass like a snake that had been straightened and lignified by some prodigious taxidermist. From the line of men came waves and fragments of conversation, restricted and broad, personal and general, fantastic and hysterical, until Pierre commanded silence from the middle and Michele echoed the order with a voice full of catarrh even at the height of summer. Then one could catch the tiny, uneasy movements of the birds in their temporary refuge on

rifugio sui rami piú alti. Nulla era ancora visibile sulla dirimpettaia collina di Valdivilla, armonica e funzionale come un membro umano. Su tutta essa la desertità[9] era verde ed il silenzio ronzava elettricamente. E nulla e nessuno, tranne un cane a spasso, di cui era visibile fin lassú l'erratica felicità, sulla strada al paese, netta e segnata come col gesso nel sodo pendio. Allora Johnny guardò di lato al paese, che pareva risentire la sua eccessiva nudità e lampantezza nella piena luce meridiana. La gente stava sprangandolo tutto, come una fortezza o un sottomarino, la chiusura delle imposte e degli usci detonava come colpi d'arma da fuoco. Si era anche taciuto il rumore del trapano elettrico. Il suo padrone falegname, un puritano, aveva lavorato fino al ragionevole ultimo, austeramente imponendo i diritti del lavoro sulla guerra e le sue partite d'armi.

Per le undici i fascisti vennero in vista: indossavano già le mimetiche, ma non sfuggivano neppure di un attimo o di un dettaglio ai giovani occhi dei partigiani. Erano molti, piú di un battaglione, l'ultima curva li stava eruttando a fiotti continui. Poi lasciarono la strada, balzando agilmente oltre i fossi e salirono per il pendio, lenti e rannicchiati. Al di sopra di essi Johnny colse, molto lontano, un gruppo di autocarri, probabilmente con le riserve di munizioni, un drappello della sanità e pochi altri uomini di retroguardia. Ed il suo cuore volò laggiú: ecco la soluzione, sparirgli di fronte come per un incantesimo, aggirare la collina a corsa forzata, piombare alle spalle dei camions: uccidere gli uomini, saccheggiare i mezzi, poi appiccargli fuoco. Con questa cocente nostalgia, con questa disperazione di forse non testimoniabili tempi futuri, con gli occhi alla sollevata figura di Pierre che stava per dare il segnale del fuoco, Johnny spallò il moschetto verso i fascisti.

Ma si facevano aspettare, salivano lentissimi, applicando ogni norma di sicurezza, capaci di fronteggiare e vigilare per cinque lunghissimi minuti il piú immoto e vuoto ed innocente cespuglio, perlustrando minuziosa-

the highest branches. Nothing was yet visible on the opposite hill of Valdivilla, harmonious and functional as a human limb. All over it was green and deserted, and the silence hummed electrically. Nobody and nothing, except a dog out for a stroll on the track to the village, whose wandering happiness could be felt even from up there, standing out against the solid slope as if marked with chalk. Then Johnny looked sideways at the village, which seemed conscious of its excessive nakedness and brightness in the full midday light. The people were sealing it up like a fortress or a submarine, the closing of shutters and doors resounded like gun-shots. Even the noise of the electric drill had ceased. Its owner, a puritanical carpenter, had worked right up to the last reasonable moment, austerely asserting the right of work before war and its shooting matches.

By eleven o'clock the Fascists came into sight: they were already wearing camouflage, but not a single detail escaped the partisans' youthful eyes for a moment. There were a lot of them, more than a battalion, erupting in continuous waves from the last bend in the road. Then they left the road, leapt athletically over the ditches, and came up the slope, slow and crouching. Over their heads Johnny saw in the distance a group of lorries, probably with extra ammunition, a medical unit and a few more rearguard men. And his heart flew there: that was the solution, to disappear from in front of them as if by magic, make a forced march round the hill, and swoop on the lorries from behind to kill the men, plunder the vehicles, then set fire to them. With this burning desire and desperate longing for a probably unrealizable future, with his eyes on the raised form of Pierre who was about to give the order to fire, Johnny shouldered his rifle and aimed at the Fascists.

But they were taking their time, climbing very slowly, applying every safety procedure, prepared to confront and watch the most motionless, empty and innocent bush for

mente i filari delle vigne, come se per loro il tempo non contasse.

Era inteso che si sparava a comando, ma alcuni minorenni non ci resistettero e spararono a modo loro non appena credettero di aver nel mirino delusiva carne di fascisti. Allora spararono tutti e da un gasp di Michele si capí che il Breda era già inceppato. Il sergente stava già lavorando a disincepparlo, con dita già sanguinanti.

Dopo la scarica i fascisti si erano del tutto, perfettamente annullati in terra e dalla loro vaga linea veniva soltanto, per ora, un trillar di fischietti. Poi scaricarono una grossa salva che morse il parapetto di terra davanti ai partigiani. Michele aveva riparato il Breda e risparò al ciglione della strada da dietro il quale i fascisti sparavano come da una trincea. «Sei alto, Michele.» Il sergente chiese scusa e subito dopo avvertí che il Breda si era nuovamente inceppato. Una nuova scarica dei fascisti rasò la cima degli alberi sopra le loro teste. I partigiani rispondevano con un fuoco intuitivo. Era chiaro che i fascisti non stavano subendo perdite piú di quante ne infliggessero ai partigiani, ma tutti gli uomini erano posseduti dalla libidine del fuoco, dalla sua compagnia morale. Certamente era già mezzogiorno passato, i fascisti inchiodati in basso, Pierre stringeva il suo corto Mas della polizia francese e la fida gioia di mantenere inviolato il paese. Johnny soffriva atrocemente di sete. I fascisti, senza avanzare di un passo, insistevano con quel loro fuoco tanto massiccio e composto quanto nullo. Vi era all'opera qualche centinaio di fucili e qualche mitragliatrice, ma la conca rendeva un frastuono da grande battaglia. Il tiro troppo alto dei fascisti potava netti i rami sulle loro teste con un crack atroce e insieme festoso.

L'erroneità del sistema e la scarsezza dello spirito di corpo erano dolorosamente lampanti. Ora sarebbe bastato che una qualunque formazione partigiana si fosse vistosamente spiegata su una qualsiasi delle alture

five dragging minutes, meticulously searching the rows of vines as if time had no meaning for them.

It was understood that the partisans were to shoot only when ordered, but some youngsters could not hold out and fired in their own time as soon as they thought they had elusive Fascist flesh in their sights. Then everyone fired, and a groan from Michele indicated that the Breda had already jammed. The sergeant was already working to free it with fingers already bleeding.

After the shooting the Fascists had completely and utterly vanished into the ground, and for the moment all that came from their hidden line was a warbling of whistles. Then they fired a heavy volley which bit into the earth parapet in front of the partisans. Michele had repaired the Breda and fired back at the bank of the road from behind which the Fascists were shooting as if from a trench. 'You're too high, Michele.' The sergeant apologized, and then immediately reported that the Breda had jammed again. A second volley from the Fascists shaved the tops of the trees above their heads. The partisans replied, shooting by guesswork. It was clear that the Fascists were suffering no more casualties than they were inflicting on the partisans, but both sides were gripped by a lust for fire, by the moral support it afforded. Certainly it was already past midday; the Fascists were pinned down below; Pierre was hugging both his short, French, police-issue Mas and his zealous joy at keeping the village inviolate. Johnny was suffering terribly from thirst. The Fascists, without moving a step forward, kept on with their fire, which was as massive and leisurely as it was ineffective. Only a few hundred rifles and a few machine guns were involved, but the bowl of ground gave off enough noise for a full-scale battle. The Fascists fired too high pruning branches neatly down onto their heads with a frightening yet festive 'crack'.

The misjudged organization and the lack of group spirit were sadly obvious. All that was now needed was for some other partisan formation to deploy itself conspicuously over one of the hills on the flank, create panic in the Fascist

laterali per piombare in orgasmo la massa fascista e costringerla al ripiegamento, ma non un uomo si stagliava sulle nitide creste, come incise nel cielo. Si mosse invece uno di quei loro camions, avanzò verso la linea lentissimo, quasi avesse il motore guasto o temesse il terreno minato. «Purché non portino avanti mortai,» disse Pierre. L'aviatore temeva dannatamente quell'arma squisitamente terrestre.

Johnny si avvide allora che il sole non filtrava piú tra i rami e nel verde si era fatta una sorta di liquido oscuramento. Guardò su al cielo che stava vertiginosamente perfezionando il suo mutamento. Masse compatte di nere nubi serravano al centro del cielo, dove una pozza di livida luce segnava il punto del naufragio del sole. Johnny sperò nel temporale, ma il temporale abortiva, sebbene il cielo si torcesse nelle doglie.

In quel momento si intese dai margini della conca la partenza della prima coppiola di mortaio: quel casalingo ma tremendo consuonare di grossi coperchi. La pelle di Pierre si fece grigia come la sua pupilla. Il colpo era corto, prevedibilmente, sconquassò i cespugli anteriori, levando un'ondata di terra polverizzata. Ma tutta la linea partigiana si sommosse, i piú degli uomini sguisciarono animalmente sui ginocchi, cercando, studiando un miglior posto. Partí il secondo colpo e questo, pure prevedibilmente, andò lungo, raspò sordamente la pendice retrostante. Poi atterrò la terza coppiola, ancora inesatta, ma ranging inesorabilmente. La quarta approdò quasi esattamente all'angolo di sinistra, lo scroscio vegetale si mischiò all'urlo degli uomini. Ma nel polverone ricadente un uomo restò alto, atletico, e urlava col suono alto e fermo di una sirena avviata. Una scheggia di mortaio gli aveva enucleato un occhio ed il piccolo globo, simile a una noce di burro, stava colandogli sulla guancia. Poi cascò a terra e nello scalpitare degli uomini che si ritiravano, Michele raccolse l'occhio e lo involse nel suo fazzoletto azzurro da battaglia. Il ferito, con mani compresse sul viso, venne portato al paese, da dove qualche

concentration and force it to pull back; but not one man showed in outline on those crests sharply engraved against the sky. Instead one of their lorries moved forward towards the front, very slowly, as if the engine were faulty or it feared the ground was mined. 'Let's hope they aren't bringing up mortars,' said Pierre. As an airman he was damnably afraid of that essentially ground-based weapon.

Johnny noticed then that the sun was no longer filtering through the branches, and that a kind of liquid darkness was forming in the green. He looked up at the sky, reeling as it accomplished its transformation. Compact masses of black clouds clustered in the middle of the sky, where a pool of livid light marked the place where the sun had been shipwrecked. Johnny put his hopes in the storm, but the storm was stillborn, even though the sky writhed in labour.

At that moment from the edge of the depression, came the launching of the first mortar shell: like a homely but overwhelming clash of enormous metal lids. Pierre's skin went as grey as his eyes. The shot fell short, predictably, and shattered the bushes in front of them, raising a shower of pulverized earth. But the whole line of partisans heaved, as most of the men slithered in animal fashion onto their knees, urgently looking around for a better place. The second shot went off, and this, also predictably, went too far, grating dully against the slope behind. Then the third shell landed, still not on target, but homing inexorably in. The fourth arrived almost exactly on the left-hand corner, and the tearing of vegetation mingled with the screams of the men. But in the settling dust one man stayed poised and erect, and screamed with the high, steady sound of a ringing siren. A shell-fragment had gouged out his eye, and the little globe was running down his cheek-bone like a blob of butter. Then it fell to the ground and in the trampling of retreating men Michele picked up the eye and wrapped it in his blue battle handkerchief. The wounded man, his hands pressed to his face, was taken to the village, from where one of the villagers would transport him to the

borghese l'avrebbe trasportato all'ospedale di Santo Stefano. Il sergente gli aveva ficcato l'involto nella tasca.

Stavano ritirandosi al poggio della Torretta, asperso dalla guasta luce del contrastato sole. Johnny e Michele di retroguardia si voltavano spesso, ma le mimetiche non albeggiavano ancora fra il verde abbandonato. Poi, salendo per il colle costoluto di pietre, ebbero ampia visione dei fascisti che sciamavano verso il paese. Si sedettero sul nudo ciglio e li osservarono in dettaglio e con comodo. Lentissimamente consumavano l'ultima erta, tastando ogni centimetro quadro di terra, soltanto qualche trillo di fischietto imperioso e meschino violava l'immobile atmosfera. Poi gli esploratori dovettero segnalare la nudità del paese, perché accelerarono tutti e scomparvero rapidamente alla vista, ora il paese albergandoli tutti con la sua sorte. «Che faranno al paese?» domandò Pierre. «Niente.» «Come niente?» «Niente. Requisiranno pane e salame, avranno il rancio sulla piazzetta, faranno la predica ai borghesi . . .» E aggiunse il sergente: «Imbratteranno i muri con le loro solite scritte con la vernice nera.»

Aspettarono a lungo un segno di male nel paese, ma non echeggiò uno sparo né si spiralò un ricciolo di fumo. Poi Johnny vide scendere a valle per una segregata stradina un carro agricolo, l'uomo a cassetta[10] tutto giacca e cappello come uno spaventapasseri e guidava la bestia in calma, abbozzando solo di cozzonarla;[11] il corpo del ferito giaceva tra le due sponde, su una delle quali sedeva, inclinato e come predicante, il giovane curato di Mango. L'aria era cosí ferma e tenue, nella sua trasparenza senza sole, che potevi cogliere o arguire il reale attrito di quelle ruote lontane sui banchi petrosi che emergevano da quella strada di scampo e di pace.

Poi alcuni fascisti uscirono dal chiuso dei muri e apparvero sulla strada al colle, ma non con l'aria di riprendere la battaglia, no, erano careless e strolling come in un footing di dopobattaglia. Si sarebbero detti

hospital at Santo Stefano. The sergeant had slipped the little wrapping into his pocket for him.

They were retreating to the Torretta hill, which was sprinkled with uncertain light from the half-obscured sun. Johnny and Michele in the rear kept looking behind, but the camouflages were not yet showing bright against the abandoned green. Then, climbing the stone-ribbed hill, they had an ample view of the Fascists swarming towards the village. They sat down on the bare ridge and watched them in detail and at leisure. Very slowly, they covered the last slope, probing every square inch of ground, the motionless atmosphere violated only by the occasional mean, imperious trill of a whistle. Then the scouts must have signalled that the village was bare, because they all speeded up and disappeared rapidly from sight, the village now embracing them along with its fate. 'What will they do to the village?' asked Pierre. 'Nothing.' 'What do you mean, nothing?' 'Nothing. They'll requisition bread and salami, have their rations in the square, give the villagers a telling-off . . .' And the sergeant added, 'They'll mess up the walls with their usual slogans in black paint.'

They waited for a long time for a sign of suffering from the village, but no shots echoed and no curls of smoke spiralled upwards. Then Johnny saw a farm wagon going down to the valley by a side road, the driver all jacket and hat like a scarecrow and guiding the horse quite calmly, hardly bothering to touch it with his whip; the body of the man who had been wounded lay between the sides of the cart, on one of which sat the young priest from Mango, bent over as if in prayer. The air was so still and thin, in its sunless transparency, that you could pick up or deduce the actual grating of those distant wheels on the stony kerbs which protruded from that peaceful escape road.

Then a few Fascists came out of the walled enclosure and appeared on the road to the hill, but not with the air of re-starting the fight; no, they were careless and strolling as if on an after-battle constitutional. You would have taken

turisti in sopralluogo[12] nemmeno tanto interessato al quotidiano ambiente dei loro mortali nemici, ad ogni passo e punto chiedentisi ciò che essi potevano farci in un qualsiasi momento di un giorno di quella guerra. Ma il sergente si infuriò, disse con quella sua voce sinistra che non sopportava quella vista ed ora si prendeva un pugno di volontari e scendeva a contrarli sulla stradina, a troncare nel sangue quel loro offensivo passeggio. Ma l'imboscata in periferia significava autorizzare i fascisti a mettere a ferro e fuoco il paese, e Michele riandò giú alla terra, con quel suo forte e povero corpo di beduino.[13] Johnny lo toccò sulla schiena. «Sergente, facciamolo stasera, quando se ne andranno via. Hanno poco trasporto e i camions saranno cosí zeppi che non potranno nemmeno manovrarci un braccio. Li sorprenderemo come altrettanti uomini che si beccano il pugno quando hanno la giacca a metà sfilata.» Il sergente capiva. «Potranno solo abbozzare e passar via. Facciamogli un morto e la giornata è nostra. Per chi se ne intende. Lo capirà anche quello di loro che se ne intende. E si mangerà il fegato per tutto il ritorno e per tutta la notte.»

Pierre accettò, ma restava col grosso. Balzò su il sergente, aggruppando le poche piastre residue e quattro altri. I restanti mostrarono le loro saccheggiate giberne o la faccia stanca e scettica.

Si precipitarono per il rovescio del colle e poi a un sostenuto passo di marcia per una stradina, affogata nella forra, parallela alla strada grande, verso il punto di mattutina comparsa dei camions. La conformazione della collina era tale che la stradina sviluppava una lunghezza piú che tripla della strada principale. Johnny però aveva tempo davanti, e conduceva a un passo normale. Contadini apparivano repentini e fissi, come statue che camminando scopri negli interstizi di un giardino. Solo piú avanti, un contadino giovane e critico salí al ciglio della stradina a domandare se scappavano e passando Michele lo schiaffeggiò. La botta partí di

them for tourists on a not very interested inspection of the daily background of their mortal enemies, wondering at every step what they were doing there in a random moment of one day in that war. But the sergeant grew angry, and said in that sinister voice of his that he couldn't bear that sight, and that he was going to take a handful of volunteers and go down to meet them on the road, and bring a bloody interruption to that insulting stroll. But an ambush on the outskirts would be equal to authorizing the Fascists to burn and sack the village, and Michele came back to earth again with his strong spare Bedouin's body. Johnny touched him on the shoulder. 'Sergeant, let's do it this evening, when they are going away. They haven't much transport, and the lorries will be so packed that they won't be able to lift an arm. We'll catch them like a load of men taking it on the chin with their jackets half off.' The sergeant understood. 'They can only fold up and go away. If we kill one of them we've won the day. Anyone who knows what's what will understand. Any one of them who knows his way around will understand. And he will eat his heart out all the way home and all night afterwards.'

Pierre agreed, but stayed with the main body. The sergeant jumped up, collecting the few remaining magazines and four other men. The remainder displayed their empty ammunition pouches, or their tired, sceptical faces.

They dropped down the other side of the hill, and then marched steadily along a track immersed in a ravine, parallel to the main road, towards the point where the lorries had appeared that morning. The formation of the hill was such that the track was more than three times as long as the main road. But Johnny had plenty of time and took them at a normal pace. Peasants appeared, still and sudden, like statues you come across in niches when walking through a garden. Only once, further on, a critical peasant youth climbed to the bank of the track to ask if they were running away, and Michele slapped him as he passed. The

sottobraccio, veloce al punto dell'invisibilità, l'uomo crollò di schiena sulle sue biolche.[14]

Johnny passò in testa, egli stesso meravigliato allo sviluppo della sua falcata. Un uomo si lamentò di male alla milza, il rumore dei camions ancora non viaggiava nell'aria ingrigente, ma non bisognava poi perder troppo tempo a cercare il posto buono dell'agguato. Il sergente conosceva bene la strada e i paraggi? Sí, ma ora era come se tutto gli si fosse cancellato dalla mente. In quel momento sorse sulle colline il rumore della partenza, ma cosí lontano ancora da suonare sottile e giuggiolante.

Salirono sul tufo e vi si appostarono sul ventre. Dopo la scarica si sarebbero lasciati scivolar giú e via per il ritano, ma con cura abbastanza per non slogarsi o rompersi la caviglia. L'immobilizzato sarebbe stato il maggior martire della guerra: avrebbe dovuto morire mille volte in olocausto al fascista ucciso. Alle loro spalle, sull'altro ciglio del ritano,[15] fra i vapori della guazza e lo scuro delle macchie una casa solitaria sbianchiva e fumava nella sera, le voci degli ignari abitanti come pigolio di uccelli nel nido già oppresso dal buio.

L'esposizione sulla strada era orribilmente diretta, benché dal tufo non emergessero che le loro fronti febbricitanti. Il sergente disse: «Perdonate, ma debbo farlo», e si voltò di fianco e orinò, il liquido frisse sul calcare. Gli altri erano della campagna, stolidi e fissi, stringevano i fucili quasi a sformarli.

Erano ancora lontani, ma il rumore era già tanto e tale che Johnny ebbe tutti i capelli ritti in testa all'idea del volume totale in transito. Disse con voce stentata: «All'ultimo camion, eh? All'ultimo.» Era difficile, l'ultimo camion: o la colonna ti immobilizza di terrore al punto che tutti i camions, l'ultimo incluso, ti passa sotto il naso o l'orgasmo ti fa sparare addirittura al primo della colonna. Michele disse con angoscia del Breda: «Mi si incepperà dopo tre colpi.»

Il rumore si avvicinava, ed era terribile come e piú

blow came from the shoulder, so fast as to be invisible, and the man collapsed backwards onto his acres.

Johnny moved up front, himself amazed that his encircling thrust was actually coming off. One man complained of a stitch, the noise of the lorries was not yet travelling through the greying air, but they mustn't waste too much time finding the best place for the ambush. Did the Sergeant know the road and surroundings well? Yes, but right now everything seemed to have been blotted from his mind. At that moment over the hills rose the noise of the troops' departure, but still so far away as to sound thin and wavering.

They climbed onto the tufa rock, and lay down there on their stomachs. After firing they would slide down and be off along the gully, taking care not to dislocate or break an ankle. Anyone immobilized would be the biggest martyr of the war: he would have to die a thousand times as a sacrifice for the dead Fascist. At their backs, on the other edge of the gully, among the swirls of mist and the dark of the undergrowth, a solitary house showed white, smoking in the evening, the voices of its unheeding inhabitants like the chirping of birds in a nest already wrapped in darkness.

Their exposure towards the road was horribly direct, although only their feverish foreheads stood out from the rock. The Sergeant said: 'Sorry, but I've got to', turned sideways and urinated; the liquid hissed on the limestone. The others were countrymen, stolid and motionless, gripping their rifles almost hard enough to bend them.

They were still a long way away, but the noise was already so loud that Johnny's hair was all standing on end at the thought of the total number being transported. He said in a strained voice: 'The last lorry, eh? The last.' It was difficult, the last lorry: either the convoy paralyses you with terror so that all the lorries, including the last, pass under your nose; or else you shoot in a spasm of nervousness at the first of the convoy. Michele said of the Breda, in anguish: 'It'll seize up on me after three shots.'

The noise drew nearer, and it was terrible how, more than

che un rumore di motori fosse uno strepito di armi. A tutti stavano rizzandosi i capelli in testa, con una gelida vitalità in punta e alle radici. Dal forsennato rombo si enucleava anche un cantare dei soldati, urlato e dopolavoristico. «Imbecilli,» pensò Johnny e stette ragionevolmente calmo.

Uscirono dalla curva, a fari spenti, lemuri[16] d'urto nell'incredula sera. I cinque stavano sul tufo come affacciati alle sponde stesse dei camions, sentendosi nudi ed esposti per la trafissione. La colonna era tutta sbucata, le macchine a gli uomini larvali, dai bordi emergevano anche macchie biancastre come di bestiame requisito. Gli uomini cantavano a squarciagola, e le disgregate e note parole piú del rombo dei motori ventavano con ala letale in faccia agli imboscanti.

Quello era certamente l'ultimo camion di coda. Spararono con tutte le armi nella linea di spettri affacciata alla sponda. Due, tre si contorsero, uno cadde in strada, come se il colpo fosse una proditoria mano di vento che l'avesse afferrato e sbalzato. Il camion sussultò, ebbe un impulso e una remora, come se il conducente avesse frenato e poi l'ufficiale in cabina gli avesse urlato di accelerare, in una macinata agonia di ruote e terreno.

Mentre rotolavano lungo il tufo spettrale verso il ritano già tenebroso, sentirono il fracasso d'arresto di tutta la colonna, i trilli di fischietto che punteggivano l'universale clamore di odio e spavento, qualche fucilata ed il tonfo di qualche bomba a mano azzardata.

I cinque se ne andavano leggieri e tranquilli via per il nero ritano, dopo un po' Johnny ed anche il sergente accendendosi una sigaretta. Si era sentita la generale rimessa in moto, verso la pianura, i motori stessi intonandosi al vano odio e vendicatività degli uomini. Solo dopo un lungo tratto salirono alla strada principale per tenerla fino in paese. Il Breda era inceppato ma per festeggiamento Michele l'avrebbe riparato soltanto domattina.

a noise of engines, it sounded like the clash of weapons. Everyone's hair was standing on end, with an icy vitality at the tips and the roots. Amidst the insane roaring one could also make out the soldiers singing in an abandoned off-duty howl. 'Idiots,' thought Johnny, and he stayed reasonably calm.

They came out round the bend with their headlamps off, antique ghosts quite out of tune with the incredulous evening. The five men lay on the rock almost peeping over the sides of the lorries, feeling naked and quite open to the first piercing bullet. The convoy had all emerged, vehicles and eerie men together; white patches stuck out from the sides, probably requisitioned animals. The men were roaring out their song, and the disjointed, familiar words even more than the rumble of the engines were blown on lethal wings into the faces of the ambushers.

This was certainly the last lorry in the line. They fired all their weapons into the row of phantoms looking over the side. Two, three of them crumpled up, one fell into the road, as if the shot were a treacherous gust of wind that had seized and whisked him over. The lorry jerked, at once leaping forward and hesitating, as if the driver had braked and then the officer in the cab had yelled at him to accelerate, in a jarring agony of wheels and earth.

As they rolled down the spectral rock towards the already dark gully, they heard the noise of the convoy stopping, the whistle-notes punctuating the general clamour of hatred and panic, a few rifle shots and the boom of a few hand-grenades thrown at random.

The five men slipped lightly and quietly down the black ravine, and after a while both Johnny and the sergeant lit cigarettes. They had heard the column move off again towards the plain, even the engines seeming to echo the vain hatred and vindictiveness of the men. Only after a long stretch did they climb to the main road and follow it back to the village. The Breda had jammed, but to celebrate Michele was going to leave mending it until the morning.

Si sentiva il paese rioccupato da Pierre, ed esso luceva di molte luci nell'alta sera, come se, dopo aver fronteggiato i fascisti, si sentisse di sfidare anche gli aeroplani notturni. Molto probabilmente, in quel momento tutti i paesi circostanti e coscienziosamente oscurati, stavano domandandosi che mai facesse Mango. Piú dappresso, si sentiva un sussurrio concitato e trepido, critico ed orgoglioso, che disse a Johnny nulla essere assolutamente accaduto al paese. Tutta la gente si era riversata nella strada che taglia il paese da un capo all'altro, e si era miscelata ai reduci partigiani, nell'alone grezzo e casalingo delle luci interne, in una confortante specie di pubblica conversazione festiva. Johnny mandò il sergente a riferire a Pierre e attraversò l'ibrida ressa. La gente era straordinariamente loquace ed euforica, di chi è uscito egregiamente da una prova ineluttabile e temuta e può ora sperare in un lungo periodo di untriedness.

I fascisti si erano fermati per ore, ma non avevano combinato nulla. Avevano sí requisito un sacco di roba, rimandando per il pagamento al maresciallo Badoglio (a proposito, il governo di dopo avrebbe riconosciuto anche questo tipo di danni?), avevano consumato un ricco e comodo rancio sulla piazza del Comune, poi piú che terrorizzato avevano burlato e schernito la rigida abbottonata gente per aver puntato e puntare sulla sconfitta degli invincibili Mussolini e Hitler e infine si erano messi a lordare i muri per l'edificazione dei partigiani: viva il Duce, viva il maresciallo Graziani,[17] viva il loro comandante di battaglione, morte ai partigiani, formale promessa a Nord[18] di tornare a catturarlo e scuoiarlo vivo. Pierre aveva già spedito una staffetta a Nord e se ne attendeva l'arrivo da un'ora all'altra, a prendere diretta visione della scritta che lo riguardava. Johnny andò a vederla, i caratteri balenavano nel malfermo alone, neri, laccati e corposi.

Il sergente stava urlandogli da qualche angolo che venisse a mangiare, ma non ci andò direttamente.

You could tell that the village had been re-occupied by Pierre, it shone with many lights in the deep evening, as if after facing up to Fascists it felt up to challenging night planes as well. Very probably at that moment all the surrounding villages, conscientiously blacked out, were wondering what on earth Mango was up to. From closer in one could hear a murmur of agitation and nervousness, complaint and pride, which told Johnny that absolutely nothing had happened there. Everybody had poured out into the street, which cuts through the village from one end to the other, and mingled with the returned partisans, in the crude, homely glow of the lights from the houses, all in a kind of comforting, festive public conversation. Johnny sent the sergeant to report to Pierre and passed through the hybrid throng. The people were amazingly talkative and euphoric, as though they had passed honourably through an unavoidable and dreaded ordeal, and can hope for a long period of 'untriedness'.

The Fascists had stayed for hours but had done nothing. Yes, they had requisitioned a load of stuff, referring them to Marshal Badoglio for payment (come to that, would the post-war government recognize this type of loss too?), they had had a plentiful, comfortable meal in the Town Hall square, then they had teased and mocked rather than terrorized the stiff, buttoned people for having bet and betting still on the defeat of the unconquerable Mussolini and Hitler; and finally they had soiled the walls for the edification of the partisans: long live the Duce, long live Marshal Graziani, long live their battalion commander, death to the partisans, and a solemn promise to Nord to come back, capture him and skin him alive. Pierre had already sent a runner to Nord, and expected him to arrive at any moment to see for himself the inscription concerning him. Johnny went to see it; the letters stood out in the uncertain light, black, lacquered and solid.

The sergeant was shouting from a corner for him to come and eat, but he did not go straight away. He lit a cigarette,

Accesasi una sigaretta, andò a un limite del paese. E andando, ripensava all'agguato: aveva fatto un'imboscata ed aveva sicuramente ucciso: era un gran passo avanti ed un compenso e rimerito per la sua propria morte.

Sordo al replicato richiamo di Michele, stava ad un muricciolo, alto sulla voragine della valle, già colma di notte. Dove egli stava era l'ultimo lembo di atmosfera immota, la soglia di una zona fornace di venti, da dove saliva un oceanico rifischiare di vortici. Tremò largamente e a lungo.

and walked to the edge of the village. As he walked he thought of the ambush: he had lain in wait and he had certainly killed: it was a big step forward, a consolation and a revenge for his own eventual death.

Deaf to Michele's repeated calls, he leaned by a low wall, high above the gulf of the valley already filled with night. Where he stood was the last edge of motionless atmosphere, the threshold of a blazing belt of wind, from which rose an oceanic screeching of tornadoes. He shivered hard for a long time.

THE TART

PIER PAOLO PASOLINI

Translated by John Higgitt

(Outline for a film producer)

MIGNOTTA

(Relazione per un produttore)[1]

Con la schiena contro un muricciolo, Mario un po' mangiava un po' cantava.

Davanti a lui, sul marciapiede ancora di terra battuta, stavano i tre napoletani;[2] e, intorno, sparsi tra gli sterri, tutti gli altri operai, sui fogli ciancicati delle loro colazioni, o sull'erba bianca, sotto il sole dell'una, che non faceva ancora venir sonno, ma metteva addosso l'allegria come ai ragazzi che aspettano davanti alle scuole, correndo e scherzando.

Mario e i tre napoletani stavano discutendo, con quell'allegria addosso, su chi di loro quattro era il più bello.

«Mo perchè me vedete così,» faceva Mario, «ma si me venite, a vede' de domenica, appena m'acchitto, faccio 'na rapina a tutta Centocelle, 'o sapete, sì?»

«Hè!» fece il più giovincello dei napoletani, mentre tutti tre continuavano a ciancicare il loro sfilatino con la mortadella come cani. «Perchè, noi no?» disse poi a suo comodo, il più grosso. Mario fece ciac con la lingua, come se avesse sentito in bocca un sapore, rattristante, di amaro. «Ma se nun pagate manco li ciechi,» disse poi amaramente ridendo.

«Se, se,» ribattè il più giovincello, «beato te!». «Nun ce guardà così,» fece Gennarino il mezzano, guardandosi la canottiera trucida sopra le sua quattr'ossa, e i calzonacci bianchi di calce, con sopra l'ombra del berretto di carta di giornale, «guàrdace in fotografia!» Mario fu preso da uno scoppio di risa, che sputò a tre metri il boccone che stava masticando: e rise fermo gonfiandosi tutto in faccia, come se lo scuotesse una scarica elettrica. «Guarda un po',» fece allora Alfio, il più piccoletto e cattivo: e

THE TART

(Outline for a film producer)

Mario was leaning against a wall, sometimes eating, sometimes singing.

Standing in front of him on the pavement, still made of beaten earth, were the three Neapolitans; and around him dotted about among the heaps of earth were the other workmen, some sitting on the crumpled bits of paper in which their lunches had been wrapped and some on the bleached grass under the one o'clock sun, not yet strong enough to make you sleepy but which made you happy as it does boys running around and playing, while waiting outside school.

Mario and the three Neapolitans were arguing in the same cheerful way about who was the best-looking of the four.

'Now you see me looking like this,' said Mario, 'but s'pose you came and saw me on Sundays when I'm dressed up. I'd beat them all hollow in Centocelle, I'm telling you.'

'You what!' exclaimed the youngest of the Neapolitans, while all three went on gnawing their bread and mortadella like dogs. 'What? so we wouldn't then?' said the biggest of them, when he was ready. Mario clicked his tongue, as if put off by a nasty taste in his mouth. 'But you wouldn't even attract a blind man,' he said with a bitter laugh.

'Yeah,' replied the youngest of them, 'it's all right for you.' 'We're no good like this,' said Gennarino, the middle one, looking at the ragged vest hanging from his bony shoulders and his old trousers white with chalk, his face shaded by his hat of folded newspaper, 'but you should see a photo of us!' Mario burst out laughing which made the bite he was chewing shoot out three yards. He laughed hard, his face swelling, as if shaken by an electric shock. 'Take a look at this,' said Alfio, the shortest and most devilish of the

cacciò dalla saccoccia di dietro dei calzoni, un vecchio portafoglio tubercoloso.[3] «'Mbe'?» fece Mario che aveva subito smesso di ridere, facendo l'innocente: e s'accucciò, da seduto che stava, mettendo la faccia tra le schiene dei tre napoletani, in fila sull'orlo del marciapiede.

Soli o in gruppo, incravattati o in canottiera, col vestito a righe, o i panni malandrini di lavoro, a San Giovanni la notte della festa, o sull'arenile di Ostia in mutandine, i tre napoletani non scherzavano proprio. Ma nemmeno Mario, però, scherzava: aveva cacciato subito le fotografie pure lui, e prima di tutte quella, con la pettinata alla ghigo e il bocchino, ch'era rimasta esposta per tre mesi nella vetrina del fotografo sotto casa, a via dei Faggi. Guardandosi l'un con l'altro le fotografie dovettero ammettere che la lotta era dura, e farsi tanto di cappello. Per decidere chi era più bello allora chiamarono a far da giudice un certo Cecione, un ciccione cattivo, con la faccia da culo,[4] che stava un po' più in là parlando minacciosamente della Roma.[5] Questo s'accostò, stette a sentire com'era la questione, tanto più nero in faccia quanto più si sentiva lusingato per l'incarico: e cominciò a fare le cose con serietà. Si prese i portafogli di Mario e dei napoletani, e cominciò a osservare con aria competente, guardando le fotografie un po' da lontano, con la testa piegata da una parte.

Ma tutt'a un botto, com'è come non è, saltò in piedi, strillando: «Ammazza, òuh»:[6] e come gli altri cercavano di avvicinarsi per vedere o avere spiegazioni, lui li spingeva via a gomitate e a spinte, tenendosi stretta davanti agli occhi la fotografia che gli aveva dato quell'attacco di petto. Poi andò a rannicchiarsi, col suo fisico di balena e le basettone sulle guance arrossate, contro una ramata: pareva un masso di cemento, e chi poteva accostarglisi e vedere che cosa teneva tra le

three, and he pulled out from the back pocket of his trousers an old, consumptive wallet. 'What's that then?' said Mario who had at once stopped laughing and was playing the innocent. He bent forward from where he was sitting, looking over the shoulders of the three Neapolitans, who were in a row on the edge of the pavement.

The three Neapolitans were deadly serious about their photographs – individually or in groups, wearing a tie or in their vests, in a striped suit, or in their scruffy, old working clothes, in San Giovanni on the night of the dance, or in their bathing trunks on the beach at Ostia. But Mario wasn't joking either – he had at once pulled out some photos of his own and first of all the one with his hair smarmed down in a Rudolph Valentino style and with a cigarette holder, which had been on show for three months in the window of the photographer's under their flat in the Via dei Faggi. Passing the photos to each other, they had to admit that it was a close matter and had to take their hats off to one another. To decide who was the best-looking, they then called over someone called Cecione to act as judge. He was a nasty, fattish kind of a man with a face like the back-end of a bus, who was a little way off, talking aggressively about Roma. This Cecione came over to hear what it was all about; he looked more and more gloomy, as he felt more and more flattered by his task. He opened the proceedings with gravity. He took the wallets off Mario and the Neapolitans and began his inspection in a professional manner, looking at the photos, holding them a little away from himself, with his head on one side.

But all of a sudden, inexplicably, he jumped up yelling 'Christ!' And as the others tried to get near to see what he was on about, he elbowed and pushed them away, holding the photo which had given him this apoplectic fit up to his eyes. He then went and crouched down against a wire-netting fence – a whale-like form with great side-boards on his red cheeks. He looked like a block of concrete, and no one would have dared to come up and see what he could be holding that interested him so much. 'What is it,

mani e lo interessava tanto? «Che c'è, a Cecione? Ah Cecioneeee . . .» faceva Mario, incuriosito come un ragazzino. Ma quello niente. Finalmente, dopo un bel po', il Cecione cantò: «A pazzi,» fece, «stanno a ffà chi è er più bello fra loro, 'sti becaccioni!» Fece anche «pct» con la lingua, come sentendo pure lui nella bocca un sapore amaro che lo rattristava. E mostrò a tutti, in giro, la fotografia che l'aveva tanto arrazzato.

Alfio, Gennaro e Santino Postiglione era poco più d'un anno che stavano a abitare a Roma. Abitavano in uno di quei villaggetti fuori legge che i napoletani costruiscono in una notte,[7] immigrando; e che poi lasciano ai loro parenti. E così appunto aveva fatto loro zio, che ora s'era fatto il soldo, prima col traffico delle Americane, e poi accroccando, a Centocelle,[8] una di quelle salette trucide col calcio-balilla, ritrovo dei pischelli più malandri di via delle Robinie, di via dei Castani, di via dei Ciliegi, di via delle Mimose, di via dei Geranei e di via degli Oleandri.[9]

La fotografia di Nannina era del più piccolo. Così, come tornarono al lavoro, fino a sera, Mario l'arruffianò con lui: ci buttò mezzo pacchetto di Nazionali.[10] L'altro fumava e taceva, con aria brava: e la fotografia ben infilata nella saccoccia interna. Come staccarono, Mario fece tutto con loro: si lavò alla fontanella, si pettinò, uscì dal cantiere, e, appena fuori, gli volle offrire il caffè al Bar 2000. Parlavano già come gente che sta facendo un affare, e tira, con la massima cortesia, a fregarsi a vicenda.

Mario arrivò al punto che la sera dopocena andò con Alfio a giocare al calcio-balilla: e fu lì, solo con lui, che girò le cose in modo da rivedere la fotografia. Era di una bellezza, questa Nannina, da far fiorire le margherite a Natale.[11] Pure i pischelletti lì intorno l'avevano svagato, quei «fiji de 'na mignotta»,[12] come li chiamò Alfio, facendo una gran caciara intorno a Mario, che

Cecione? Cecione . . .' said Mario, full of boyish curiosity. But the other said nothing. At last, after a long time, Cecione sang out: 'These idiots are trying to find out which one of them is the best-looking!' He also clicked his tongue, as if he too had been put off by a bitter taste in his mouth. And he showed the photograph which had so excited him to everyone in turn.

It was little more than a year that Alfio, Gennaro and Santino Postiglione had lived in Rome. They lived in one of those little outlaw villages which the Neapolitans build in the space of a night, when they come up from the South, and which they then leave to their relations. And that was just what their uncle had done – he had now made some money, first selling American cigarettes on the black market and later building up in Centocelle one of those delapidated little bar-football places, which had become the meeting place of the roughest boys from Via delle Robinie, Via dei Castani, Via dei Ciliegi, Via delle Mimose, Via dei Geranei and Via degli Oleandri.

The photo of Nannina belonged to the smallest of the three and so, while they went back to work and up until the evening, Mario made up to him – he used half a packet of Nazionali in the process. The other smoked in silence, looking smug, the photograph tucked well away in his inside pocket. As they knocked off, Mario did everything with them: washed with them at the fountain, combed his hair with them and left work with them and, when they were outside, he offered them a coffee at the Bar 2000. They were already talking as if transacting some business and very politely trying to swindle each other.

Things progressed so far that Mario met Alfio in the evening after supper for a game of bar-football, and it was there, alone with him that he managed to get another look at the photograph. This Nannina was so beautiful that she would have made the flowers bloom in winter. Even the kids around them had gathered what was going on. Those 'little bastards', as Alfio called them, started making a great din

s'era subito impeciato. Alfio si riprese la fotografia, chè aveva capito benissimo che la cosa andava sfruttata: e le dosi dovevano esser piccole. Era stabilito – malgrado quella piccola, innocente concessione al capriccio di Mario – che sua sorella non si toccava.

A chi gliel'avesse detto quel giorno e i giorni appresso, a Mario, ch'era innamorato come un poeta antico, lui gli avrebbe riso in faccia; e così i tre napoletani, con quell'aria di gente che fiuta un affare in cui non ha niente da perdere, e che ha tutto il tempo dalla parte sua. Mario non se la passava male; abitava in un appartamentino di Centocelle – in coabitazione, magari – con la madre e le sorelle che lavoravano. I tre napoletani non avevano la residenza a Roma; abitavano in una baracca: e lo zio non cacciava una brecola. Così entrando in rapporto d'affari con Mario e la famiglia – che non ci capiva niente – avevano trovato un tetto. Il fatto è che più stava più Mario pensava a quella fotografia, diventata presto celebre nei dintorni: sicchè finalmente l'affare un po' alla volta, per farla breve, si concluse, primo, col passaggio della fotografia dalle saccocce dei tre fratelli a quelle di Mario; secondo col permesso di scrivere a Nannina – che era, del resto, analfabeta, e gli faceva rispondere da uno del suo paese; e infine col fidanzamento per corrispondenza:

> E lo mi Ammore sta a Centocelle:
> me manda li saluti pe le stelle,
> je li rimanno pe le rondinelle.

Nannina arrivò a Roma un mattino di primavera. L'aspettavano alla stazione i tre fratelli e il fidanzato, belli come nelle fotografie. Lei scese dall'accelerato,[13] spaventata e cattiva, con dietro la madre piena di ceste, e lei stessa piegata sotto i fagotti. Era ancora più bella di come il fidanzato se l'immaginava. Le presentarono subito Mario, che s'era tutto gonfiato, per farla restare subito impeciata di lui: arruffata e sudata, Nannina gli

around Mario, who at once became embarrassed. Alfio took back the photograph, because he realized that the situation was to be exploited – and anyway the doses had to be small. It was clear – in spite of that little, innocent concession to Mario's whims – that his sister was to be left alone.

If anybody then or in the next few days had told Mario that he had got it as bad as the average poet of long ago, he'd have laughed in his face. The three Neapolitans, who looked as if they could smell a deal in which they couldn't lose and in which time was on their side, would have done the same. Mario was not badly off. He lived in a small flat in Centocelle, even though he shared the place with his mother and sisters who went out to work. The three Neopolitans didn't have a proper address in Rome – they lived in a shack and their uncle didn't give them a penny. And so by doing business with Mario and his family, who did not know what was going on, they had got themselves a roof. The fact is that as time went by Mario thought more and more about the photograph, which was soon famous all around. The result was that at last, perhaps a bit suddenly, to speed things up, the deal was concluded: first with the passing of the photograph from the pockets of the three brothers to those of Mario; secondly with their permission to write to Nannina, who was, anyway illiterate, and who got someone from her village to write back to him; and lastly with a postal engagement:

> My sweetheart lives in Centocelle,
> And sends me messages by the stars,
> And the swallows carry back word from me to my love.

Nannina arrived in Rome one spring morning and waiting for her at the station were her three brothers and her fiancé, all looking as good as in their photographs. She got off the slow train and looked nervous and sulky; her mother was following her, laden with baskets and she herself was bent under her bundles. She was even more beautiful than her fiancé had imagined. At once they introduced her to Mario, who had drawn himself up, so that she would im-

diede appena retta, tutta presa dal grande incontro famigliare: madre, fratelli e lei stessa che strillavano come al mercato di Benevento.[14] Così cominciò la loro vita in comune. Uscirono dalla stazione con Mario che cercava di rendere pubblico il suo possesso su di lei, prendendola solennemente a braccetto, e lei, selvatica, che gli sfuggiva. Gli amici di Mario esprimevano alla luce del sole il suo stato interiore: «Ammazzate, che burina,» si dicevano fra loro, e subito dopo: «Ma quant'è bbona!»

Si cominciò infatti con una scazzottatura. Nel tranvetto. Era pieno di gente; e alcuni giovanotti di Torpignattara,[15] vedendo quella bellezza, con la madre intontonita, non accorgendosi, nella ressa, che c'era il corpo di guardia, avevano cominciato a alzar moina e a marciarci. Finirono col fare le loro scuse. Ma pure stavolta furono gli amici di Mario che definirono la situazione: «È come si ne sposassi venti!»

Non parliamo dell'incontro con la famiglia di Mario. Nell'appartamentino di Centocelle ci capivano[16] appena: benchè i coabitanti se la fossero discretamente squagliata, accroccandosi in una camera.

La madre di Mario era una tardona, grossa grossa: fruttarola a piazza Vittorio da trent'anni. Una dritta[17] che non finiva mai. Non ci si seppe vedere fin dal primo momento con quelle due burine per casa. Ancora più dritte, le due figlie minori: a cui non c'era nessuno al mondo che fosse in grado di tappare la bocca: e mica erano poco sboccate, soprattutto quando si trattasse di sfottere, e ancor più quando si trattasse di far valere i propri sacrosanti diritti. Se le guardarono, la cognata e la madre, e per poco non sbottarono sotto i loro occhi a sbudellarsi dal ridere: ma adottarono per sfotterle una tecnica leggera, vigliacca – per quanto in fondo bonacciona. La terza figlia faceva invece l'aristocratica: dato ch'era impiegata alla Banca d'Italia: amava i vestiti grigi, di taglio serio – e da questa sua predilezione era

mediately fall for him. Nannina was all ruffled and sweaty and scarcely noticed him, because she was quite taken up with the great family reunion – her mother, brothers and herself were shouting as they do in the market at Benevento. And that was how their life together began. They left the station with Mario trying to broadcast that she was his, taking her solemnly by the arm, and with her bashfully trying to get away from him. Mario's friends expressed openly what he felt inside: 'My God, what a yokel!' they said to each other, and then they would immediately follow this with: 'but she's quite something to look at!'

They started off in fact with a fight. It was in the tram, which was full of people. Some youths from Torpignattara, seeing this beauty with her bewildered mother and not noticing in the crowd that she was being guarded, started to pass comments and show off in front of her. They ended up by apologizing. But this time too Mario's friends summed up the situation: 'It's as if you were marrying twenty of them!'

We will pass over the meeting with Mario's family. In the little flat in Centocelle there was hardly room for everybody, although the other residents of the flat had discreetly got out of the way and were piled into one bedroom.

Mario's mother was a big, fat, frumpy woman, who had been selling fruit on Piazza Vittorio for thirty years. She was exceptionally well able to look after herself. From the first moment she could not stand the idea of having the two country women around the house. The two younger sisters were even sharper than their mother. No one in the world was able to shut them up and they didn't half use bad language, especially when they were taking the micky out of them and even more so when they were insisting on their own precious rights. Whenever they looked at their sister-in-law and her mother, they could scarcely stop themselves from bursting out into helpless laughter in front of them. But they went about mocking them in a subtle, cowardly way – even if it was at bottom good-natured. The third daughter, however, put on airs, because

continuamente messa in uno stato d'animo offeso contro il cattivo gusto dei residenti a Centocelle – parlava in francese per telefono col parrucchiere di via Veneto[18] che la pelava; e per tutto l'anno viveva in vista dei quindici giorni di ferie a Cortina – dove quasi sempre pioveva: era la cognata che meno ci voleva per una pecorara.[19]

I tre giorni che precedettero le nozze furono però completamente dedicati all'organizzazione: s'era accesa una specie di lotta sorda, ma feconda, tra i romani – compresi i coabitanti – e i burini, nella ricerca di un compromesso tra i due mondi. Nannina e sua madre, intanto, erano state sistemate nel tugurio dei tre fratelli maschi: la prima in via provvisoria, la seconda definitivamente. Ci si erano trovate subito come a casa loro. Lì si faceva tutto all'aperto, fra grandi strilli, risate e litigi: la vecchia madre, Assunta, esaltata dal matrimonio, e priva del senso del mutamento geografico, si comportava come se fosse rimasta al paese: urtando i suoi figli e conterranei, che si sentivano smascherati da lei, ricondotti ai primi tempi dell'immigrazione – e eccitando il senso umoristico degli indigeni della borgata – sfrattati – che, in stretta intesa tra loro, la inchiodavano con due sparate secche a mezza voce. Il destino di Assunta era quello di esser ridotta poco a poco al completo silenzio.

Nannina, per intanto, condivideva il suo entusiasmo di sistemazione: e era così distratta da questo, che Mario, sempre più accanito a sentirsene e a mostrarsene possessore, era sempre meno filato da lei. D'altra parte anche Mario era completamente immerso nel lavoro organizzativo. Alle nozze, tra i parenti di lui e di lei, nella pizzeria di via delle Genziane dove si fece il pranzo, c'era quasi un intero paese: fatto il calcolo, che in precedenza era stato fatto approssimativamente, risultarono presenti alle nozze sessanta ragazzini.

she worked in the Banca d'Italia. She liked grey clothes of a sober cut – and this preference of hers was always being offended by the bad taste of those who lived in Centocelle. She spoke French over the telephone to the hairdresser on the Via Veneto who always charged the earth. She lived the whole year for her two-week holiday in Cortina – where it nearly always rained. She was the least likely person to be the sister-in-law of a peasant girl.

The three days before the wedding, however, were completely taken up with making the arrangements. A sort of silent but very fertile feud had opened between the Romans – including the other tenants – and the peasants, in the search for a compromise between the two different worlds. In the meanwhile, Nannina and her mother were put up in the hovel where the three brothers lived – the former only temporarily, the latter for good. There they had at once felt themselves at home. Everything was done there out in the open, amid shouting, laughter and quarrelling. The old mother, Assunta, excited by the marriage, and not appreciating the geographical change, behaved just as at home, irritating her sons and the others from where she came, who felt that she was unmasking them, and as if they were newly arrived immigrants all over again. And she aroused the sense of humour of the natives of the town, who had been evicted and who collaborated closely in shutting her up by muttering a few sarcastic remarks. It was Assunta's fate to be reduced little by little to complete silence.

Meanwhile Nannina was busy sharing her mother's enthusiasm for getting organized. She was so taken up by this that she paid less and less attention to Mario who was growing ever more eager to feel and show his possession of her. Besides Mario was also completely wrapped up in organizing things. At the wedding, what with his relations and hers, there were enough people to make up a small village in the pizzeria on Via delle Genziane, where they had the feast. When they had worked out the numbers, as they had done roughly beforehand, it turned out that there were sixty children alone at the wedding.

La sera Nannina fece il suo ingresso ufficiale nell'appartamentino di via dei Sambuchi.

L'appartamentino consisteva in quattro camere, la cucina, il bagno, l'ingresso e uno sgabuzzino: due camere erano occupate dalla famiglia di Mario, le altre due e lo sgabuzzino dai coabitanti – che erano otto – e la cucina in comune. Delle due camere a cui aveva diritto la famiglia di Mario, in una dormivano le donne, nell'altra i maschi, ossia Mario e l'ultimo figlio, giusto nell'età in cui i pischelli cominciano a lavorare: faceva il garzone[20] del lattaio di via dei Faggi. In seguito al matrimonio, fu spostato e sistemato nell'ingresso. E la camera fu libera per i due sposi.

La faccenda diventò molto imbarazzante, quando venne il momento di andare a dormire – imbarazzante per tutti fuorchè per Nannina. Alduccio, il fratello piccolo, e gli altri ragazzini della casa, avevano certe facce che prenderli a schiaffi era poco: gli altri manifestavano chiaramente di fare un sacrificio, ma di sacrificarsi volentieri, con tutto l'appoggio e la simpatia. Nina, la sorella impiegata, era sostenuta, il signor Finamore, il capo famiglia dei coabitanti, era scherzoso, insomma nessuno riusciva a staccare il pensiero da lì.

Quando Mario e Nannina entrarono in camera, era la prima volta in vita loro che stavano insieme da soli. Mario, tanto malandrino di solito, fece pena a se stesso: «Me sputerebbe in un occhio,» pensava, mentre tentava in qualche modo di entrare in confidenza con la sposa. Questa era un capolavoro misto di goffaggine e di lenzaggine, di impazienza e di rassegnazione, con quegli occhi che un po' luccicavano d'ironia e disprezzo, un po' fissavano ingenui e infantili. Mario fece di tutto per farla un po' parlare, prima. ... Diceva «sì» o «no» oppure «mannaggia». Lui tentò tutte le strade: cercò perfino di mettersi, lui!, sotto una luce romantica, a proposito della fotografia; finì addirittura col cantare, a mezza

That evening Nannina officially entered the little flat in Via dei Sambuchi.

The flat consisted of four bedrooms, a kitchen, a bathroom, a hall and a small box-room. Two bedrooms were occupied by Mario's family, the other two and the box-room by the other tenants – who numbered eight. They shared the kitchen. Of the two bedrooms allotted to Mario's family one was used by the women, the other by the men – that is, Mario and the youngest brother, who was just the age when boys first start work. He worked at the dairy on Via dei Faggi. Because of the marriage he was moved out and put in the hall. The bedroom was free for the bridal couple.

It all became very embarrassing, when it was time to go to bed – embarrassing for everyone except Nannina. Alduccio, the youngest brother, and the other children in the house exchanged significant looks so that they seemed at the very least to be asking for a slap round the face. The others made it very clear by their assistance and kindness that they were making a sacrifice, but that they were doing so gladly. Nina, the sister who worked at the bank, behaved stiffly. Signor Finamore, the head of the family that shared the flat, was being jolly. In short no one could take their minds off the subject.

When Mario and Nannina got into their bedroom, it was the first time in their lives that they had been alone together. Mario, who was usually so sure of himself, now felt embarrassed. 'She would spit in my face if she could,' he thought, while he tried to find a way to win over his bride. She was a prize example of clumsiness and native wit, of impatience and resignation; her eyes sometimes sparkled ironically and scornfully and sometimes stared with childlike ingenuousness. Mario did everything possible to get her talking a bit, before. . . . She would say, 'Yes' or 'No' or perhaps 'Heavens'. He tried every possible way. He tried too to show himself – he of all people – in a romantic light with the story about the photograph. He even ended up singing

voce, ma con tutto il sentimento, una canzone napoletana – che lei non sapeva: – niente. Nannina cadeva dal sonno, e finì con l'appennicarsi. Un po' ubriaco, Mario s'appennicò pure lui. Dormirono mezzi vestiti.

La seconda notte di nozze non fu meglio. I signori Finamore, i coabitanti, avevano l'aria di chi sta sempre sul punto d'andarsene via – a star meglio, naturalmente, in un appartamento da quarantamila lire![21] – e ciò in base alla genialità del signor Roberto Finamore, il quale lavorava in una ditta come disegnatore, ma la sua vocazione era altra: lo scrittore, per esempio, o l'inventore. Anzi, da più di due anni, la famiglia Finamore puntava tutto su un suo brevetto riguardante un cappelletto automatico per i tubi di dentifricio, tanto che viveva già nell'aria di agio e buongusto che, alla fine delle laboriose trattative con importanti enti e persone, quel brevetto le avrebbe procurato. Il fatto è che non se ne andavano mai. E anzi, proprio quella notte, con due mesi d'anticipo, la signora Finamore fu presa dalle doglie e diede alla luce il settimo Finamore.

Il giorno dopo era domenica. Aspettando con impazienza la sera, Mario si portò la sposa dentro Roma, a spasso; prima su e giù per via Veneto, poi all'Ambra Jovinelli, dove si videro lo spettacolo due volte. Nannina era ora chiusa e sorda come un riccio, ora espansiva come una bambina, ridicola almeno quanto era bella. Mario – specialmente nel difficile frangente dell'entrata all'Ambra Jovinelli, che c'era tanta gente che dovette intervenire la Celere – godette tutte le possibili gioie della vanità e tutte le possibili amarezze delle magre.... Quando finalmente arrivarono a casa, trovarono che la «loro» camera era occupata. Era successo che la Nina – ch'era andata a Palestrina[22] in pullman coi suoi colleghi della Banca d'Italia – aveva avuto la fortuna di cadere e di fratturarsi un braccio. Sentendosi malata e infelice, non volle lasciarsi sfuggire nessuno dei vantaggi sentimentali che ne derivavano: aveva voluto – col generale appoggio – una camera tutta per sè, e ben rimessa in

softly though passionately a Neapolitan song, which she didn't know. It was no good. Nannina was dropping with tiredness and finally went to sleep. As he was a little drunk, Mario dropped off as well. They slept half-dressed.

The second night of their marriage was no better. The Finamores, the other tenants, appeared to be always on the point of going away – to a 40,000-lire flat, where, of course, they would be much better off! All of this was on account of Signor Roberto Finamore's genius. He worked with a firm as a draughtsman, but that was not his vocation – he wanted to be a writer, for instance, or an inventor. More than that, for over two years the Finamores had staked everything on a patent for an automatic toothpaste tube cap. And so they already lived in an atmosphere of comfort and good taste, which, after the laborious negotiations with important organizations and people, the patent would have afforded them. The truth is that they never left. On the contrary, on that very night and two months early, Signora Finamore went into labour and brought the seventh Finamore into the world.

The next day was Sunday. Waiting impatiently for evening to come, Mario took his bride for a walk round Rome; first up and down the Via Veneto and then to the Ambra Jovinelli, where they saw the film twice. Nannina would one moment close in on herself like a hedgehog and seem deaf and the next would be as expansive as a little girl and at least as ridiculous as she was beautiful. Mario – especially during the difficult moment going into the Ambra Jovinelli, when there were so many people that the police had to intervene – went through all the joys of vanity and all the bitterness of humiliation. . . . When they finally got back home, they found that 'their' room had been taken. It had so happened that Nina – who had gone by coach to Palestrina with her friends from the Banca d'Italia – had happened to fall and break her arm. As she felt sad and ill, she did not want to let slip any of the sentimental advantages which she could draw from this situation. She had asked – with general support – for a bedroom all to

ordine, dove ricevere il dottore e le colleghe. Ne aveva per una trentina di giorni.

Nannina andò a dormire in comune con le altre sorelle, Mario nel corridoio con Alduccio, il quale gli sbottò a ridere in faccia, e allora Mario lo menò tanto che svegliò tutta la casa.

Il giorno dopo ci fu il sopralluogo di Mario nei prati verso Tor de' Schiavi. In fondo a via dei Sambuchi, dopo qualche terreno lottizzato e due o tre cantieri, cominciava la campagna, intorno alla Casilina. A sinistra c'era appunto la borgata di Tor de' Schiavi, a sinistra il Quarticciolo; e in mezzo grandi praterie, tutte piene di montarozzi, ch'erano i resti di vecchie cave di tufo, e con qua e là degli spiazzi dove i ragazzi andavano a giocare al pallone, e, negli angoli, gli spazzini svuotavano l'immondezza. Mario tornò a casa abbastanza soddisfatto del suo giro. Dopo cena, con un certo sforzo invitò Nannina a scendere a prendere il caffè. Uscirono e lui la portò verso «il prato»: ma arrivarci fu una parola! Prima incontrarono i fratelli di lei, lì sotto la saletta del calciobalilla; poi gli amici di lui, al Bar 2000. Non fu tanto facile liberarsi nè dai primi nè dai secondi: i primi avevano cominciato una lotta clandestina alla lontana coi Finamore, avendo come ideale da realizzare la propria installazione al posto dei Finamore nell'appartamento di via dei Sambuchi; ai secondi poi, come tutte le sere, sorrideva la vita, e avevano fiato da buttare.

Quando poi finalmente restarono soli, al di là dei terreni lottizzati, dovettero fare i conti con una ripparolata[23] di pischelli in cerca d'avventure. Mario dovette litigarci. Quelli scapparono, ma ripiombarono subito dopo sui montarozzi circostanti, come indiani. Mario dovette mettersi d'accordo e distribuire un pacchetto di Nazionali. Se ne andarono in fondo a un prato dove di giorno i ragazzini giocavano al pallone. Ma laggiù era il regno della Adele – ch'era, fra l'altro, vicina di casa dei fratelli di Nannina – con, lontano,

herself and nicely tidied up where she could receive the doctor and her girl friends. She was set up for about a month.

Nannina went to sleep with the other sisters and Mario slept in the corridor with Alduccio, who burst out laughing at him, and then Mario hit him so hard that he woke the whole house.

The next day Mario carried out an inspection in the fields over towards Tor de' Schiavi. At the bottom of Via dei Sambuchi, after some building plots and two or three building sites, the country began, around the Via Casilina. Just on the left was the village of Tor de' Schiavi and also on the left Quarticciolo. In the middle there were great fields full of humps, which were the remains of old tufa quarries, and here and there were open spaces, where the boys went to play football and in odd corners dustmen came to tip their rubbish. Mario went home, well pleased with his tour of inspection. After supper, with some effort, he invited Nannina to come out and have a coffee. They went out and he took her towards 'the meadow' – but getting there was another matter! First they met her brothers down outside the bar-football place, then his friends by the Bar 2000. It was not so easy getting rid of either the one or the other. The brothers had begun a clandestine struggle from afar against the Finamores and were aiming at installing themselves in the place of the Finamores in the flat on Via dei Sambuchi. And life smiled on his friends, as it did every evening, and they had plenty to say.

When they were finally alone on the other side of the building plots, they had to contend with a gang of pubescent boys in search of adventure. Mario had to argue it out. They ran off, but straight away they came rushing down again onto the surrounding humps, like a band of Indians. Mario had to come to an agreement and hand round a packet of Nazionali. They went off to the bottom of a field where in the daytime the boys played football. But down there was Adele's territory – she was, among other things, a neighbour of Nannina's brothers. In the distance was

Aurelio il pappone –[24] altro vicino di casa – e intorno, a gruppi minacciosi, si parava la clientela.

Allora nuova ritirata e nuova ricerca, con Nannina insospettita, ma anche, – questa volta – insospettatamente tenera e complice. Tutto era inteso, fra loro due, malgrado il più casto silenzio. Trovarono finalmente un posticino, tra il fango e gli zeppi. Nasceva la luna.

Breve fu la tranquillità. Arrivarono dalla vicina strada due vecchi zozzi e ubbriachi cantando ora Bandiera Rossa ora la Marcia Reale.

Stretti, finalmente come due innamorati, ma inquieti e colpevoli in mezzo a tanti impicci, e mortificati, giunsero sulla strada lì vicino. Nannina aveva una faccia come se sentisse intorno un cattivo odore, tutta sospettosa. Si chinò e si guardó le scarpe, le sue scarpine nuove. Che macello! «Qua vicino ce sta 'na funtanella,» fece avvilito Mario, gliele sfilò e andò a lavargliele. Quando tornò, vide Nannina che piangeva.

Nei giorni che seguirono – quelli della degenza romanzesca della Nina – si delinearono e presero corpo questi tre fatti: primo, l'adattamento di Nannina a Centocelle. Fu una cosa miracolosa: dal suo disperato[25] salernitano, intanto, era passata prima a un linguaggio misto, che stuzzicava il genio dei famigliari più prossimi; figurarsi poi gli amici di Mario e gli estranei! Poi, si era messa a parlare un romanesco perfetto, che pareva nata e cresciuta a Centocelle. E, insieme al dialetto e al gergo cominciava a prendere gli atteggiamenti e a imparare le norme della dritteria. Non tutto in una volta, si capisce, ma man mano che si svolsero gli avvenimenti successivi. Da principio la sua intraprendenza non fu che ingenuità di paesana, che non si rende conto del diverso modo di pensare: poi fu quella di una drittarella romana, quasi senza soluzione di continuità.[26]

Secondo – e anche questo fatto si sviluppò con gli avvenimenti: il cambiamento del suo rapporto con

Aurelio, her protector, another neighbour, and all around in threatening groups appeared her clientele.

Another retreat then and a new search, with Nannina growing suspicious but also – on this occasion – surprisingly tender and cooperative. It was all understood between the two of them, in spite of their chaste silence. At last they found a small corner, among the mud and sticks. The moon was coming up.

Their peace was short-lived. Two filthy old drunks came from the near-by road, singing alternately the Red Flag and the Royal Anthem.

Embraced at last like two lovers but nervous and guilty among so many obstacles, and mortified, they walked to the road near by. Nannina looked as if she could smell something unpleasant, and seemed suspicious. She lent forward and looked at her shoes, her new shoes. What a mess! 'There's a fountain near here,' said Mario dispiritedly. He took them off her feet and went over to wash them for her. When he came back, he noticed that Nannina was crying.

During the following days – those of Nina's romantic convalescence – three facts appeared and took shape. First Nannina's adjustment to Centocelle. It was quite miraculous. She had in time progressed from her hopeless Salerno dialect, first to a mixed language which amused her closest relatives – you can just imagine then the reaction of Mario's friends and of outsiders! Then she began to speak perfect Roman, so that she seemed to have been born and bred in Centocelle. And along with the dialect and slang, she began to pick up the attitudes and learn the rules of urban cunning. Not all at once, you understand, but gradually as successive events unfolded. At first her shrewdness was only that of a naïve peasant woman, who does not appreciate the different way of thinking; later it became that of a sharp little Roman woman, almost without a period of transition.

Second – and this fact too developed with events – the change in her relationship with Mario. She found herself

Mario. Si trovò innamorata di lui senza accorgersene. Dalla schiavitù tradizionale, era passata prima a un vero e proprio attaccamento, e poi proprio all'amore. E anche lui, un po' alla volta passava all'amore – dal capriccio: forse anche perchè doveva sempre così accanitamente desiderarla, e difenderla: dal ridicolo e dalle tentazioni dei compari.

Terzo: la notte, la loro notte che non arrivava mai.

E purtroppo Mario era svelto d'amore, come i colombi. E un colombo appunto pareva: di quei colombi col collo spiumacciato controvento, chè Mario – la sua famiglia – veniva dal Monte Amiata,[27] e era un po' barbaro, come gli antichi toscani: e così, per quanto si tosasse, la testa tonda era sempre piena di capelli, capelli alti, come un cespuglio d'erbasaetta,[28] d'un color grigiopiombo venato di giallo. E, sotto, gli occhietti celesti – sotto quell'aureola di santo amoroso. Due occhietti celesti ma torbidi, che specchiavano il profondo istinto del suo amore con le donne: tanto e svelto. Così gli zigomi, alti sotto quegli occhietti, di pelle bruna e pallida, erano sempre tirati e un po' smunti. Con un simile carattere gli era duro vivere accanto a quella colombella selvatica ch'era Nannina, senza montarci ogni momento sopra, biondo colombo pieno d'amore com'era.

Quello che ci voleva insomma, ecco, era un appartamento. Nannina se ne rese conto, e subito, con l'incoscienza che solo lei poteva avere, ma anche con tenacia e con la decisione di riuscirci, cominciò a darsi da fare per raggiungere lo scopo. Cominciò per la strada più semplice e paesana: metter da parte del denaro: «moneta» come disse lei, «grana»,[29] come la corresse Mario, che ogni volta che si presentava l'occasione le dava lezione di lingua. Andò a lavorare con le sorelle e la madre di Mario, al banco di piazza Vittorio. Ma era ancora nella fase linguistica meno adatta allo scopo e all'ambiente. Gridava alla maniera del suo paese, tra il divertimento indescrivibile delle fruttarole a destra e dei pesciaroli a

in love with him without noticing it happening. She had progressed from the traditional slavery first to a real attachment and later to love itself. And he too, a little at a time, was moved to love – from caprice, perhaps also because he had always to desire her so furiously and defend her, from ridicule and from the temptation of friends.

Third, their wedding night, the night that never came.

Unfortunately Mario was made for loving, like the dove. And he looked like a dove, too, one of those doves with their puffed-out necks facing into the wind, for Mario's family came from Monte Amiata, and was a little barbarous, like the Tuscans of old. And so no matter how much it was sheared, his round head was always covered in hair, hair standing on end, like an arrow-head bush, of lead-grey streaked with yellow. And under that were his blue eyes – under that halo of a loving saint. Two small blue but clouded eyes, which mirrored the depth of his instinctive love for women, which was so great and natural. So too the high cheek-bones, with their pale brown skin, under those small eyes, were always drawn and a little wan. Being of such a character it was hard for him to live by his little wild dove Nannina, without mounting her at every moment, blond love-bird that he was.

In short, what they needed was a flat. Nannina realized this and at once, with that ingenuousness which only she could have had, but also with tenacity and the determination to succeed, started to do what was necessary to reach her aim. She started in the simplest and most peasant-like way – to put aside money, 'cash' as she called it, 'dough', as Mario corrected her. He never missed an opportunity to give her lessons in the language. She went to work with Mario's mother and sisters on their stall on the Piazza Vittorio. But she was still at the phase of linguistic development least suitable for the purpose and surroundings. She called out as they did in her village, to the indescribable amusement of the fruit-women on the right and the

sinistra. Finì con un litigio generale di donne, a graffi, e ciavattate:[30] e quella lite fu per vari giorni l'argomento dei discorsi delle due sorelle minori di Mario. Comunque, a piazza Vittorio, Nannina non se la fece più.

Ora accadeva che, come s'è detto, i fratelli di Nannina e sua madre, tenessero gli occhi sull'appartamento di via dei Sambuchi: e, se non se ne andavano i Finamore, essi nascostamente contavano che, quanto meno, cominciassero con l'andarsene Mario e Nannina. Fu facile perciò dato il generale accordo famigliare, che lo zio accettasse di mettere come cassiera la Nannina nella sua saletta del calcio-balilla. Nannina vi si installò, nuda come la miseria.[31] La voce a proposito di quell'eccezionale cass ieradi Don Ciccillo, corse subito tra i giovinotti della borgata. Una sera, mentre tornava dal lavoro, Mario fu fermato da un amico suo: «Permetti, a Ma' te vorrebbe dì 'na parola,» gli fece. Era tutto pieno del sentimento dell'onore, della lealtà e dell'amicizia. La «parola» fu rimandata a più tardi. Intanto, tra proteste di reciproca amicizia e dritteria,[32] entrarono in una pizzeria, bevvero, si fecero dichiarazioni d'amore, e altre prefazioni e preamboli. Poi, già un po' sbronzo, l'amico, con la massima diplomazia, a metà strada tra il gergo e le sparate napoletane, gli fece la sua cantata. Era successo che da qualche tempo i giovanotti del vicinato avevano scoperto che il calcio-balilla era un gioco molto spassoso: un po' alla volta avevano cacciato ragazzini e pischelli dal loro regno e vi si erano fatti clienti fissi, occupando tutti i tavoli del gioco. Nannina, lei, se ne stava al banco, un po' da burina tonta com'era, a non capire le frecciate nei suoi riguardi un po' a non capire gli sviscerati complimenti alla sua bellezza. Ma veramente non capiva? Quand'era in ultimo, sia nel primo che nel secondo caso, finiva col fregare tutti, con un gesto, una parola, un lampo malandrino dello sguardo. Ci si divertiva, faceva la tonta, e instanto sparampiava grana per l'appartamento. Mario tagliò corto con quella

fishmongers on the left. It ended in a general squabble among the women, who set about each other with their finger nails and their shoes. This fight was for several days the subject of conversation of Mario's two younger sisters. Anyway Nannina gave up going to the Piazza Vittorio.

Now it happened that, as has been said, Nannina's brothers and mother had their eyes on the flat in Via dei Sambuchi. And, even if the Finamores were not leaving, they secretly expected that Mario and Nannina would at least go away first. It was easy therefore, given that the family was agreeable, for the uncle to take on Nannina as cashier in his bar-football place. She installed herself in the bare room. The news about Don Ciccillo's exceptional cashier at once ran round the young men of the neighbourhood. One evening on his way home from work Mario was stopped by a friend of his. 'Wait a moment, Mario, I want to tell you something,' he said. He was full of the sentiments of honour, loyalty and friendship. The 'something' was postponed until later. Meanwhile, amid protestations of mutual friendship and admiration, they went into a pizzeria, drank, declared their affection for each other, and made other such prefatory remarks and preambles. Then, by now a little drunk, the friend, with very great diplomacy, in a mixture of slang and Neapolitan witticisms, told him his tale. As a matter of fact some time ago the youths of the neighbourhood had discovered that bar-football was a very good game. Gradually they had chased the young kids from their territory and had become regulars, taking up all the football tables. Nannina remained behind the counter, like the dense peasant that she was, not understanding the rude remarks in her direction and equally failing to understand the passionate compliments on her beauty. But did she really not understand? When it came to it, in both cases she ended up taking everyone in, with a gesture, a word, a wicked flash of her eyes. She was enjoying it, she was playing thick and in the meantime was putting aside dough for the flat. Mario put an end to this, and, what

faccenda; e anzi, per l'occasione, sebbene con discrezione, la menò.

Il giorno dopo si decise che Nannina doveva imparare a leggere e a scrivere. Fu incaricata la Nina, che però si stufò subito: provvidero a completare l'istruzione le due sorelle più piccole: su *Grand Hôtel.*[33] Con un po' di dispiacere del signor Finamore, che avrebbe desiderato molto intervenire in quella faccenda. Ma il rapporto di coabitazione era in quel periodo molto teso: le donne lottavano sotto traccia, esplodendo di tanto in tanto. Ancora più grande fu però il disappunto del primogenito, Romolo Finamore, che, fin dai primi tempi su Nannina aveva fatto un pensiero. E, siccome il giorno di lavoro tutti lavoravano, succedeva che per lui e Nannina si presentasse spesso l'occasione di restare soli, e di avere tutto un appartamento a loro disposizione.

Romolo Finamore era ragioniere da un anno: ed era, con la sua compagnia di studenti o figli di papà, l'altra faccia della vita sociale di Centocelle. Aveva scarpine a punta, cravatta, cappotto sale e pepe e calzoni a tubo: il centro della lotta tra le due famiglie in fondo era lì. E aveva se mai propaggini nei bar frequentati dagli amici di Mario e dagli amici di Romolo.

Nannina, di Romolo, non s'era neanche accorta: lui era come un cane senza padrone che ogni tanto le veniva tra i piedi. Del resto Nannina passava quasi l'intera giornata nel villaggio di tuguri, con la madre e i conterranei. La madre era sempre più sordida e antica: altro mezzo di adattamento non aveva che il silenzio: un silenzio espressivo e umido come quello dei cani o degli accattoni. Tanto più che anche la figlia, ormai si andava trasformando: nel fare, nel parlare. Sapeva anche leggere. . . . Fu leggendo con Adele, la zoccola, e su consiglio di Adele, che durante il giorno era una brava donna di famiglia, gli annunci pubblicitari del «Messaggero»,[34] che Nannina, con tutta la sua incoscienza di burina, concepì nuovi tentativi di lavoro e di guadagno . . .

is more, for just that once, although not too hard, he beat her.

The next day it was decided that Nannina should learn to read and write. Nina was entrusted with this; however, she got fed up at once. The two younger sisters arranged for the completion of her instruction, with copies of *Grand Hôtel*. This upset Signor Finamore a bit, as he would have liked very much to help in his matter. But the relations between the tenants were at this time very tense. The women quarrelled restrainedly, exploding every now and then. Even greater, however, was the disappointment of the eldest son, Romolo Finamore, who, since Nannina's first days in Rome had had her on his mind. And, because on workdays everyone was working, Nannina and he often had an opportunity of being alone together and having the whole flat to themselves.

Romolo Finamore had been a qualified book-keeper for a year and made up, along with the company which he kept of students and spoilt young men, the other side of the social life of Centocelle. He had winkle-pickers, a tie, a speckled coat and drain-pipe trousers. This was really the centre of the feud between the two families, and it was bound to have its ramifications in the bars frequented by Mario's friends and by Romolo's friends.

Nannina had not even noticed Romolo. He was like a stray dog, which every now and again got between her feet. Anyway Nannina spent nearly the whole day in the shanty town with her mother and fellow southerners. Her mother was growing ever more filthy and ancient. She had no other way of adapting except by silence, an expressive and moist-eyed silence, like that of dogs and beggars. Even more so now that her daughter was also changing in her manner and speech. She could even read. . . . It was by reading the small ads in the *Messagero* with Adele, the tart, and on the advice of Adele, who during the day was a good family woman, that Nannina, with all her country innocence, conceived new ways of working and earning . . .

Gli unici a parte del segreto delle sortite di Nannina – Mario sarebbe stato messo al corrente a cose fatte – erano i naturali difensori del suo onore, erano i tre fratelli, che, con la speranzella dell'appartamento, sulla faccenda dell'onore avevano chiuso un occhio . . . e anche due: sempre più malandrini che mai, però. Mario, poveraccio, era tutto il giorno allo sgobbo, faceva un mazzo così a lavorare l'intera settimana: la domenica, con due o tre piotte[35] in tasca, e la sposina da portare a spasso – a divertirsi – si limitava ogni tanto a diventar nero in faccia e dire con una voce da far gelare le ossa «Si ciavesse un mitra ammazzerebbe tutti . . . e nun risparmierebbe manco Gesù Cristo.» Lei capricciosa e golosa come una ragazzina, teneva duro: con un'ostinazione misteriosa e commovente come la sua razza. Era capace pure di rifiutare un gelatino da venti lire.

Fu quello sderenato del Finamore, che mise Nannina, date le sue relazioni coi più bei giovanotti del quartiere, sulla strada di Cinecittà.[36] E fu per colpa sua che stette per scoppiare una vera tragedia. Quella volta Nannina ne prese poche de botte. Ma non si mise l'anima in pace: vedeva i biglietti da mille a portata di mano, dietro un muretto, dietro una sbarra bianca e rossa. E proprio non capiva che cosa andasse cercando suo marito: «nun ciaveva er senso der raccionamento», come diceva lui. Lei, intanto, non si sognava manco per niente di aver paura di tutti quegli uomini che, smandrappati o acchittati come figurini, bazzicavano da quelle parti, gridando fra di loro come se fossero sempre allegri, anche quelli con la faccia da smidollati o da morti di fame. Se proprio non pensava a «'u curtiello», come i giovincelli di Torpignattara dicevano con aria paragula, sapeva bene come difendersi. E poi lei ci andava per lavorare: di tutto ciò che non riguardava la grana per farsi la casa non gliene importava un cavolo. La seconda volta che Mario sgamò, furono dolori.

Nella casa di Torpignattara e nei tuguri del Man-

The only people to share the secret of Nannina's expeditions – Mario was to be informed of what was happening after it had happened – were the natural defenders of her honour, the three brothers, who, hoping for the flat, had turned a blind eye to the matter of her honour . . . in fact had turned two blind eyes. They were more scheming than ever. Poor Mario spent the whole day slaving and wore himself out like this, working the whole week. On Sundays with two or three hundred lire in his pocket, and while taking his wife for a walk, to enjoy themselves, he would do nothing but frown every now and again and say in a spine-chilling tone, 'If only I had a submachine gun, I would kill the lot . . . and I wouldn't spare anyone, not even Jesus Christ.' She was capricious and greedy like a little girl but held hard, with an obstinacy as mysterious and touching as everything about her people. She was even capable of refusing a twenty-lire ice-cream.

It was that degenerate Finamore boy who, with his contacts with the best-looking young men in the area, put Nannina onto the road to Cinecittà. And it was his fault that a real tragedy was on the point of erupting. This time Nannina got away with a small beating. But this did not calm her down. She could see 1,000-lire notes within easy reach behind a wall, the other side of a red and white barrier. And she really didn't understand what her husband was after: 'There was no sense in it', as she would say. On the other hand, it didn't occur to her at all to be frightened of all those men who, some messy and others as smart as tailors' dummies, haunted those parts, shouting to one another, as if all the time they were feeling cheerful, even those who looked weak or dead with hunger. Even if it didn't occur to her to think of ''u curtiello' – the knife – as the boys of Torpignattara said mockingly, she knew how to defend herself. And later she went there to work. She didn't give a damn for anything which was not connected with getting money for their house. The second time that Mario got the message there was trouble.

In the house in Torpignattara and in the hovels on the

drione si passò una domenica di fuoco. Mario e i due fratelli – quello di mezzo era partito in quei giorni per la naja – urlavano, come scellerati;[37] le donne ancor più di loro, affiancate dalla Adele e da altre due o tre zoccolette, che strillavano, povere creature con certe facce che avrebbero fatto lacrimare pure i sassi.

Senonchè quella settimana Mario fece un dodici al totocalcio, guadagnò quasi trecentomila lire, e tutto si mise a posto. I due sposini già si vedevano nella camera, nella cucina e nel bagno che sognavano: Nannina impazziva dalla gioia, parlò e canterellò tutto il giorno, cominciò a darsi arie, ad avere un contegno sostenuto. . . . Occorreva fare delle spese: per comune accordo e approvazione generale, sia lei che lui erano ridotti senza un vestito e coi piedi nudi – le scarpine di Mario erano sfondate, Nannina non poteva proprio più andare avanti con quei due o tre straccetti che aveva addosso: sicchè il giorno appresso, Mario fece sega, e andò con Nannina a piazza Vittorio. Fu un giorno vissuto come in delirio, passarono tutti i negozi, a uno a uno, con mille giudiziosi ragionamenti, sudando di emozione davanti alle vetrine. . . . Tornarono a Torpignattara verso sera, nel tranvetto carico fin sui tetti completamente sfiniti e col portafoglio di Mario che piangeva. In compenso Mario indossava uno sfolgorante maglione a strisce rosse, turchine e nere, come un tappeto persiano, che gli era costato dieci sacchi.[39] Avevano tutti e due il cuore spezzato: storditi dall'ebbrezza degli acquisti, massacrati dalla felicità sorseggiata tra boccate di fiele. . . . Si consolavano pensando che in fondo gli[38] rimanevano altre duecento saccate.

Invece, con quelle duecento saccate, Mario si comprò il Rumi. Per Nannina, poverella, fu un brutto colpo. Ma come? dopo tanto che s'era parlato della casa . . . della casa per far l'amore in pace . . . per la umile sposina era

Mandrione, Sunday was a rough day. Mario and the two brothers – the middle one had just gone off to do his military service – yelled at each other like devils. The women did so even more than them and were backed up by Adele and two or three other members of her profession, who screamed like the poor creatures they were, with expressions which would have made the stones weep.

But that week, Mario had won the pools and got nearly 300,000 lire and everything settled down again. Husband and wife could already see themselves in the bedroom, kitchen and bathroom that they had longed for. Nannina went mad with joy, chattered and hummed all day long. She began to give herself airs and to behave haughtily. . . . They needed to buy some things, by common agreement and with general approval; both of them found themselves with nothing to wear and no shoes on their feet – the soles of Mario's shoes were dropping off, and Nannina couldn't really go round in the few rags that she had on her back. So the next day Mario took the day off and went with Nannina to Piazza Vittorio. They spent the day in a delirious fever and went past every shop, one by one, with a host of reasonable arguments, sweating with emotion in front of the shop-windows. . . . When they went back to Torpignattara in the evening in the tram, which was packed right up to the roof, they were quite worn out and Mario's wallet was sadly depleted. To make up for this, Mario was wearing a dazzling pullover with red, blue and black stripes, like a Persian carpet, which had cost him 10,000 lire. The experience had broken both their hearts. They were stunned by the excitement of buying things and shattered by their sips of happiness between the draughts of gall. . . . They comforted themselves with the thought that after all they still had another 200,000 lire.

But instead Mario bought himself a Rumi motorbike with the 200,000 lire. It was bad luck for poor Nannina. What could he mean? – after talking for so long about the house . . . the house where they could make love in peace.

un vero mistero, che l'umiliava ancora più, che la faceva tornare al suo antico stato di pecorara rifatta. . . . Non diceva niente. Il fatto è che il Rumi era nel cuore di Mario da molto tempo prima di Nannina. Era la sua vera, grande passione: quella che lo faceva essere come gli altri – i dritti, si capisce, di Torpignattara, – il barlume di un ideale di vita, la possibilità di realizzare solidamente qualcosa nel mondo.

Mario comparve un martedì sera, per le strade di Torpignattara, col maglione nuovo e il Rumi: a cento all'ora. Era già sul tardi; il semaforo all'incrocio di via dell'Acqua Bullicante era fermo all'arancione, e in giro c'erano solo i perditempo, o gli ultimi treppi di lavoratori ammucchiati alle fermate del tranvetto. Mario scaricò la sera stessa i suoi vecchi compagni, quelli del Bar 2000, del Bar della Pugnalata, delle partite, a biliardo e alla zecchinetta.[40] Si promosse ad amico dei motorizzati, e si accatenò a loro. Quelli, ogni sera, combinavano sfide e carosielli[41] che assordavano tutto il quartiere, finchè non partivano a tutto gas verso Tivoli o Grottaferrata, per tornare dopo la mezzanotte, ubriachi e rossi in faccia come il fuoco. Erano vestiti da meccanici, chè i capi della banda lavoravano poco più su per la Casilina, davanti al monumentino ai caduti, in un'officina; ma c'erano anche quelli acchittati, padroni di Guzzetti, Lambrette, vecchie MB per sport, come Mario: ma, se non erano neri in faccia di catrame o olio di macchine, non parevano meno degli altri appena usciti dall'inferno. Neri e caldi ancora delle fiamme del diavolo.

Quella sera stessa Mario cominciò le sfide. Meticolosamente preparate sui cronometri degli amici portati sul sellino posteriore. Facevano dei circuiti, partendo a intervalli, secondo la potenza del motore, attraverso la Borgata Gordiani, o giù per il Pigneto. Poi si stufarono, e sparirono come una mandria di scellerati, giù verso il Mandrione.

. . . It was a real mystery for his humble wife, a mystery which humiliated her even more, and which took her back to her former state as a thinly disguised country girl. . . . She did not say anything. The truth of the matter is that the Rumi had been in Mario's heart much longer than Nannina. It was his true, great passion – the one which made him like the others – that is, the ones that counted in Torpignattara – the glimmer of an ideal in life, the chance of achieving something solid in this world.

Mario appeared one Tuesday evening on the streets of Torpignattara, in his new pullover and on his Rumi – going sixty miles an hour. It was already getting late. The traffic light at the crossroads on Via dell' Acqua Bullicante was fixed on amber, and the only people around were the lay-abouts or the last groups of workers crowding by the tram stops. That very evening Mario dropped his old friends, his friends at the Bar 2000, at the Bar della Pugnalata, and with whom he had played billiards and cards. He had promoted himself to being one of the ton-up boys and he latched onto them. Every evening they would deafen the whole neighbourhood with dares and competitions that they arranged, until they set off at full throttle towards Tivoli or Grottaferrata, coming back after midnight, drunk, and as red as fire in the face. They dressed as mechanics because the leaders of the gang were working in a workshop a little further up the Via Casilina in front of the little war memorial. But there were also some smarties, who owned Guzzettis, Lambrettas and old sports-model MBs, like Mario, and even if their faces weren't black with tar or car oil, no less than the others they seemed newly arrived from hell – still hot and black from the devil's flames.

That very evening Mario began to take part in the dares, which were prepared meticulously on the stop-watches of friends riding pillion. They rode round circuits, setting off at intervals, according to the capacity of their engines, through Borgata Gordiani, or down through Pigneto. Then they got fed up with this and disappeared like a band of robbers down towards the Mandrione.

Quella fantomina[42] durò tutta la settimana: Nannina vedeva Mario, disteso a pancia in giù sul Rumi, sparire di sotto la porta di casa: e non lo rivedeva fino alla mattina dopo. Il sabato sera, la banda motorizzata, coi calzoni nuovi, e certi maglioni tutti lavorati come pianete – eccetto gli sciammannati che non lasciavano mai – per vanità, poi – le tute impiastricciate – decisero di farsi una corsa fino a Ostia. Andarono, bevvero un bicchierino di liquore, rifurono a Torpignattara. Comparvero giù per l'Acqua Bullicante dalla parte del Mandrione, imboccarono Torpignattara sotto il semaforo, voltarono su a destra, verso il Bar della Pugnalata. Mario era, per colpa di un furgoncino, in coda, e per raggiungerli filava ai cento sui sampietrini sconnessi. Dietro c'era il tranvetto, a destra, davanti, veniva un autotreno, quando dei ragazzini, uscendo di corsa dal Due Allori,[43] attraversarono la strada. Mario rasentò il tranvetto, andò a finire sotto le ruote dell'autotreno. Restò lì, vicino al Rumi squarciato, in una pozzanghera di sangue, così maciullato che era impossibile riconoscerlo. Lo ricoprirono con dei fogli di giornale.

Quando lo vide lì, morto sotto quei pezzi di carta insanguinati, Nannina capì quanto ormai volesse bene a quel ragazzo. E come ormai tutto per lei fosse finito. Durante i primi mesi di lutto, infatti, fu tollerata in casa della famiglia di Mario; poi le cose si misero piano piano in modo che lei se ne dovette andare. Era ridiventata una sconosciuta, occupava un posto non suo; nessuno non solo non le voleva bene, ma nemmeno quasi le parlava. Lei tentò in principio di giocare la carta della memoria di Mario, chiusa nel suo lutto di burina; ma poi dovette arrendersi e se ne andò. Andò nel tugurio dei fratelli e della madre, al Mandrione.

Conobbe a poco a poco la vita che si svolgeva lì, in una crosta di polvere e sporcizia, in quelle povere baracche addossate ai muraglioni dell'Acquedotto; fino a notte alta, con la luce rossiccia che rigava il fango dalle fessure delle porte, qua e là, in quelle casupole dove le zoccole

This craze went on the whole week. Nannina saw Mario disappear from the door of the house, lying stomach downwards on his Rumi, and she would not see him again until the next morning. On Saturday evening the motorbike gang in new trousers and pullovers, as ornately patterned as priestly vestments – except for the more slovenly ones who never got out of their dirty overalls and now wore them out of vanity – decided to arrange a race down to Ostia. They went there, drank a glass of spirits and got back to Torpignattara. They came out some way down the Acqua Bullicante near the Mandrione, they entered Torpignattara below the traffic lights, turned up right, towards the Bar della Pugnalata. Because of a small van, Mario had got behind and he was doing a good sixty over the loose cobbles to catch up with them. Behind him was the tram, in front on his right a lorry was coming and just then some boys ran out of the Due Allori across the road. Mario grazed past the tram and ended up under the wheels of the lorry. He lay there near the twisted Rumi in a pool of blood, so disfigured that he was unrecognizable. They covered him with sheets of newspaper.

When Nannina saw him there, dead and covered by those bits of bloody newspaper, she realized how much she loved him now and that for her now everything was over. For the first few months as a widow Mario's family put up with her around the house; but then things gradually forced her to leave. Once again she was a stranger and was occupying a place which was not hers. Not only did no one love her, but scarcely anyone even spoke to her. At first she tried to play the card of the memory of Mario, wrapped up, as she was, in her peasant-like mourning; but later she had to give in and she left. She went to the hovel where her brothers and mother lived on the Mandrione.

Little by little, she got to know the kind of life that you lead there, under a layer of dust and filth, in those shacks built up against the walls of the old Roman aqueduct. Later at night, there would be the reddish light from the cracks in the doors furrowing the mud here and there in the

vegliavano aspettando gruppi sbandati di clienti, con la capa, la più vecchia di loro, che invitava spudorata i giovanotti che si riducevano lì; coi letticcioli grigiastri che s'intravedevano per le finestrelle storte con dei fondi di casse per imposte; e tutto accadeva come in un lungo cortile, in un budello, con gli ardenti sereni delle notti estive che si spalancavano sopra, al di là degli archi dell'Acquedotto, nell'aria limpida e sonora. E poi i desolati risvegli al primo mattino, con la luce calcinante che cadeva sul fango secco, sui bambini coperti di stracci e le donne che andavano a far la spesa. La gente che abitava lì intorno ora si vendicava su Nannina: ora che la ragazza era dei loro, decaduta, miserabile. La sua bellezza la rendeva ancora più antipatica alle donne, che aspettavano che quella bellezza si infangasse nel loro fango. Ma lei non si lasciò mettere sotto i piedi: e quanto a vivere, lavorò.

Intanto il fratello più anziano ebbe un colpo di fortuna: un amico suo di Torpignattara aveva fatto, in modo poco pulito, un po' di grana, e voleva investirla; Santo era, in provincia di Benevento, barbiere: sicchè quel suo amico pensò di comprarsi un negozietto di barbiere – in società con lui – mettendolo a lavorare. Trovarono il negozietto a Forte Boccea, che è come dire in un'altra città. Da principio Santo scese abbastanza di frequente giù al Mandrione, se non altro per vanità: poi, man mano che la prima ingenua vanità fu sostituita dal senso di dignità di chi si è innalzato nella scala sociale, le sue visite si fecero sempre più rade. Arrivava vestito di scuro, con una faccia da usciere, la cravatta con lo spillo, i baffetti e i capelli duri di brillantina sulla sua grossa testa di cafone. Parlava poco, per non compromettere la sua dignità, finchè, diventato del tutto una persona seria, un professionista che pensa a metter su famiglia scomparì del tutto.

Del resto, anche le prime volte, quando scendeva per

hovels in which the prostitutes were waiting up for the straggling groups of clients and the tart-in-chief, who was the oldest of them, brazenly inviting in young men who ended up there. And the greyish little beds, which you caught a sight of through the misshapen little windows with shutters made out of old packing-cases. Everything happened as in a long courtyard or in an alley with the blazing clear skies of the summer nights which gaped above them beyond the arches of the aqueduct in the limpid, resonant air. And then the gloomy awakening in the early morning and the burning light which fell on the dry mud, on the ragged children and the women going off to do their shopping. The people who lived around there now were getting their own back on Nannina – now that the girl was one of them, fallen, wretched. Her beauty made her even more hateful to the women, who were waiting for her beauty to become muddied in the slough of their world. But she did not let people walk over her and, as for earning a living, she worked.

In the meantime the eldest brother had a bit of luck. A friend of his from Torpignattara had made a bit of cash by crooked means and he wanted to invest it. Santo had been a barber down in Benevento, and so this friend of his thought of buying a little barber's shop – together with him – getting him to work in it. They found the shop in Forte Boccea, which really means in another town altogether. At first Santo went down quite often to the Mandrione, out of vanity as much as anything else. Then, gradually, as the first ingenuous vanity was replaced by the sense of dignity of someone who has gone up a rung in the social ladder, his visits became more and more rare. He would arrive dressed in dark suits, with a bailiff-like expression, a tie and pin, a small moustache and hair stiff with brilliantine on top of his big southern peasant's head. He spoke little, so as not to compromise his dignity, until, by now a completely serious person, a professional man, thinking of setting up a family, he completely disappeared.

Anyway, even the first few times that he came down for

la visita domenicale ai parenti, era difficile che incontrasse Nannina; perchè Nannina, pur conservando un lutto tenace, se ne andava al cinema, con Romolo Finamore, l'unica relazione che avesse conservato del mondo superiore da cui era stata respinta e rifiutata. Il giovanotto era innamorato perso di lei; erano mesi che non desiderava e non pensava altro che averla, preso dal più peccaminoso degli amori. Il povero ragionierino ancora disoccupato, e con tre o quattro piotte in saccoccia, altre donne non aveva avuto che le zoccolette di Torpignattara. Nannina era il suo grande amore.

Ma non gli disse bene, era destino. Già da qualche tempo, quando veniva dalle parti del Mandrione, con gli scarpini bianchi bucherellati e la maglietta gialla, a prendere Nannina, vedeva, appoggiato allo stipite di una porticina sfondata, o dritto in mezzo alla fanga, con le mani in saccoccia, Aurelio, il magnaccia dell'Adele,[44] che lo guardava con uno stuzzicadenti in bocca. Da principio si limitò a guardarlo, duro e inespressivo come una bestia, grosso e quadrato dentro i suoi calzoni nocciola e la camicia grigia di zella; poi ci fu una smorfia, con un rumore di saliva tra i denti: è vero che poteva essere il semplice bisogno imperioso di sputare di chi ha appena mangiato: ma c'era in esso qualcosa di insolente e significativo, che Romolo capì benissimo – era vecchio a queste moine – ma finse di non capire. Una domenica, il magnaccia disse pure qualcosa, una frase rapida e ironica, come pronunciata al vento, assoluta e rassegnata come un proverbio: poi entrò dentro la casupola dell'Adele, sbattendo la povera porticina. La volta seguente, Romolo non potè fare il distratto,[45] perchè lo sguardo del faciolo lo fissava, fin da quando egli era comparso in fondo alla strada, con troppa insolenza: era un'ironia mista e corretta da una interna rabbia, un gelo feroce che prendeva quasi sfumature confidenziali e amichevoli. Tutto era predisposto per la cerimonia della lite. Infatti, pigramente, il faciolo si staccò dallo stipite a cui era

the Sunday visit to his relations, it was difficult for him to meet Nannina, because Nannina, although persistently continuing to observe her period of mourning, went off to the cinema with Romolo Finamore, the only contact she had kept with the upper world, by which she had been refused and rejected. The young man was hopelessly in love with her; for months, seized by the most culpable of loves, he had wanted and thought of nothing but having her. The poor little book-keeper, still without a job and with three or four hundred lire in his pocket, had had no other women besides the tarts at Torpignattara. Nannina was his great love.

But things did not go well for him; that was fate. For some time already, when he came down towards the Mandrione, with his white shoes full of holes and wearing a yellow pullover, to get Nannina, he had seen Aurelio leaning against the frame of a broken-down door or standing in the middle of all the mud, with his hands in his pockets, the man who was Adele's protector, who was watching him with a tooth-pick in his mouth. At first he only watched him, hard and expressionless like an animal, and big and square in his brown trousers and shirt which was grey with dirt. Then there came a grimace, with the sound of saliva running between the teeth. It might indeed just have been the imperious need to spit of someone who has just eaten, but there was in it something insolent and meaningful, which Romolo very well understood – he was experienced in this type of bravado – but he pretended not to be able to understand. One Sunday the pimp did indeed say something, a short, sarcastic remark, which seemed to have been said to no one in particular, a remark as absolute and full of resignation as a proverb. Then he went into Adele's shack, slamming the wretched little door. The next time Romolo could not ignore it, because the pimp's gaze had followed him too insolently from when he had appeared at the bottom of the road. In his gaze there was an irony mingled and supported with inward rage, an icy ferocity with an almost confidential and friendly note in it. Everything was ready

rimasto ammucchiato con aria stanca, e sputando lo stuzzicadenti si mise a gambe larghe, compatto e rilasciato, in mezzo alla strada. Aspettava Romolo guardandolo con aria equivoca: come se avesse intenzione di battergli una mano sulla spalla e farsi una risata con lui, o come se conoscesse un suo segreto e stesse lì per ricattarlo. Fatto sta che Romolo, come gli giunse faccia a faccia, non potè far a meno di dirgli, con un tono di voce disposto ancora a tutte le inflessioni: «Che cc'è?» L'altro aveva le battute pronte e consacrate: «Come sarebbe a dì che cc'è,» fece. «Me stai a guardà,» disse, un po' con un'aria da ragazzino Romolo. L'altro ghignò: «Ma come! Tu te permetti de venì a prenne de petto 'a ggente pecchè se ne sta in mmezzo a la strada? A morè,»[46] aggiunse con voce più bassa, come chi dà un buon consiglio, «bada che qqua caschi male!» Romolo cercò di buttare la cosa in ridere. «E va bbè,» fece, ritraendo allegramente la testa fra le spalle. L'altro s'incupì. Gli si accostò, gli prese delicatamente un pizzico della majetta gialla tra le dita e si accinse a fargli un lungo discorso. Dopo qualche preambolo – qualche smorfia, tra un «a morè» e un altro, due battute con le dita contro il naso,[47] qualche considerazione di carattere generale sui propri principi . . . – avvertì Romolo ch'era meglio per lui che non si facesse più vedere da quelle parti.

In quei giorni, la madre se ne andò. Dopo aver taciuto per giorni, mesi e anni, una mattina cominciò a parlare, in salernitano. Era alla fontanella, dopo un temporale, e stava piovendo ancora; le viottole intorno ai tuguri erano scivoli di fango; la pioggia veniva giù storta, portata da un vento tiepido. Tuonava vagamente, da qualche parte, dietro i muraglioni dell'acquedotto, negli sprofondi della ferrovia, sugli attici del Quadraro, tutti in fila, bianchi come tombe, contro un cielo azzurro, una sperduta di cielo, pulito, sereno, sgombro come in un sogno.

for the full ceremony of a fight. Indeed the pimp lazily pulled himself away from the door-post, against which he had sleepily propped himself, and, spitting out his toothpick, he went and stood, legs apart, compact and relaxed, in the middle of the road. He was waiting for Romolo, looking at him in an ambiguous way, as if he wanted to slap him on the shoulder and fool around with him, or as if he knew a secret of his and was there to blackmail him. It so happened that, as he came face to face with him, Romolo could not avoid saying to him, in a tone still open to any interpretation: 'What's up?' The other knew the time-honoured, quick replies: 'What do you mean, "What's up?"' he said. 'You're looking at me,' Romolo said, a little childishly. The other leered: 'What? You think that you can go around assaulting people just because they're in the middle of the street? Look here, my dark-haired friend,' he added more quietly, as if giving a bit of advice, 'you'd better watch it or it won't be healthy for you around here!' Romolo tried to make a joke out of it. 'Thanks for the advice,' he said, cheerfully throwing back his head. The other began to look nasty. He went up to him, carefully took a bit of his yellow pullover between his fingers and prepared to deliver him a long lecture. After a few opening remarks – a grimace or two between each 'Look here', two occasions on which he tapped his nose with his fingers and a few remarks of a general nature on his basic premises . . . – he warned Romolo that it would be better for him, if he wasn't seen around there again.

It was at that time that the mother died. Having remained silent for days, months, years, one morning she started talking in the language of Salerno. It was at the fountain after a storm and it was still raining. The alleys between the shacks were slippery with mud. The rain fell crookedly, blown by a warmish wind. There was indistinct thunder, somewhere, behind the walls of the aqueduct, far away among the railway cuttings around the penthouses in Quadraro, which were lined up, as white as tombs, against a blue sky, an infinite sky, clean, serene, clear as in a dream.

La vecchia cominciò a cioccare come una matta; svelta come una bambina; tanto svelta che non finiva neanche le parole, le finali delle frasi le restavano in bocca, col fiatone; poi corse in casa con la secchia vuota, e là ricominciò a parlare, da sola, chè non c'era nessuno.

Parlava dentro, uscendo ogni tanto col naso fuori dall'usciolo sfondato, e ritirandosi subito, nel buio della bicocca. Le sue parole andavano e venivano, come portate anche loro, con la pioggia, dal vento tiepido, l'ultimo dell'estate. Parlò tutta la mattina, con le altre donne intorno – alla fontanella, sulla fanga, tra le casupole sventrate, sotto i bandoni – che facevano le facce balorde di chi bada ai fatti suoi, pur capendo i fatti degli altri, ma non se ne vuole impicciare. Già, su quelle facce balorde, era dipinto tutto quello che stava per accadere.

Tornò Nannina, tornò Alfio, verso sera – lavorava a un cantiere a Monte Sacro[48] – e se finora nessuno aveva capito che cosa dicesse la vecchia in quella lingua sconosciuta, adesso, i figli che la capivano, non riuscirono a capacitarsi come una donna di settant'anni parlasse come una bambina di sei, senza che avesse la febbre – benchè, rientrando, l'avessero trovata tutta vestita sulla sua cuccia nera di zella, in fondo alla stanzuccia gocciolante, che parlava al soffitto, gettando ogni tanto verso chi l'ascoltava occhiate disperate e non finite, come le parole.

Così prima anche Nannina, e poi Alfio, fecero le facce balorde. La vecchia parlò di seguito di tutte quelle sue cose da bambina, per una settimana, poi stirò le gambe, nella sua cuccia. Lì rimase in silenzio, ad aspettare che la portassero via.

Così con Gennaro soldato, Santo passato di rango a Forte Boccea, restarono soli nella baracca Nannina e il fratello più piccolo, Alfio.

Proprio il giorno dei funerali della madre, al ritorno

The old woman began to yell like a mad-woman. She babbled like a small child, so quickly that she did not even finish her words, and the ends of the phrases remained in her mouth, she was so breathless. She then ran into the house with the bucket empty, and there began again to talk, alone, for there was nobody else.

Inside she talked, putting her nose out of the broken-in door every now and again and withdrawing immediately into the darkness of her hovel. Her words came and went, as if they too were, like the rain, borne on the warm wind, the last of the summer. She spoke the whole morning, with the other women around – at the fountain, in the mud, among the broken-down shacks, beneath the corrugated iron – making stupid faces like someone minding his own business while he understands that of others, but does not want to get involved. Already those stupid faces showed everything that was about to happen.

Nannina came back and so did Alfio in the evening – he was working on a site at Monte Sacro – and if up till now nobody had understood what the old woman was saying in that unknown language of hers, now her children, who understood it, could not imagine why a woman of seventy was speaking like a little girl of six, without being feverish – even so, when they came back in, they had found her completely dressed on her wretched bed which was black with filth, at the far end of the dank little room, talking to the ceiling, every now and then casting towards her listeners desperate glances, incomplete like her words. And so too, first Nannina and then Alfio looked on stupidly. The old woman talked without stopping about all those things from her childhood for a week and then she stretched out her legs in her dirty little bed. She remained there in silence, waiting for them to carry her away.

So, with Gennaro in the army and Santo having moved up in the world in Forte Boccea, only Nannina and her youngest brother, Alfio, were left in the shack.

On the very day of his mother's funeral on the way back

dal Verano,[49] che scendeva la sera come una tempesta, sull'Acqua Bullicante, su Torpignattara, sulla Casilina, dove il giorno finito restava come un fantasma, e decine di migliaia di persone, tornando dal lavoro, passavano nella sua luce invetrita, come di Carnevale – Alfio se ne andò al cinema con un suo compare trovato per caso da quelle parti, da Gara o al Bar Flamengo. Al cinema Due Allori. Il pidocchietto. Che ciaveva ancora di qua e di là dello schermo, il sipario rosso tirato, ridotto a uno straccio con un palmo di polvere secca. La platea era fatta di seggiolette di quelle d'una volta, tutte rotte. E il pavimento era segnato dalle pisciate che i bravi facevano senze muoversi dal loro posto, per sfregio, e che si radunavano tra le cartine, le cicche, i pezzi di giornali, le cocce delle noccioline, sotto lo schermo. Una quarantina di spettatori erano sbragati contro gli schienaletti che scricchiolavano, i più malandri, quelli sotto i vent'anni, con le ginocchia puntate sullo schienaletto davanti, e la pancia messa in mostra e offerta a tutti i venti. I venti del cesso. La cui porticella s'apriva e si chiudeva in continuazione, come un faro: una sbarbagliata e una zaffata fetente, e un gniiiiu gnnnnnau, seguito da un pac, che voleva dire che la porta si era rinchiusa sull'ultimo atto rituale, e sulla sacra sosta là dentro, tra la lastra e le cellette, tra muri più pieni d'iscrizioni e disegnetti che il coppone di Dio Padre. Tre o quattro pischelletti, uno roscio di capelli e rosso di faccia, come un burino, uno delicatuccio come un grillo, che facevano i venditori di noccioline, gelato e mostaccioli, e erano quindi di casa, avevano preso il vizio di baciarsi come le coppie. E il roscio baciava il morettino, sulla bocca; e il morettino voleva ancora. Questo si vedeva contro lo schermo, dove facevano a pistolettate; ma sotto, dietro lo schienaletto lavorato dalla zella come un orefice, non si sapeva cosa facevano le mani zozze. Alfio e il compare innominato, andarono anche loro sulle loro seggiolette, fumando come dannati, con le bocche disgustate, gustandosi il filmetto di banditi. Poi cominciarono a prender parte alla

from Verano, as evening was falling like a storm, over the Acqua Bullicante, over Torpignattara and over the Via Casilina, where there remained the ghost of the dying day, and tens of thousands of people, coming back from work, passed through its glassy, Carnival light, Alfio went off to the cinema with a friend of his that he had met by chance around there, at Gara's or at the Bar Flamengo. To the Due Allori cinema, a real flea-pit. On each side of the screen it's got its stretched-out red curtains, worn ragged and with inches of dry dust on them. The stalls were made up of the small seats which used to be common and they were all broken. For the hell of it the local toughs, without leaving their seats, urinated onto the floor which was marked by pools of urine, which in their turn collected among the cigarette-papers, fag-ends, bits of newspaper and nut-shells under the screen. There were about forty people there, sprawled in their creaking seats. The worst of them, those under twenty, had their knees over the backs of the seats in front of them, displaying their stomachs for all to see. And the stink of the Gents. Its door didn't stop opening and closing. Like a lighthouse it sent out a swinging beam of light and a fetid stench, its door creaked as it swung to and fro and then banged, which meant that the door had closed in again on the last ritual act and on the hallowed stay within – between the urinals and the cubicles – between walls covered with more inscriptions and drawings than there are creases and wrinkles on the pate of God the Father. Three or four little kids, one with red hair and a rosy complexion, like a farmer's boy, and one as frail as a cricket, who sold nuts, ice-creams and lollipops and were therefore at home there, had picked up the habit of kissing each other like courting couples. The red-haired one was kissing the dark one on the mouth; and the dark one wanted more. You could see this against the screen, where there was a gun fight going on; but down below, behind the back of the seat which was ornamented with dirt as if it had been worked by a jeweller, you could not see what their filthy little hands were up to. Alfio and his nameless friend also

cerimonia dell'andata al cesso. E fu lì che Alfio trovò il suo soggetto.

Era uno sulla trentina, la faccia spaventata, la cadoppa[50] tosata, e il trench da impiegato, bluastro – che se ne stava incollato contro la lastra bluastra e rigata d'acqua impestata, guardando il cielo.

Dopo una decina di minuti, Alfio e il disperato, se ne andarono fuori dal Due Allori, imboccarono prima la Casilina, dov'era già notte, poi quella strada stretta e lunga, che parte dalla Casilina come un vicoletto, e, dopo essersi infossata tra due o tre case di quelle rimaste in piedi da quando lì era ancora campagna, va su su, tra muretti, ammucchiamenti di baracche, salite e discese, tra i campi, e arriva alla Borgata Gordiani. A metà di quella strada c'era un prato, che arrivava in discesa a un fosso pieno di frattacce, e qualche vecchia pianta abbandonata di frutta con a sinistra dei cantieri, a destra dei campi ancora coltivati, coi mucchi di letame, rimestati dall'ultimo venticello dell'estate.

I due si fermarono, vicino a quel fosso, sulla fanga. E fu breve la gioia che Alfio potè dare al disperato: perchè era debole di reni, e caldo come tutti i maschi nati dalle bande di Benevento.

«Mezzo sacco, e che ce faccio co' mezzo sacco, me ce compro i bruscolini,» fece poi. Il fatto era che, Alfio, non s'accontentava – nell'animo suo, dentro quell'anima, o animaccia sua – perchè di quell'uomo caduto dal cielo, o composto da chissà che casi del povero mondo zozzo e cane, non aveva saputo vedere che un trench bluastro: non s'accontentava nè di mezzo sacco, nè di un sacco, nè dei due o tre sacchi che quello poteva avere in saccoccia; ma voleva entrare in possesso, nè più nè meno che del trench, con la stessa disperazione con cui il disperato aveva voluto entrare in possesso di quello che lui aveva sotto, dentro la cova dei calzonacci da lavoro. E allora lo toccò, strinse tra le dita il bavero, lo alzò

went to their seats, smoking like chimneys, screwing up their faces, and enjoying the gangster film. Then they too joined in the ceremonial visit to the Gents. And it was there that Alfio found his man.

He was about thirty, with a frightened-looking face, shorn hair and a bluish, office-worker's trench-coat – standing glued against the bluish urinal, which was streaked with foul water, looking at the sky.

About ten minutes later Alfio and his sorry companion left the Due Allori and first entered the Via Casilina, where it was already night, then that long, narrow street which turns off the Via Casilina like an alley and, after going down between two or three of those houses still left standing from the time when it was still country there, goes on between low walls, groups of shacks, up and down, between the fields, and comes out at Borgata Gordiani. Half-way along that road there was a field, which went down to a ditch full of brambles, and some old, abandoned fruit-bushes; on the left there were building sites, and on the right fields which were still cultivated with their heaps of manure, stirred by the last summer breeze.

The two of them stopped near the ditch in the mud. But Alfio could only give the poor fellow brief satisfaction, because he was weak and excitable as were all the men born within the bounds of Benevento.

'Five hundred lire, what am I going to do with five hundred lire? A fat lot I'll be able to do with that,' he then said. The fact of the matter was that Alfio was not satisfied – in his heart of hearts, in his soul, in his wretched soul – for in this man, fallen from the sky and made up of heaven knows what accidents of this poor, dirty, bestial world, he could see nothing more than a blue trench-coat. He wasn't content with 500 lire, nor with a thousand, nor with the two or three thousand that the man probably had in his pocket, but he wanted to possess nothing less than the coat, with the same desperation with which the man had wanted to possess what was there underneath, hidden by his old working trousers. So he touched it, felt the lapel

come si alza la sottana di una donna per esaminare con occhio sorridente la fodera: come se quel trench non fosse infilato a una creatura, ma appeso a un attaccapanni.

Basta: Alfio voleva entrare in possesso del trench, se non con le buone, anche con le cattive. Ma quello, il farlocco, non ci stava: come un bambino, si attaccava alla cosa sua, non la mollava. Alfio allora con la stessa rapidità con cui se n'era venuto, ora s'incazzò, sbattè a terra il farlocco – che cominciò a piangere e a strillare, gridando aiuto, quello stronzo, come se preferisse finire in camera di sicurezza da Baffetti[51] piuttosto che ammollare quello straccetto che aveva addosso. Così per farlo star zitto, Alfio prese una pietra, ch'era lì sulla fanga, e gliela sbattè in fronte, tre quattro volte: quello tacque. Alfio gli sfilò il trench e si diede.

Tre quattro giorni dopo lo beccarono, da Gara, insieme al compare innominato, con su tutto arioso il trench bluastro del destino; se lo bevettero e lo portarono al Coeli[52] per un pelo, chè Alfio aveva compiuto diciott'-anni da un mese, e forse meno.

Nannina era sola, a Roma e a Salerno, a Centocelle e al Mandrione. Sola in tutto il mondo. Il ragionierino non s'era più fatto vivo. Si fece vivo invece Aurelio, come un pitone che dorme anche quando si muove. Per qualche mese si mosse così: con l'occhio lontano, distratto, il baffetto nero cadente. La domenica mattina, che l'Adele non lavorava, e s'alzava tardi, Nannina andava alla loro baracca, e beveva il vermut. Faceva la serva in quel periodo, e aveva le mani rosse, a forza di lavare piatti nella casa di un certo mandrucone impiegato a un Ministero; e siccome l'aveva già capito d'un pezzo come sarebbe finita, aveva già cominciato ad ammollarsi, e più d'un giovanotto s'era accontentato di quelle mani rosse, dopo il ballo alla sala Bruscolotti o al Nilo. Una mattina, l'Adele non c'era. C'era solo Aurelio, che s'era risvegliato dal lungo sonno: l'occhietto nero di siciliano

between his fingers, raised it as you raise a woman's skirt to examine, smilingly, the lining, as if the coat was not worn by a living creature, but was hanging from a peg.

That was enough. Alfio wanted that coat and if not by fair means then by foul. But the other, the stranger, was not having it. Like a child he clung to his possession and would not let go. Alfio then, with the same speed of passion as before, now grew angry, flung the stranger down on the ground – this last began to cry and to scream, calling for help, the idiot, as if he would prefer to end up in a cell at Baffetti's, rather than release the rag which he was wearing. And so, to shut him up, Alfio picked up a stone, which was there in the mud, and smashed it against his forehead three or four times. The man lay quiet. Alfio took off the coat and cleared off.

Three or four days later they got him at Gara's, along with his nameless friend, proudly wearing the fateful bluish trench-coat. They arrested him and took him off to the Regina Coeli – but only just, for Alfio had only been eighteen for a month or perhaps less.

Nannina was alone, in Rome and in Salerno, in Centocelle and on the Mandrione. Quite alone in the world. The little book-keeper had not turned up again. Aurelio was around, however, like a python that sleeps even when moving. For some months he moved like this with a distant, absent-minded look and a drooping, black moustache. On Sunday mornings, when Adele was not working and got up late, Nannina went to their hut and drank vermouth. She was working as a servant at this time and her hands were red as a result of doing the washing-up in the house of some old fogey who was working for a minister. As for some time she had already gathered how things would end up, she had already begun to give way, and more than one young man had found those red hands pleasing enough after the dance at the Sala Bruscolotti or at the Nilo. One morning Adele was not there. There was only Aurelio, who had

gli brillava come una stella, nell'espressione materna di tutto il viso. Abbracciò Nannina come solo una madre può abbracciare – protettore come un santo. La distese, delicatamente, come un prete tocca un'ostia e la sposta sul tabernacolo, sopra il lettone dell'Adele la Dentona, e le fece sentire quella cosa che dai tempi di Mario, ormai, Nannina non conosceva più.

Nannina cominciò la vita una sera d'inverno inoltrato, che su Roma, il giorno prima era caduta un po' di neve: e rimaneva bella bianca solo sui cornicioni della fontana e degli archi del Mandrione. All'Acqua Santa, sulla Tuscolana, dove Nannina andò a lavorare, era già nera. E poi piovvicicava un po'. Le altre donne avevano acceso un fuocherello, lì dove Aurelio la lasciò, proprio al margine dei pratoni dell'Acqua Santa, che si alzavano neri di gobbe e di grotte, contro il cielo sparso di nubi bianchicce. Nel cuore dell'inverno, con la neve qua e là, benchè sporca, già si sentiva qualcosa della primavera.

Le mignotte stavano intorno al loro fuocherello, e si eccitavano come ragazzine a cercar legna e carta per tenerlo acceso: era proprio un fuocherello da niente, che il vento gelato di primavera muoveva appena, tra i piedi delle mignotte e quelli di qualche cliente bonaccione o di qualche pischello tenero – venuto lì con loro a scaldarsi e a tenergli un po' di compagnia.

woken from his long sleep. His small, black, Sicilian eyes shone like stars in the motherly expression of his whole face. He embraced Nannina with a mother's embrace – as protective as a saint. He laid her out, delicately, like a priest touching the host and removing it from the tabernacle, on the great bed of Toothy Adele and made her feel something which, since the days of Mario, Nannina had not known at all.

Nannina began her new life one evening in late winter. A little bit of snow had fallen on Rome the day before, and it remained beautiful and white only on the ledges of the fountain and of the arches across the Mandrione. At the Acqua Santa by the Via Tuscolana, where Nannina went to work, it was already dark. And then it was drizzling a bit. The other women had lit a small fire, where Aurelio left her, just on the edge of the fields by the Acqua Santa, which rose up black with mounds and caves, against the sky scattered with off-white clouds. In the heart of winter, with patches of snow here and there, even if dirty, there was already a feeling of spring.

The prostitutes were standing around their little fire, running around excitedly like little girls looking for wood and paper to keep it alight. It was really an insignificant little fire, which the icy wind of spring scarcely moved, down there between the feet of prostitutes and those of some good-natured client or some young kid, who had come there with them to warm himself and to keep them company for a while.

OVERTAKING

ALBERTO MORAVIA

Translated by Brian Cainen

IL SORPASSO

Non si possono avere due passioni nello stesso tempo. La passione per la macchina, che ero riuscito alfine di comprare, mi distrasse in quei giorni dalla passione per Ines, la ragazza con la quale pensavo di fidanzarmi. Tanto bastò perché Tullio, l'amicone mio, si intrufolasse tra Ines e me e tentasse di soffiarmela. Eh, gli amici, è meglio non parlarne. E se proprio bisogna parlarne, allora dobbiamo riconoscere che l'amicizia è bella e buona finché non c'è la donna. Guardate un pollaio: due galli beccano insieme, cantano insieme, dormono insieme; fate che sopravvenga una gallinella di primo pelo, di quelle tutte bianche con la crestina rossa, e addio pace, i due galli si azzuffano e si cavano gli occhi con le beccate.

Che cos'è un pensiero: qualsiasi cosa uno faccia, passeggi o lavori, stia solo o in compagnia, quel pensiero si affaccia come qualche cosa che non si capisce e che, appunto perché non si capisce, si gira e rigira da ogni parte e non si finisce mai di rigirare. Non si capisce perché si ama. Questo mi avveniva con Ines finché non comprai la macchina; una volta comprata la macchina, cominciò ad avvenirmi con la macchina. Va' a capire certe cose:[1] Ines era di carne e ossa, la macchina di ferraccio; Ines ci aveva una bella faccia tonda con gli occhi neri e dolci e la bocca ridente, la macchina un muso coi paraurti che sembravano i denti di un mastino; Ines, benché piccola, era fatta al tornio[2] per tutta la persona, la macchina era fatta come tutte la macchine, in fondo un cassone; eppure, pian piano, il pensiero della macchina scacciò il pensiero di Ines. E mi fossi contentato di pensarci. Il guaio è che ne parlavo: e gli altri lo notavano più di quanto avessi creduto. Tullio me lo disse un giorno,

OVERTAKING

You can't be passionately in love with two different things at the same time. At that time the love for my car, that I'd finally managed to buy, was distracting me from my love for Ines, the girl I was thinking of getting engaged to. That was enough to make Tullio, my best friend, poke his nose in between Ines and me and try to get her away from me. Friends? It's best not to talk about them. And if you've really got to talk about them, well then you've got to realize that friendship is all very well, as long as there are no women around. Take a poultry-run for example: two cocks peck together, crow together, sleep together; let a young hen in her prime come along, one of those ones white all over with a red comb, and it's good-bye to peace: the two cocks quarrel and peck each other's eyes out.

Look what a thought can do: whatever you do, whether you're going for a walk or working, alone or with friends, that thought comes into your mind like something you don't understand, and precisely because you can't understand, it keeps on coming and going and you never stop turning it over. You can't understand why you're in love. This happened to me with Ines until I bought my car; once I'd bought the car, it began to happen to me with the car. Some things I'll never understand: Ines was made of flesh and blood, the car of scrap-iron; Ines had a nice round face with soft black eyes and a laughing mouth, the car had a mug with bumpers that looked like a mastiff's teeth; although Ines was small, she was beautifully fashioned; the car was made like any other car, basically a box; and yet, slowly but surely, thoughts about the car drove out thoughts about Ines. If only I'd been content with thinking about it. The trouble is, I talked about it; and other people noticed more than I thought. One day, with Ines there, Tullio said

presente Ines: «Tu, Gigi, ormai non pensi piú che alla macchina. Ines, io al tuo posto sarei geloso.» Ines, sorridendo, disse allora: «Gigi, chiudi gli occhi e dimmi che vedi: due gambe o quattro ruote?» Risposi, naturalmente: «Due gambe»; ma in realtà mentivo: avevo visto quattro ruote, quattro belle ruote con i copertoni nuovi che, come sapevo, mi aspettavano all'angolo della strada per portarmi dove volevo io.

Basta, una di quelle mattine, che era domenica, telefonai ad Ines che sarei venuto a prenderla per andare al mare; avvertendo che volevo star solo con lei: volevo parlarle del fidanzamento. Contento e leggero, discesi al garage sotto casa mia, tirai fuori la mia bella bicolore grigia e blu[3] e per prima cosa andai dal benzinaro, all'angolo di via Candia,[4] dove mi feci fare il servizio completo: benzina, acqua, olio, gomme, perfino l'acqua distillata della batteria, nonché una ripulita al vetro del parabrezza. Salgo, metto la prima, passo alla seconda, ingrano la terza, finalmente faccio tutto viale Giulio Cesare in quarta: una meraviglia. La macchina non correva, addirittura si beveva la strada; con il motore che faceva un ronzio d'amore come le api a primavera su un prato fiorito. Ma come svoltai in piazza della Libertà, vidi da lontano che Ines non era sola.

Ci rimasi male, anche perché l'avevo avvertita che volevo restar solo con lei; tanto piú male ci rimasi quando vidi che l'altro era Tullio. Già ce lo sapevo[5] che Tullio, amico mio e socio nel commercio di accessori, occhieggiava Ines; la sua presenza, quella mattina, fu per me una conferma. Debbo aggiungere che tra di noi, il forzuto, il bello era Tullio: alto, le spalle larghe, la testa piccola piantata su un collo di toro. Io, invece, basso e striminzito, non ci avevo che gli occhi, intensi e intelligenti, a ricordare che dopo tutto non c'è soltanto la forza a questo mondo. Notai con antipatia che Tullio ci aveva la maglietta a strisce rosse e blu e i pantaloni uso mare,[6] turchini: piú bullo[7] del solito. Come fui all'altez-

to me: 'Gigi, you think of nothing but your car these days. In your place, Ines, I'd be jealous.' So, with a smile, Ines said: 'Close your eyes, Gigi, and tell me what you can see: two legs or four wheels?' 'Two legs,' I replied, of course; but in fact I was lying: I'd seen four wheels, four lovely wheels with new tyres that I knew were waiting for me at the street corner to carry me off to wherever I wanted.

Enough of all that, one of those mornings, a Sunday, I phoned Ines to say that I would be coming to take her to the seaside; telling her that I wanted to be alone with her: I wanted to talk to her about our engagement. Happily and light-heartedly I went down to the garage below my house, got out my beautiful two-tone, blue and grey car and first of all went to the petrol station at the corner of Via Candia, where I had a complete check done: petrol, water, oil, tyres, even the distilled water in the battery, and had the windscreen cleaned as well. I got in, put her into first, moved into second, engaged third and finally went down the whole of Viale Giulo Cesare in fourth – marvellous. The car wasn't running, it was really drinking the street up; and the engine was humming with love, like bees in spring over a flowery meadow. But, as I turned into the Piazza della Libertà, I saw from a distance that Ines wasn't alone.

I was annoyed by this, especially as I'd told her that I wanted to be alone with her; I was even more annoyed when I saw that the person she was with was Tullio. I already knew that Tullio, my friend and colleague in the car accessories business, had his eye on Ines; his presence there that morning confirmed this for me. I should add that of the two of us, the strong one, the good-looking one was Tullio; he was tall and broad-shouldered, with a small head and a bull neck. I, on the other hand, am small and thin, with only my intense, intelligent eyes to remind you that after all strength isn't the only thing that counts in this world. I noticed with irritation that Tullio was wearing a red and blue striped shirt and dark blue light-weight

za di quei due, aprii la portiera, fermandomi, e dissi asciutto: «Addio Tullio.» Ines, allegra, spiegò: «Tullio mi aveva telefonato e allora gli ho detto di venire anche lui.» Tullio disse, sfacciato; «Non ti fa niente, eh? Tanto per te l'importante è guidare la macchina, no?» Parole imprudenti che mi andarono subito in tanto veleno. Risposi, da finto tonto: «E come no. L'importante per me è la macchina, il resto non conta. Su, salite.» Salirono dunque, Ines sul sedile di dietro, Tullio accanto a me. Questa disposizione lí per lí mi piacque; ma poi ben presto, mi accorsi, che non avevo di che stare allegro. Tullio, infatti, si girò subito dalla parte di Ines, lei si sporse verso Tullio; e cosí, mentre badavo a guidare, loro cominciarono una conversazione fitta fitta, proprio da innamorati o che ci tirano a diventarlo. Che si dicevano? Eh, di tutto un po', scherzi, allusioni, complimenti, insinuazioni, mezze frasi, parolette in aria. Quello che, però, mi dava piú fastidio era il tono: eccitato, entrante, malizioso, proprio di due persone che se la intendono e poco importa quello che si dicono, tanto, sotto sotto, c'è l'intesa.

Intanto eravamo usciti da Roma e filavamo sull' Aurelia.[8] L'idea era di andare a Santa Marinella,[9] era tardi ormai, presi a correre. Correre, però: una parola. Per quanto era lunga la strada, le macchine si seguivano alle macchine: grandi e piccole, italiane e straniere, di lusso e utilitarie. Ogni tanto qualche camion del latte, qualche autocarro delle colonie marine guidato da un pazzo che faceva i sorpassi come se avesse avuto sotto mano una motoretta. Presi a tenere una marcia bassa, e forse avrei continuato se quei due accanto a me non mi avessero dato sui nervi col loro chiacchericcio. Non so come, non so perché, il nervoso della gelosia si comunicava alla mia guida e cosí accelerai, forse con l'idea di giungere al piú presto a Santa Marinella e interrompere quella loro conversazione troppo confidenziale. Presi perciò a sorpassare le macchine, una dopo l'altra, come

trousers: more cocky than usual. When I got up to them, I slowed down, opened the door and said dryly: 'Goodbye, Tullio.' Cheerfully Ines explained: 'Tullio phoned me so I told him to come too.' 'You don't mind, do you?' said Tullio brazenly, 'anyway, what matters to you is driving the car, isn't it?' Stupid words, which immediately got my back up. Pretending to be a bit slow, I replied: 'Of course. The important thing for me is the car, nothing else matters. Come on, get in.' So they got in, Ines in the back, Tullio next to me. At first I liked this arrangement, but pretty soon I realized I had nothing to be pleased about. In fact, Tullio immediately turned round towards Ines, and she leaned forward towards him; and so, while I was paying attention to the driving they began a very cosy conversation, just like people in love or about to fall in love. What were they saying to each other? Well, a bit of everything, jokes, hints, flattering remarks, innuendoes, half-sentences, words left hanging in the air. But what annoyed me most was their tone: excited, full of insinuations, mischievous, just like two people who have an understanding with each other, and it doesn't matter what they say, since underneath it all there is this mutual understanding.

Meanwhile we had left Rome and were going along the Via Aurelia. The idea was to go to Santa Marinella; by now it was late and I began to speed along. Speed along – mere words. For the whole length of the road the cars followed on one after the other: big and small, Italian and foreign, de-luxe models and cheaper ones. Every so often there came some milk lorry, some lorry from one of the seaside resorts driven by a fool who was overtaking as if he were driving a scooter. I began keeping in a low gear and perhaps I would have stayed in it if those two next to me hadn't got on my nerves with their stupid chattering. I don't know how, I don't know why, but the irritability caused by jealousy was transferred to my driving and so I accelerated, perhaps with the idea of getting to Santa Marinella as soon as possible and of interrupting that over-confidential conversation of theirs. So I began overtaking

si infilano le perle. Al mio strombettamento insistente, ce n'erano che si mettevano subito da parte, macchine buone che osservavano le regole della strada; ma c'erano pure le macchine che non volevano farsi sorpassare a nessun patto. Feci l'osservazione: le macchine piú educate erano le piú potenti, i macchinoni grossi, di lusso, guidati da gente che se ne infischiava dei sorpassi, tanto ce lo sapevano che, se volevano, correvano piú di tutti: le macchine piú tignose erano invece le utilitarie, piene di donne e di bambini, con il padre di famiglia al volante. Ai figli, alla moglie, quei disgraziati che avevano passato la settimana col sedere nella poltrona, volevano dimostrare di essere sportivi, dritti, gagliardi; e cosí, al momento del sorpasso, invece di rallentarsi e mettersi da parte, acceleravano. Li avrei ammazzati; tanto piú che mentre loro, gravi, compresi, imperturbabili, spingevano al massimo della velocità la macchinetta a rate, la famiglia intera mi considerava da dietro i vetri con certe facce canzonatorie e trionfanti, come a dire: «Te l'abbiamo fatta. Papà è piú forte di te.» Io li guardavo e mi domandavo perché mai facce, se le avessi viste al negozio o per strada, mi sarebbero sembrate indifferenti o magari simpatiche, viste dietro i vetri di un'automobile, mi parevano tanto odiose. Intanto avevamo passato il bivio di Fregene e ci dirigevamo verso Ladispoli.[10]

Oltre al chiacchericcio di Ines e di Tullio e alle facce antipatiche delle famiglie indomenicate, c'era un'altra cosa che mi urtava i nervi: il fatto che Tullio interrompesse ogni tanto di civettare con Ines per incitarmi, bontà sua, a fare i sorpassi. Mi diceva: «Sotto, Gigi, passami quella utilitaria;» oppure: «Dàgli, passala, che aspetti?» Oppure ancora: «Vai, di che hai paura? Metti la terza e passala.» Fossimo stati soli, pazienza: qualche volta può essere anche divertente fare le corse. Ma c'era Ines; e nessuno mi toglieva dalla testa che Tullio mi spingesse a fare i sorpassi per tenermi occupato e distrarmi in modo che potesse fare i comodi suoi con lei. Con in

the other cars, one after the other, just like stringing pearls. When they heard me persistently sounding the horn, some cars immediately drew in, good cars that observed the highway code; but there were others that didn't want to be overtaken at any cost. This is what I noticed: the best-behaved cars were the most powerful ones, the big, de-luxe cars driven by people who couldn't care less about being overtaken, since they knew that if they wanted to they could go faster than everyone else. But the most niggardly cars were the cheap ones, full of women and children with father at the wheel. These wretches, who had spent the week with their backsides in an arm-chair, wanted to show their children and wives that they were sporty, manly and strong; and so, just when they were being overtaken, instead of slowing down and moving over, they accelerated. I could have killed them; the more so because while they, serious, concentrating and stolid, pushed their little cars bought on the never never to their highest speed, the whole family would stare at me from behind the windows with jeering, triumphant faces, as if to say: 'We beat you. Dad's stronger than you.' I stared at them and wondered why on earth faces that would have seemed to me indifferent or even pleasant had I seen them in a shop or on the street, seemed so hateful behind the windows of a car. Meanwhile we had passed the junction at Fregene and were making for Ladispoli.

As well as the stupid chattering of Ines and Tullio and the horrible faces of these families on their Sunday outings, there was something else that was getting on my nerves: the fact that every so often Tullio would stop flirting with Ines to egg me on, which was very nice of him, to overtake someone. 'Come on, Gigi,' he'd say, 'Overtake that cheap one for me'; or 'Go on, overtake him, what are you waiting for?'; or again 'Go on, what are you frightened of? Put her into third and overtake him.' If we'd been on our own, O.K. having races can sometimes be quite good fun. But there was Ines; and no one could have put it out of my head that Tullio was pushing me on to overtake so as to keep me

piú, forse, una punta di canzonatura. Un po' come gli innamorati, ai giardini pubblici, che dicono al bambino importuno: «Su, bravo, va a giocare a palla.» Ci sformavo; ma invece di rallentare e guidare con calma come avrei dovuto, per la rabbia mi sentivo portato a seguire gli incitamenti e a fare i sorpassi; e piú li facevo e piú mi arrabbiavo al pensiero che cosí davo ragione a Tullio il quale mi considerava un giocherellone che bastava metterglì tra le mani il volante perché si lasciasse soffiare la ragazza.

Però li tenevo d'occhio. Tullio stava girato sul sedile, una gamba ripiegata sul cuscino, le due mani aggrappate alla spalliera; Ines si piegava verso di lui, e teneva anche lei la mano sulla spalliera, benché non ce ne fosse bisogno. Ad un certo momento senza parer di nulla, aggiustai lo specchietto in modo che adesso non vedevo piú la strada dietro di me, ma quella parte del sedile dove loro appoggiavano le mani. Dopo un poco vidi, cosí, la mano di Tullio avvicinarsi, strisciando piano piano, a quella di Ines, e poi, ad una svolta ricoprirla. Nello stesso momento Tullio disse: «Sotto, Gigi, sorpassami quell'utilitaria, che aspetti?» Guardai alla strada: la macchina di cui parlava Tullio mi stava davanti e correva forte. Era una vecchia giardinetta, con una carrozzina da lattante legata sul tetto. Dentro si vedeva il solito groviglio di donne e di bambini; alla guida il solito padre di famiglia, il testone affondato nel collo, grasso, inquartato, le mani nere e pelose aggrappate al volante: un pupazzo. Ma togliendo gli occhi dalle mani di Tullio e di Ines e guardando alla giardinetta, la prima cosa che vidi non fu il guidatore, bensí, dietro il vetro posteriore, la faccia di un ragazzino di forse sei anni, brutta e pallida, con le orecchie a sventola, che mi faceva le boccacce, e mi tirava la lingua. Il bambino mi faceva le boccacce perché pensava che io ci sformassi ad essere stato sorpassato dal padre; ma io, non so perché, pensai che mi facesse le boccacce per canzonarmi sul

occupied and distracted so that he could get on better with her. And perhaps there was also a touch of mockery. A bit like lovers in a park who say to a troublesome child: 'Come on, be a good boy, go and play ball.' I was getting angry; but instead of slowing down and driving calmly as I should have done, because of my anger I got carried away into doing what he urged and overtaking; and the more I overtook, the angrier I got, realizing that by doing this I was admitting Tullio was right, Tullio who saw me as a mere play-thing in whose hands you only had to put a steering-wheel to get his girl off him.

But I kept an eye on them. Tullio had turned round with one leg bent underneath him and was holding on to the back of the seat with both hands; Ines was leaning towards him and she too had her hand on the back of his seat, although there was no need for it. At one point, without seeming to give it much attention, I adjusted the mirror so that now I no longer saw the road behind me, but instead that part of the seat where they were resting their hands. In this way, after a while I saw Tullio's hand sliding very slowly along and getting nearer to Ines's, and then at a bend in the road, cover it. At the same time Tullio said, 'Come on Gigi, overtake that cheap one for me, what are you waiting for?' I looked at the road: the car Tullio was talking about was in front of me and travelling very fast. It was an old estate car, with a baby's pram tied onto the roof. Inside you could see the usual mass of women and children; at the wheel, the same old head of the family, with his large head sunk into his neck, fat, stolid, his black, hairy hands gripping the wheel: a puppet. But as I took my eyes from Tullio's and Ines's hands the first thing I saw wasn't the driver, but behind the back window the ugly, pale face of a little boy, perhaps six years old, with flapping ears, who was pulling faces at me and sticking out his tongue. The boy was making faces because he thought I was getting angry at being overtaken by his father; I don't know why, but I thought he was pulling faces to make a fool of me because of Tullio and Ines. I frowned at him; with his

fatto di Tullio e di Ines. Lo guardai aggrottando le sopracciglia; lui, che aveva il braccio della madre girato intorno il petto e schiacciava il naso contro il vetro, mi guardò anche lui e poi tirò di nuovo la lingua. Alzai gli occhi allo specchietto e vidi che, adesso, Tullio risaliva dalla mano di Ines al polso, e dal polso al braccio. Tullio disse, ipocrita: «Ahò, ma ti sei incantato? Accelera.» Ines, con la voce dolce del turbamento d'amore, confermò: «Andiamo troppo piano... cosí non ci arriviamo piú a Santa Marinella.»

Risposi: «Ah sí, non corro abbastanza? mo'[11] vedrete.» Eravamo su un rettifilo che, in fondo, finiva in una salita. Sul lato destro avevo una siepe in cima ad un rialzo del terreno, sul sinistro una fila di platani inchinati verso la strada, coi tronchi fasciati di bianco. Misi la terza, premetti a fondo l'acceleratore, schiacciai il clackson e via di gran corsa, strombettando, con un ruggito potente del motore. Ci credereste? Il padre di famiglia, al mio strombettamento, invece di mettersi a destra come avrebbe dovuto, si piazza in mezzo alla strada e accelera anche lui. Fui, cosí, costretto ad accodarmi; Tullio disse: «Ahò, ma che fai, non ti vergogni?» poi alzai gli occhi e vidi il ragazzino che mi tirava la lingua. Allora mi gettai di nuovo sulla sinistra e sempre strombettando cominciai a correre a paro alla giardinetta. Eravamo ormai quasi in fondo al rettifilo dove la strada si arrampicava per la salita, il padre di famiglia accelerava, io non ce la facevo e crepavo dalla rabbia; poi, tutto ad un tratto, presi a guadagnare terreno. Ma ecco, proprio in quel momento, sbucò alla voltata una macchina che mi veniva incontro a velocità moderata ma sempre sufficiente ad impedirmi di compiere il sorpasso. Avrei dovuto rinunziare, accodarmi di nuovo; ma non so che diavolo mi suggerí di sorpassare. La macchina del padre di famiglia accelera anche lei, faccio appena in tempo a gettarmi tutto a sinistra, nel fosso, per evitare il cozzo, e vedo il tronco di un platano venirmi incontro.

mother's arm round his chest and rubbing his nose against the window he looked back at me and then stuck his tongue out again. I looked up at the mirror and saw that Tullio was now moving up from Ines's hand to her wrist, and from her wrist to her arm. 'Come on then,' said Tullio hypocritically, 'are you dreaming? Accelerate.' With her voice made sweet by the excitement of love Ines agreed: 'We're going too slowly . . . at this rate we'll never get to Santa Marinella.'

'Oh, I see,' I replied, 'I'm not going fast enough, am I? Well, you'll soon see.' We were on a straight stretch of road that rose slightly at the end. On the right there was a hedge on top of an embankment, on the left a row of plane trees that bent over towards the road, painted white round their trunks. I put the car into third, pushed the accelerator right down, pressed the horn and away we went with the horn blaring and the engine roaring powerfully. Would you believe it? As my horn blared out, instead of pulling into the right as he should have done, the father of the family planted himself in the middle of the road and accelerated as well. So I was forced to fall in behind him; 'Come on, what are you doing?' said Tullio, 'aren't you ashamed of yourself?'; then I looked up and saw the little boy sticking his tongue out at me. So I threw myself to the left again and with the horn blaring all the time began to run level with the estate car. By now we were almost at the end of the straight stretch where the road began to climb; the father of the family accelerated, but I couldn't keep up and was fuming with rage; then suddenly I began to gain ground. But just at that moment a car coming from the opposite direction drew out on the bend fairly slowly but fast enough to stop me finally overtaking. I should have given up, drawn back again, but some evil spirit urged me on to overtake. The family man's car accelerated as well; I had hardly had time to throw myself right over to the left into the ditch, to avoid the collision, when I saw the trunk of a plane tree

Mi parve di udire la voce di Tullio che gridava: «Frena, frena»; e poi non sentii piú niente.

Inutile raccontare quello che avvenne dopo: andate a prendere il giornale del lunedí e ci troverete tutti i particolari. Voglio soltanto dire che io fui il solo che me la cavai con poco: dieci giorni salvo complicazioni che per fortuna non ci furono. Ma Tullio ebbe una gamba rotta e stette due mesi all'ospedale dove io l'andai a trovare tutti i giorni. Ines, lei, si fratturò proprio quel braccio che con tanta docilità aveva abbandonato alla carezza di Tullio e se lo portò al collo piú di un mese. Della macchina, poi, meglio non parlarne: uno di questi giorni la venderò come rottame di ferro. Ma lo sapete piuttosto quel che mi disse il dottor Frontini, un giovanotto sveglio che curava Tullio, al quale raccontai per filo e per segno come era avvenuto il fatto? «Lei, nel suo subconscio voleva distruggere la macchina che le impediva di voler bene a Ines, ammazzare per gelosia il suo amico, ammazzarsi per la disperazione di non essere piú amato e punire la sua ragazza per il tradimento. In parte c'è riuscito.» Domandai: «Ma si può sapere che cos'è questo subconscio?» E lui: «Quello che noi non sappiamo di noi stessi.» Dissi allora: «Sarà; ma io ho voluto fare un sorpasso e non ci sono riuscito, ecco tutto.» Però, dopo l'incidente, ho rinunziato a guidare e mi sono fidanzato con Ines. E Tullio? Tullio ed io siamo di nuovo amici come prima.

coming towards me. I seemed to hear Tullio's voice shouting 'Brake, brake!'; and then I heard nothing more.

There's no point in going into what happened afterwards: go and buy that Monday's paper and you'll find all the details there. I only want to say that I was the only one to come out of it without much harm: ten days, unless there were complications, which luckily enough there weren't. But Tullio had a broken leg and spent two months in hospital, where I went to see him every day. Ines fractured that very arm that she had so easily let Tullio caress, and she carried it in a sling for more than a month. As for the car, I'd rather not talk about it; one of these days I'll sell it for scrap-iron. But, more important, do you know what Dr Frontini, a smart young chap who was looking after Tullio, said to me when I told him in great detail how the accident had happened? 'In your subconscious you wanted to destroy the car that stopped you from loving Ines, to kill your friend through jealousy, to kill yourself through despair at not being loved any more and to punish your girl-friend for her betrayal. You've partly succeeded.' 'But tell me what this subconscious is?' I asked him. 'What we don't know about ourselves,' he replied. So I said. 'That's as may be; but I wanted to overtake and I didn't make it, that's all.' Still, after the accident I gave up driving and got engaged to Ines. And Tullio? Tullio and I are friends again, just like before.

THE ORIGIN OF THE BIRDS

ITALO CALVINO

Translated by Richard Andrews

L'ORIGINE DEGLI UCCELLI

L'apparizione degli Uccelli è relativamente tarda, nella storia dell'evoluzione: posteriore a quella di tutte le altre classi del regno animale. Il progenitore degli Uccelli – o almeno il primo di cui i paleontologi abbiano trovato traccia – l'Archaeopteryx (ancora dotato di alcune caratteristiche dei Rettili da cui discende), rimonta al Giurassico, decine di milioni d'anni dopo i primi Mammiferi. È questa l'unica eccezione alla successiva comparsa di gruppi animali sempre piú evoluti nella scala zoologica.[1]

Erano giorni in cui non ci aspettavamo piú sorprese, – *raccontò Qfwfq*, – come sarebbero andate[2] le cose ormai era chiaro. Chi c'era c'era, dovevamo vedercela tra noi: chi sarebbe arrivato piú lontano, chi sarebbe rimasto lí dov'era, chi non ce l'avrebbe fatta a sopravvivere. La scelta era tra un numero di possibilità limitate.

Invece, una mattina, sento[3] un canto, da fuori, che non avevo mai sentito. O meglio (dato che il canto non si sapeva ancora cosa fosse): sento fare un verso che nessuno aveva fatto mai. M'affaccio. Vedo un animale sconosciuto che cantava su di un ramo. Aveva ali zampe coda unghie speroni penne piume pinne aculei becco denti gozzo corna cresta bargigli e una stella in fronte. Era un uccello; voi l'avevate già capito; io no; non se n'erano mai visti. Cantò: «Koaxpf ... Koaxpf ... Koaaaccch ...», sbatté le ali striate di colori cangianti, s'alzò a volo, tornò a posarsi un po' piú in là, riprese il canto.

Adesso, queste storie si raccontano meglio con dei fumetti che non con un racconto di frasi una dopo l'altra. Ma per disegnare la vignetta con l'uccello sul ramo e io affacciato e tutti gli altri a naso in su, dovrei

THE ORIGIN OF THE BIRDS

The appearance of the Birds is relatively late in evolutionary history: later than that of any other class in the animal kindgom. The ancestor of the Birds – or at least the earliest one of which palaeontologists have found traces – Archaeopteryx, still bearing some characteristics of the Reptiles from which it descends, dates from the Jurassic period, tens of millions of years after the first Mammals. This is the only exception to the progressive appearance of animal groups each more evolved than the last in the zoological scale.

They were days when we had stopped expecting surprises – *recounted Qfwfq* – it seemed clear now how things were going to turn out. Those who existed, existed; we had to sort out on our own which of us was going to develop further, who would remain where he was, who would not manage to survive. The choice was between a limited number of possibilities.

But instead, one morning, I heard some singing outside which I had never heard before. Or rather (given that we didn't yet know what singing was), I heard a noise that nobody had ever made before. I looked out. I saw an unknown animal singing on a branch. It had wings, feet, tail, claws, spurs, feathers, quills, talons, beak, teeth, crop, horns, crest, wattles, and a star on its forehead. It was a bird; you had already guessed; I hadn't – they'd never been seen before. It sang: «Koaxpf . . . Koaxpf . . . Koaaaccch . . .», flapped its striped rainbow-coloured wings, took flight, came down and perched further away, and began to sing again.

Nowadays these stories are better told in a comic-strip than in a narrative with sentences one after the other. But to do a drawing of the bird on the branch and me looking out at it and all the others gawping upwards, I should need

ricordarmi meglio com'eran fatte tante cose che ho dimenticato da tempo: primo, quello che io adesso chiamo uccello, secondo, quello che io adesso chiamo «io», terzo il ramo, quarto il posto dove ero affacciato, quinto tutti gli altri. Di questi elementi ricordo solo che erano molto diversi da come li rappresenteremmo adesso. È meglio che cerchiate voi stessi d'immaginare la serie di vignette con tutte le figurine dei personaggi al loro posto, su uno sfondo efficacemente tratteggiato, ma cercando nello stesso tempo di non immaginarvi le figurine, e neppure lo sfondo. Ogni figurina avrà la sua nuvoletta con le parole che dice, o con i rumori che fa, ma non c'è bisogno che leggiate lettera per lettera tutto quello che c'è scritto, basta che ne abbiate un'idea generale a seconda di come vi dirò.

Per cominciare, potete leggere tanti punti esclamativi e punti interrogativi che zampillano dalle nostre teste, e ciò vuol dire che stavamo guardando l'uccello pieni di meraviglia – festosa meraviglia, voglia anche noi di cantare, d'imitare quel primo gorgheggio, e di saltare, al vederlo alzarsi a volo –, ma pure pieni di sbigottimento, perché l'esistenza degli uccelli mandava all'aria il modo di ragionare in cui eravamo cresciuti.

Nella striscia di fumetti che segue, si vede il piú sapiente di tutti noi, il vecchio U(h), che si stacca dal gruppo degli altri, dice: «Non guardatelo! È un errore!» e allarga le mani come volesse tappare gli occhi dei presenti. «Adesso lo cancello!» dice, o pensa, e per rappresentare questo suo desiderio potremmno fargli tracciare una riga in diagonale attraverso la vignetta. L'uccello sbatte le ali, schiva la diagonale e si mette in salvo nell'angolo opposto. U(h) si rallegra perché con quella diagonale in mezzo non lo vede piú. L'uccello dà una beccata contro la riga, la spezza, e vola addosso al vecchio U(h). Il vecchio U(h) per cancellarlo cerca di tracciargli addosso due fregacci[4] incrociati. Nel punto dove le due righe s'incontrano, l'uccello si posa a fare l'uovo. Il vecchio U(h) gliele strappa di sotto, l'uovo

to have a clearer picture of all sorts of things which I have long forgotten: first, the thing which I am now calling a bird, secondly the thing I am now calling 'me', thirdly the branch, fourthly the place I was looking out of, fifthly all the others. Of all these ingredients I can only remember that they were very different from the way we should represent them today. It is better if you yourselves try to imagine the series of drawings with the figures of all the characters in their places on an effectively sketched background, but if at the same time you try not to imagine the figures or the background. Every figure will have its little balloon with the words it says, or the noises it makes, but there is no need for you to read everything that is written word for word, as long as you get the general idea according to what I tell you.

To start with you can read a lot of exclamation marks and question marks shooting out from our heads, and that means we were looking at the bird full of wonder – an exuberant wonder, an urge to join in singing to imitate that first warbling, and to jump when we saw it take flight – but yet full of bewilderment, because the existence of birds shattered the rules of logic with which we had grown up.

In the strip of cartoons which follow you see the wisest of us all, old U(h), who steps out from among the others and says 'Don't look! It's a mistake!' and spreads out his hands as if to cover the eyes of everyone present. 'Now I'll cross it out!' he says, or thinks, and to show this desire of his we could make him draw a line diagonally across the picture. The bird flaps its wings, dodges the diagonal and takes refuge in the opposite corner. U(h) cheers up because with the diagonal in between he can't see it any more. The bird gives a peck at the line, shatters it, and flies down at old U(h). To eliminate it old U(h) tries to cross it out with two heavy strokes. At the point where the two lines meet the bird settles and lays an egg. Old U(h) snatches them from under, the egg falls, the bird flies away. The next picture is completely smothered in egg-yolk.

casca, l'uccello vola via. C'è una vignetta tutta imbrattata di tuorlo d'uovo.

Raccontare con i fumetti mi piace molto, però avrei bisogno d'alternare alle vignette d'azione delle vignette ideologiche, e spiegare per esempio quest'ostinazione di U(h) nel non voler ammettere l'esistenza dell'uccello. Immaginatevi dunque un quadratino di quelli tutti scritti, che servono per informare sinteticamente sui precedenti dell'azione: *Dopo il fallimento dei Pterosauri, da milioni e milioni d'anni s'era persa ogni traccia d'animali con le ali.* («A parte gli Insetti,» può precisare una nota in calce.) Quello dei volatili era considerato un capitolo chiuso, ormai. Non s'era detto e ripetuto che dai Rettili tutto quel che poteva nascere era nato? Nel corso di milioni d'anni non c'era forma d'essere vivente che non avesse avuto occasione di venir fuori, di popolare la terra, e poi – novantanove casi su cento – di decadere e scomparire. Su questo eravamo tutti d'accordo: le specie rimaste erano le sole meritevoli, destinate a dar vita a progenie sempre piú selezionate e adatte all'ambiente. Ci aveva tormentato a lungo il dubbio su chi era un mostro e chi non lo era, ma da un pezzo poteva dirsi risolto: non-mostri siamo tutti noi che ci siamo e mostri invece sono tutti quelli che potevano esserci e invece non ci sono, perché la successione delle cause a degli effetti ha favorito chiaramente noi, i non-mostri, anziché loro.

Ma se adesso si ricominciava con gli animali strani, se i Rettili, antiquati com'erano, riprendevano a tirar fuori arti e tegumenti di cui prima non s'era mai sentita la necessità, se insomma una creatura impossibile per definizione come un uccello era invece possibile (e per di piú poteva essere un bell'uccello come questo, piacevole alla vista quando si librava sulle foglie di felce, e all'udito quando lanciava i suoi gorgheggi), allora la barriera tra mostri e non-mostri saltava in aria e tutto ritornava possibile.

I enjoy telling stories with comic-strips, but I should need to alternate action-pictures with idea-pictures, and explain for example this stubborness with which U(h) refused to admit the bird's existence. So imagine one of those frames with nothing but writing, such as they use to summarize the story so far: *After the failure of the Pterosauri, for millions and millions of years there had been no sign of any animal with wings.* ('Apart from insects,' you can add in a footnote).

The chapter of flying creatures was reckoned to be closed by now. Hadn't it been said over and over again that everything which could develop from the Reptiles had already developed? In the course of millions of years there was no form of living being which had not had the chance to appear, to populate the earth, and then – ninety-nine times out of a hundred – to decline and disappear. On this point we were all agreed: the species which remained were the only deserving ones, destined to give birth to descendants who were progressively more select and adapted to the environment. We had been troubled for a long time by the doubt about who was a monster and who was not, but for some time the question could be regarded as settled: those of us who are here are non-monsters, whereas the monsters are all those who could be here but are not, because the succession of cause and effect has clearly favoured us, the non-monsters, rather than them.

But if we were now starting up again with strange animals, if the Reptiles, old-fashioned as they were, were starting to produce limbs and coverings which had never seemed necessary up to now, in short if a creature impossible by definition like a bird turned out to be possible after all (and, what's more, could be a fine bird like this one, pleasant to watch when it balanced on the fern leaves, pleasant to listen to when it poured forth its warblings), then the distinction between monsters and non-monsters vanished into thin air and anything was possible once again.

L'uccello volò lontano. (Nella vignetta si vede un'ombra nera contro le nuvole del cielo: non perché l'uccello sia nero ma perché gli uccelli lontani si rappresentano cosí.) E io gli andai dietro. (Mi si vede di spalle, che m'inoltro in uno sterminato paesaggio di monti e di foreste.) Il vecchio U(h) mi grida dietro: «Torna, Qfwfq!»

Attraversai contrade sconosciute. Piú volte mi credetti perso (nel fumetto, basta rappresentarlo una volta) ma sentivo un «Koaxpf . . .» e alzando gli occhi vedevo l'uccello fermo su una pianta,[5] come se m'aspettasse.

Cosí seguendolo, arrivai a un punto in cui i cespugli mi impedivano la vista. M'apersi un varco: sotto i miei piedi vidi il vuoto. La terra finiva lí; io stavo in equilibrio sull'orlo. (La linea a spirale che s'innalza dalla mia testa rappresenta la vertigine.) In basso non si scorgeva nulla; qualche nuvola. E l'uccello in quel vuoto s'allontanava volando, e ogni tanto torceva il collo verso di me come invitandomi a seguirlo. Seguirlo dove, se piú in là non c'era niente?

Ed ecco che dalla lontananza bianca affiorò un'ombra, come un orizzonte di nebbia, che man mano[6] s'andava disegnando con contorni sempre piú precisi. Era un continente che veniva avanti nel vuoto: se ne scorgevano la sponde, le vallate, le alture, e già l'uccello le stava sorvolando. Ma quale uccello? Non era piú solo, tutto il cielo là sopra era uno sbattere d'ali d'ogni colore e d'ogni forma.

Sporgendomi dall'orlo della nostra terra io guardavo avvicinarsi il continente alla deriva.[7] «Ci viene addosso!» gridai, e in quel momento tremò il suolo. (Un «bang!» scritto a lettere cubitali.) I due mondi dopo essersi toccati, tornarono ad allontanarsi, per rimbalzo, e poi a ricongiungersi, a staccarsi di nuovo. In uno di questi scontri io mi trovai sbalzato di là, mentre l'abisso vuoto tornava a spalancarsi e a separarmi dal mio mondo.

Mi guardai intorno: non riconoscevo niente. Alberi,

The bird flew into the distance. (In the drawing you see a black shape against the clouds in the sky: not because the bird is black, but because that is the way to draw birds in the distance.) And I went after it. (You see me from behind, going away into a limitless landscape of mountains and forests.) Old U(h) cried after me: 'Come back, Qfwfq!'

I travelled through unexplored regions. Several times I thought I was lost (in the comic it will be enough to show this just once), but I heard a 'Koaxpf . . .', raised my eyes and saw the bird perched on a tree as if it were waiting for me.

Following it in this way, I reached a place where my view was blocked by bushes. I forced a way through: and saw a void beneath my feet. The earth ended there; I was balancing on the rim. (The spiral line going up from my head shows my dizziness.) Below nothing could be seen; just a few clouds. And the bird went flying into the distance, into that void, and every now and then it turned its head round towards me as if inviting me to follow it. Follow it where, if there was nothing beyond?

And then I saw a shadow emerging from the white distance, like a horizon of mist, which gradually revealed itself in more and more precise outlines. It was a continent coming forward out of the void: you could see its shores, its valleys, its hills, and the bird was flying over it. But which bird? It was alone no longer; the whole sky over there was a beating of wings of every colour and shape.

Leaning out from the edge of our world I watched the continent floating nearer. 'It's going to hit us!' I shouted, and at that moment the ground trembled. ('Bang!' written in huge letters.) The two worlds touched and bounced apart on the rebound, then they went on bumping and separating again. In one of these crashes I found myself bounced across, while the empty abyss yawned once again and separated me from my own world.

I looked around: not a thing was familiar. Trees, crystals,

cristalli, bestie, erbe, tutto era diverso. Non solo uccelli popolavano i rami, ma pesci (dico per dire) con gambe di ragno o (diciamo) vermi con le penne. Adesso non è che io voglia descrivervi com'erano le forme della vita, laggiú; immaginatevele come vi vien meglio, piú strane o meno strane importa poco. Quello che importa è che intorno a me si dispiegavano tutte le forme che il mondo avrebbe potuto prendere nelle sue trasformazioni e invece non aveva preso, per un qualche motivo occasionale o per un'incompatibilità di fondo: le forme scartate, irrecuperabili, perdute.

(Per rendere l'idea bisognerebbe che questa striscia di vignette fosse disegnata in negativo: con figure non dissimili dalle altre ma in bianco su nero; oppure capovolte, – ammettendo che si possa decidere, in una qualsiasi di queste figure, qual è l'alto e qual è il basso.)

Lo sgomento mi gelava le ossa (nel disegno, gocce di sudore freddo che sprizzano dalla mia figura) a vedere quelle immagini sempre in qualche modo familiari e sempre in qualche modo stravolte nelle proporzioni o nelle combinazioni (la mia figura piccolissima in bianco, sovrapposta a ombre nere che prendono tutta la vignetta) ma non mi tratteneva dall'esplorare avidamente intorno. Si sarebbe detto che il mio sguardo, anziché evitare quei mostri, li cercasse, come per convincersi che non erano mostri fino in fondo, e che a un certo punto l'orrore facesse posto a una sensazione non sgradevole (rappresentata nel disegno da raggi luminosi che attraversano lo sfondo nero): la bellezza che esisteva anche là in mezzo, a saperla riconoscere.

Questa curiosità m'aveva fatto allontanare dalla costa e addentrarmi tra colline spinose come enormi ricci marini. Ero ormai perduto nel cuore del continente ignoto. (La figura che mi rappresenta è diventata minuscola.) Gli uccelli che ora è poco erano per me l'apparizione piú strana, stavano già diventando le presenze piú familiari. Erano tanti da formare intorno a me come

animals, plants, all were different. Not only were the branches populated with birds, but there were fish (as it were) with spiders' legs, or (let's say) worms with feathers. I don't want to start describing to you now what the forms of life were actually like over there; you can imagine them any way you please, just how strange you make them doesn't really matter. What does matter is that around me were displayed all the forms which the world could have adopted during its transformations but which in fact it had not adopted, whether for some purely accidental reason or because of some basic incompatibility: the forms which were discarded, irrecoverable, lost.

(To convey the idea this strip of drawings would have to be done in negative, with figures not unlike the others, but in white on black; or upside down – granted that you can work out in any given figure which is up and which is down.)

I was chilled to the bone with dismay (in the drawing drops of cold sweat showering from my face), seeing those images always somehow familiar and always somehow distorted in their proportions or combinations (a tiny figure of me in white superimposed on black shadows which fill the whole frame) but this did not stop me from eagerly exploring my surroundings. One could say that, far from avoiding these monsters with my gaze, I sought them out, as if to convince myself that they were not really monsters underneath; and at a certain point my horror gave way to a feeling that was not unpleasant (shown in the drawing by rays of light on a black background): the beauty which existed in all this too, if one learned to recognize it.

This curiosity had led me to move away from the coast, and plunge in between spiny hills like enormous sea-urchins. By now I was lost in the heart of an unknown continent. (The little figure which represents me is now very tiny.) The birds, which a little while ago I had seen as the strangest of apparitions, were already becoming the most familiar presences. There were so many that they formed a

una cupola, alzando e abbassando le ali tutti insieme (vignetta gremita d'uccelli; la mia sagoma s'intravvede appena). Altri stavano posati al suolo, appollaiati sugli arbusti, e man mano che[8] io avanzavo si spostavano. Ero loro prigioniero? Mi voltai per scappare, ma ero circondato da pareti d'uccelli che non mi lasciavano alcun varco, tranne che in una direzione. Mi stavano spingendo dove volevano loro, tutti i loro movimenti conducevano in un punto. Cosa c'era, là in fondo? Non riuscivo a scorgere altro che una specie d'enorme uovo coricato per il lungo, che si schiudeva lentamente, come una conchiglia.

Si spalancò d'un tratto. Sorrisi. Dalla commozione gli occhi mi si riempirono di lacrime. (Sono rappresentato io solo, di profilo; quello che vedo resta fuori della vignetta.) Avevo di fronte una creatura di bellezza mai vista. Una bellezza *diversa,* senza possibilità di confronto con tutte le forme in cui era stata da noi riconosciuta la bellezza (nel fumetto continua ad essere situata in modo che ad averla di fronte sia solo io, mai il lettore), eppure *nostra,* quanto c'era di piú *nostro* del nostro mondo (nel fumetto si potrebbe ricorrere a una rappresentazione simbolica: una mano femminile, o un piede, o un seno, che spuntano da un gran manto di piume), e tale che senza di lei il nostro mondo aveva sempre mancato di qualcosa. Sentivo d'essere giunto al punto in cui tutto convergeva (un occhio, si potrebbe disegnare, un occhio dalle lunghe ciglia raggiate che si trasformano in un vortice) e in cui stavo per essere inghiottito (o una bocca, lo schiudersi di due labbra finemente disegnate, alte quanto me, e io che volo aspirato verso la lingua che affiora dal buio).

Intorno, uccelli: sbattere di becchi, ali che starnazzano, artigli protesi, e il grido: «Koaxpf . . . Koaxpf . . . Koaaaccch . . .»

«Chi sei?» domandai.

Una didascalia spiega: *Qfwfq di fronte alla bella Org-Onir-Ornit-Or,* e rende la mia domanda inutile; alla

kind of dome around me, beating their wings up and down all together (a picture crammed with birds, my own form is scarcely visible). Others were settled on the ground, perched on the bushes, moving out of the way as I went forward. Was I their prisoner? I turned to run, but I was surrounded by walls of birds which only left me a passage in one direction. They were pushing me where they wanted; all their movements were directed at one spot. What was it there at the end? I could make out no more than a kind of huge egg lying on its side, opening slowly like a seashell.

Suddenly it gaped open. I smiled. My eyes filled with tears of emotion. (You can only see me, in profile; what I am looking at is outside the picture.) The creature before me was of a beauty never before experienced. A *different* beauty, which could not possibly be compared with all the forms in which beauty had been recognized (in the picture it is still placed so that only I can see it, never the reader), and yet *familiar*, everything that was most *familiar* about our familiar world (in the comic you could resort to a symbolic representation: a feminine hand, or foot, or breast emerging from a great cloak of feathers) and such that without it our world had always been missing something. I felt I had reached the place where everything converged (an eye, you could draw, an eye with long radiating lashes which turn into a vortex) and in which I was about to be swallowed up (or a mouth, the parting of two finely drawn lips, as tall as me, and I am sucked on its breath towards the tongue which blossoms out of the dark).

All around were birds: a clatter of beaks, wings clapping, talons extended and the cry: 'Koaxpf ... Koaxpf ... Koaaaccch ...'

'Who are you?' I asked.

A caption explains: *Qfwfq before the beautiful Org-Onir-Ornit-Or*, and makes my question unnecessary; the little

nuvoletta che la contiene se ne sovrappone un'altra, anch'essa uscita dalla mia bocca, con le parole: «T'amo!», affermazione ugualmente superflua, subito incalzata da un'altra nuvoletta contenente la domanda: «Sei prigioniera?» a cui non attendo risposta e in una quarta nuvoletta che si fa strada sopra le altre, soggiungo: «Ti salverò. Stanotte fuggiremo insieme.»

La striscia che segue è interamente dedicata ai preparativi di fuga, al sonno degli uccelli e dei mostri, in una notte rischiarata da un ignoto firmamento. Un quadratino buio, e la mia voce: «Mi segui?» La voce di Or rispose: «Sí.»

Qui potete immaginarvi una serie di strisce avventurose: *Qfwfq e Or in fuga attraversano il Continente degli Uccelli*. Allarmi, inseguimenti, pericoli: lascio fare a voi. Per raccontare dovrei in qualche modo descrivere com' era Or: e non posso farlo. Immaginate una figura in qualche modo sovrastante la mia, ma che in qualche modo io nascondo e proteggo.

Arrivammo sull'orlo del baratro. Era l'alba. Il sole si levava, pallido, a scoprire in lontananza il nostro continente. Come raggiungerlo? Mi voltai verso Or: Or aprí le ali. (Non vi eravate accorti che le avesse, nelle vignette precedenti: due ali vaste come vele.) M'aggrappai al suo manto. Or volò.

Nelle figure che seguono si vede Or volare tra le nubi, con la mia testa che fa capolino[9] dal suo grembo. Poi, un triangolo di triangolini neri nel cielo: è uno stormo di uccelli che ci inseguono. Siamo ancora in mezzo al vuoto, il nostro continente s'avvicina, ma lo stormo è piú veloce. Sono uccelli rapaci, con becchi ricurvi, occhi di fuoco. Se Or fa presto a raggiungere la terra, saremo tra i nostri,[10] prima che i rapaci ci assaltino. Forza, Or, ancora pochi colpi d'ala: nella prossima striscia siamo in salvo.

Macché: ecco che lo stormo ci ha circondato. Or vola in mezzo ai rapaci (un triangolino bianco inscritto in un altro triangolo pieno di triangolini neri). Stiamo sorvo-

balloon which contains it is overlaid by another, also coming from my mouth, with the words 'I love you!' – an equally superfluous declaration, followed straight away by another little balloon containing the question 'Are you a prisoner?' which I do not wait to have answered, and in a fourth little balloon which crowds in on top of the others I add: 'I will save you. Tonight we shall run away together.'

The strip which follows is entirely devoted to the preparations for our flight, with all the birds and monsters asleep in a night lit by an unknown firmament. A black frame, and my voice: 'Are you following?' Or's voice answered: 'Yes.'

Here you can imagine a series of comic-strips full of adventure: *Qfwfq and Or escape across the Continent of the Birds.* Alarms, pursuits, dangers: it's up to you. To tell you about it I should have somehow to describe what Or was like: and that I can't do. Imagine a figure somehow overshadowing my own, and yet which I somehow conceal and protect.

We arrived at the edge of the abyss. It was dawn. A pale sun was rising, revealing our own continent in the distance. How could we get there? I turned to Or: Or opened her wings. (You hadn't realized she had any in the previous drawings: two wings as vast as sails.) I hung on to her cloak. Or flew.

In the pictures which follow you see Or flying among the clouds, with my head peeping from her lap. Then a triangle of little triangles in the sky: it is a flock of birds pursuing us. We are still in the middle of the void, our continent is getting nearer, but the birds are faster. They are birds of prey with curved beaks and fiery eyes. If Or reaches land quickly, we shall be with our side, before the raptors can attack us. Come on, Or, just a few more strokes with your wings: in the next line of drawings we shall be safe.

No use: the flock has already surrounded us. Or flies in the midst of the raptors (a little white triangle drawn in a large triangle full of little black triangles). We are flying

lando il mio paese: basterebbe che Or chiudesse le ali e si lasciasse cadere, e saremmo liberi. Ma Or continua a volare alto, insieme agli uccelli. Io gridai: «Or, abbassati!» Lei schiuse il manto e mi lasciò precipitare. (Slaff!) Lo stormo, con Or in mezzo, gira nel cielo, torna indietro, impiccolisce all'orizzonte. Mi ritrovai steso a terra, solo.

(Didascalia: *Durante l'assenza di Qfwfq, molti cambiamenti erano avvenuti.*) Da quando s'era scoperta l'esistenza degli uccelli, le idee che regolavano il nostro mondo erano entrate in crisi. Quello che prima tutti credevano di capire, il modo semplice e regolare per cui le cose erano com'erano, non valeva piú; ossia: questa non era altro che una delle innumerevoli possibilità; nessuno escludeva che le cose potessero andare in altri modi tutti diversi. Si sarebbe detto che adesso ognuno si vergognasse d'essere come si aspettava che fosse, e si sforzasse d'ostentare un aspetto irregolare, imprevisto: un aspetto un po' da uccello, o se non proprio da uccello, tale da non sfigurare[11] di fronte alla stranezza degli uccelli. I miei vicini non li[12] riconoscevo piú. Non che fossero molto cambiati: ma chi aveva una qualche particolarità inspiegabile, mentre prima cercava di nasconderla, adesso la metteva in mostra. E tutti avevano l'aria di chi aspetta da un momento all'altro qualcosa: non il succedersi puntuale di cause ed effetti, come un tempo, ma l'inaspettato.

Io non mi ci ritrovavo. Gli altri mi credevano uno rimasto con le vecchie idee, del tempo di prima degli uccelli; non capivano che a me le loro velleità uccellesche facevano soltanto ridere: avevo visto ben altro, avevo visitato il mondo delle cose che avrebbero potuto essere, e non riuscivo a togliermelo dalla mente. E avevo conosciuto la bellezza prigioniera nel cuore di quel mondo, la bellezza perduta per me e per tutti noi, e me ne ero innamorato.

Passavo le giornate in cima a un monte, a scrutare il cielo se mai un uccello lo traversasse a volo. E sul cocuzzolo d'un altro monte lí vicino, c'era il vecchio U(h),

over my own country: Or need only close her wings and drop, and we should be free. But Or continues to fly high, along with the birds. I shouted 'Or, go down!' She opened her cloak and let me fall. ('Slaff!') The flock, with Or in their midst, turns in the sky and goes back, dwindles above the horizon. I found myself lying on the ground, alone.

(Caption: *During Qfwfq's absence many things had changed.*) Since the existence of birds had been discovered, there had been a breakthrough in the ideas which governed our world. Something which everyone had thought he understood, the simple, steady rule by which things were the way they were, was no longer valid: or rather, this was only one of countless possibilities; you couldn't exclude the possibility of things happening in completely different ways. It was as if now everyone was ashamed of being what people expected him to be, as if everyone was trying to show off some irregular, unexpected feature – a bird-like feature, or if not exactly bird-like, one which would measure up to the strangeness of the birds. I no longer recognized my neighbours. Not that they had changed much: but anyone who had something inexplicable about him, instead of hiding it as he would have done before, was now putting it on display. And they all had the air of people who expect anything to happen at any moment; not the punctual progression of cause and effect, as before, but the unexpected.

I couldn't feel at home any more. The others thought that I had stuck to the old ideas from before the birds; they did not realize that to me their bird-like trappings were just laughable: I had seen something very different, I had visited the world of what might have been, and I couldn't get it out of my mind. And I had known the beauty imprisoned in the heart of that world, a beauty lost to me and to us all, and I had fallen in love with it.

I spent the days at the top of a mountain, scanning the sky in case a bird should fly across it. And on the crown of another mountain near by stood old U(h), also watching

anche lui guardando il cielo. Il vecchio U(h) era considerato sempre il piú sapiente di tutti noi, ma il suo atteggiamento verso gli uccelli era cambiato. Credeva che gli uccelli fossero non piú l'errore ma la verità, la sola verità del mondo. S'era messo a interpretare il volo degli uccelli cercando di leggervi il futuro.[13]

«Hai visto niente?» mi gridava dal suo monte.

«Niente in vista,» dicevo io.

«Eccone uno!» alle volte gridavamo, o io o lui.

«Da dove veniva? Non ho fatto in tempo a vedere da che parte del cielo è apparso. Dimmi: da dove?» chiedeva lui, tutto affannato. Dalla provenienza del volo U(h) traeva i suoi auspici.

Oppure ero io a domandare: «In che direzione volava? Non l'ho visto! È sparito di qua o di là» perché io speravo che gli uccelli mi mostrassero la via per raggiungere Or.

È inutile che racconti dettagliatamente l'astuzia con cui riuscii a tornare nel Continente degli Uccelli. Nei fumetti andrebbe raccontato con uno di quei trucchi che vengono bene soltanto a disegnarli. (Il quadretto è vuoto. Arrivo io. Spalmo di colla l'angolo in alto a destra. Mi siedo sull'angolo in basso a sinistra. Entra un uccello, volando, da sinistra in alto. All'uscire dal quadretto resta incollato per la coda. Continua a volare e si tira dietro tutto il quadretto appiccicato alla coda, con me seduto in fondo che mi lascio trasportare. Cosí arrivo al Paese degli Uccelli. Se questa non vi piace potete immaginarvi un'altra storia: l'importante è farmi arrivare là.)

Arrivai e mi sentii artigliare braccia e gambe. Ero circondato da uccelli, uno se n'era posato sulla mia testa, uno mi beccava il collo. «Qfwfq, sei in arresto! T'abbiamo preso, finalmente!» Fui chiuso in una cella.

«Mi uccideranno?» chiesi all'uccello carceriere.

«Domani sarai portato in giudizio e lo saprai,» disse quello, appollaiato sulle sbarre.

the sky. Old U(h) was still regarded as the wisest of us all, but his attitude to birds had changed. He saw birds no longer as a mistake, but as the truth, the only truth in the world. He had set himself to interpret the flight of birds in an effort to read the future.

'Have you seen anything?' he would shout from his mountain.

'Nothing in sight,' I said.

'There's one!' one of us would shout occasionally.

'Where was it coming from? I didn't have time to see whereabouts in the sky it appeared. Where, tell me?' he asked agitatedly. It was from the provenance of the flight that U(h) drew his auguries.

Or else I would ask in turn: 'Which direction was it going in? I didn't see! Did it go over here or over there?' because I hoped that the birds would show me the way to reach Or.

There is no point in telling you in detail the trick by which I managed to return to the Continent of the Birds. In the cartoon you could show it with one of those devices which only come off in drawings. (The frame is empty. I enter. I smear the top righthand corner with glue. I sit down in the bottom lefthand corner. Enter a bird, flying, from top left. As it leaves the frame its tail gets stuck. It carries on flying and pulls the frame along glued to its tail, with me riding along, seated at the bottom. Thus I arrive at the Country of the Birds. If you don't like this you can imagine another story: the important thing is to get me there.)

I arrived and felt claws seizing my arms and legs. I was surrounded by birds, one had perched on my head, another was pecking at my neck. 'Qfwfq, you're under arrest! We've got you at last!' I was shut in a cell.

'Will they kill me?' I asked the jailer-bird.

'Tomorrow you will be judged, and then you'll know,' said he, perching on the bars.

«Chi mi giudicherà?»

«La Regina degli Uccelli.»

L'indomani fui introdotto nella sala del trono. Ma quell'enorme uovo-conchiglia che si schiudeva io l'avevo già visto. Trasalii.

«Allora non sei prigioniera degli uccelli!» esclamai.

Una beccata mi colpí il collo. «Inchinati alla regina Org-Onir-Ornit-Or!»

Or fece un segno. Tutti gli uccelli si fermarono. (Nel disegno si vede una sottile mano inanellata che si leva da un trofeo di penne.)

«Sposami e sarai salvo,» disse Or.

Si celebrarono le nozze. Neanche di questo posso raccontare nulla: tutto quello che m'è rimasto nella memoria è uno spiumio[14] di immagini cangianti. Forse pagavo la felicità con la rinuncia a comprendere quello che vivevo.

Lo chiesi a Or.

«Vorrei capire.»

«Cosa?»

«Tutto, tutto questo.» Accennai intorno.

«Capirai quando avrai dimenticato quello che capivi prima.»

Scese la notte. La conchiglia-uovo faceva da trono e da letto nuziale.

«Hai dimenticato?»

«Sí. Cosa? Non so cosa, io non ricordo nulla.»

(Fumetto del pensiero di Qfwfq: *No, ricordo ancora, sto per dimenticare tutto, ma mi sforzo di ricordare!*)

«Vieni.»

Ci coricammo insieme.

(Fumetto del pensiero di Qfwfq: *Dimentico. . . . È bello dimenticare. . . . No, voglio ricordami. . . . Voglio dimenticare e ricordare nello stesso tempo. . . . Ancora un secondo e sento che avrò dimenticato. . . . Aspetta. . . . Oh!* Un lampo contrassegnato dalla scritta «Flash!» oppure «Eureka!» a lettere maiuscole).

Per una frazione di secondo tra la perdita di tutto quel

'Who will judge me?'

'The Queen of the Birds.'

The next day I was brought into the throne-room. But that huge, slowly opening seashell-egg was something I had seen before. I gave a start.

'Then you are not the birds' prisoner!' I exclaimed.

A beak struck at my neck. 'Bow down to Queen Org-Onir-Ornit-Or!'

Or made a sign. All the birds were quiet. (In the drawing you see a slim be-ringed hand rising from a trophy of feathers.)

'Marry me, and you will be released,' said Or.

The wedding was celebrated. I cannot tell you much about this either: all that remains in memory is a plumage of shifting images. Perhaps I paid for my happiness by renouncing the ability to understand what I was experiencing.

I asked Or.

'I should like to understand.'

'What?'

'Everything, all this.' I made a sweeping gesture.

'You will understand when you have forgotten what you understood before.'

Night fell. The conch-egg acted both as throne and nuptial bed.

'Have you forgotten?'

'Yes. What? I don't know, I don't remember anything.'

(Balloon with Qfwfq's thought: *No, I still remember, I am almost forgetting it all, but I am fighting to remember!*)

'Come.'

We lay down together.

(Balloon with Qfwfq's thought: *I'm forgetting. . . . It's good to forget. . . . No, I want to remember. . . . I want to forget and remember at the same time. . . . Another second and I feel I shall have forgotten. . . . Wait. . . . Oh!* A flash of lightning, identified by 'Flash!' or 'Eureka!' in capital letters.)

For a fraction of a second between losing everything I

che sapevo prima e l'acquisto di tutto quel che avrei saputo dopo, riuscii ad abbracciare in un solo pensiero il mondo delle cose com'erano e quello delle cose come avrebbero potuto essere, e m'accorsi che un solo sistema comprendeva tutto. Il mondo degli uccelli, dei mostri, della bellezza d'Or era lo stesso di quello in cui ero sempre vissuto e che nessuno di noi aveva capito fino in fondo.

«Or! Ho capito! Tu! Che bello! Evviva!» esclamai e mi levai sul letto.

La mia sposa gettò un urlo.

«Ora ti spiego!» dissi, esultante. «Ora spiego tutto a tutti!»

«Taci!» gridò Or. «Devi tacere!»

«Il mondo è uno e quel che c'è non si spiega senza. . . .» proclamavo. Or mi era sopra, cercava di soffocarmi (nel disegno; un seno che mi schiaccia): «Taci! Taci!»

Centinaia di rostri e artigli laceravano il baldacchino del letto nuziale. Gli uccelli calavano su di me, ma al di là delle loro ali riconoscevo il mio paesaggio natale che s'andava fondendo con il continente estraneo.

«Non c'è differenza! Mostri e non-mostri sono sempre stati vicini! Ciò che non è stato continua ad essere . . .» e parlavo non solo agli uccelli e ai mostri ma pure a coloro che avevo sempre conosciuto e che accorrevano da ogni parte.

«Qfwfq! M'hai perduta! Uccelli! A voi!» e la regina mi respinse.

Troppo tardi m'accorsi come i rostri degli uccelli erano intenti a separare i due mondi che la mia rivelazione aveva ricongiunto. «No, Or, aspetta, non staccarti, noi due insieme, Or, dove sei?» Ma stavo rotolando nel vuoto tra pezzi di carta e penne.

(Gli uccelli strappano a beccate e a graffi la pagina dei fumetti. Volano via ognuno con un brandello di carta stampata nel becco. La pagina che c'è sotto è anch'essa disegnata a fumetti; vi è rappresentato il mondo com'era

knew before and gaining everything I would know afterwards, I managed to embrace in a single thought the world of things as they were and the world of things as they might have been, and I realized that all was contained in a single system. The world of birds, monsters and Or's beauty was the same as that in which I had always lived, and which none of us had really understood.

'Or! I've got it! You! Marvellous! Hooray!' I exclaimed, and I sat up on the bed.

My wife cried out.

'Now I'll explain!' I said exultantly. 'Now I'll explain it all to everybody!'

'Quiet!' shouted Or. 'You must be quiet!'

'The world is one, and what exists can't be explained without . . .' I proclaimed. Or was on top of me, trying to stifle me (in the drawing, a breast crushing me): 'Quiet! Quiet!'

Hundreds of beaks and claws were tearing at the canopy of the nuptial bed. The birds swooped down on me, but beyond their wings I recognized my native landscape which was merging with the alien continent.

'There's no difference! Monsters and non-monsters have always been close together! Things which have never been continue to be . . .' and I was talking not only to the birds and the monsters but also to the people I had always known, and who were running up from every direction.

'Qfwfq – you have lost me! Birds – to work!' and the Queen pushed me away.

Too late I realized how the birds' beaks were intent on separating the two worlds which my revelation had joined together. 'No, Or, wait, don't let go, we two together, Or, where are you?' But I was tumbling in the void amidst quills and pieces of paper.

(With pecks and scratches the birds tear up the page of cartoons. They fly off, each with a shred of printed paper in its beak. The page underneath is also covered with cartoons, representing the world as it was before the birds appeared,

prima della comparsa degli uccelli e i suoi successivi prevedibili sviluppi. Io sto in mezzo agli altri, con aria smarrita. Nel cielo continuano ad esserci uccelli, ma nessuno piú ci bada.)

Di quel che avevo capito allora, ho dimenticato tutto. Ciò che vi ho raccontato è quanto posso ricostruire, aiutandomi con congetture nei passaggi lacunosi. Che gli uccelli possano riportarmi un giorno dalla regina Or, non ho mai smesso di sperarlo. Ma saranno i veri uccelli, questi che sono rimasti tra noi? Piú li osservo e meno mi ricordano quello che vorrei ricordare. (L'ultima striscia del fumetto è tutta di fotografie: un uccello, lo stesso uccello in primo piano, la testa dell'uccello ingrandita, un particolare della testa, l'occhio . . .)

with its subsequent predictable developments. I stand among the others with a bewildered air. There are still birds in the sky, but nobody pays them any more attention.)

Everything that I had understood then, I have now quite forgotten. What I have told you is as much as I can reconstruct, filling in the gaps with guesswork. I have never ceased to hope that the birds may one day take me back to Queen Or. But can these be the real birds, the ones that have stayed behind with us? The more I look at them the less they remind me of what I want to remember. (The last strip of the comic is all made up of photographs: a bird, a close-up of the same bird, the bird's head enlarged, a detail of the head, the eye . . .)

BIOGRAPHICAL NOTES ON AUTHORS

ITALO SVEVO

Italo Svevo (born Ettore Schmitz 1861, died 1928) is best known for his three major works, *Una vita* (A Life), 1892, *Senilità* (As a Man Grows Older), 1896, and *La coscienza di Zeno* (Confessions of Zeno), published in 1923. With the help and encouragement of James Joyce, he achieved a certain recognition of his work in Europe, largely based on the success of his third work, but only achieved more general admiration after his death.

Svevo grew up in a multi-lingual atmosphere. Born in Trieste and educated in Bavaria, it is probable that his first language was Triestine-Italian dialect, but it is at least definitely known that he learned literary Italian at school, and that this Italian was for him a language taught and learned rather than absorbed and grown up with. In spite of the immense differences between the languages concerned, it is not unfair to compare Svevo's Italian with Conrad's English – a language in each case grammatically faultless, but afraid to be over-flexible, with Conrad something more English than English, and Svevo something more Italian than Italian. Nabokov has shown that it is not impossible to discover the possibilities and boundaries of a language, and know them well enough to go beyond them in a way which is both striking and acceptable, but the talent is a rare one. In the case of Svevo it is on rather different grounds that his achievements as a writer may be more profitably discussed.

In 'The Mother' we have a sardonic fable in which a moral lesson is implicit, and in which the lesson itself is made more strikingly apparent than it might otherwise have been by the fact that the principal 'character' never learns what it is. The psychological implications of the tale reveal the author's preoccupation with feeling, behaviour and

motive, which appears consistently and more directly in his novels, with their exploration of personality. Here the allegorical form, and the setting of what might be called a tragedy of aspiration in a community of chicks (as a chick grows older, and thinks he grows up), add further touches of irony which would probably have had to be more baldly, and so less effectively, expressed had Svevo chosen to portray humans, instead of birds who are about as feather-brained as they are down- or feather-covered.

In this particular tale what is basically a limitation in Svevo's Italian, can be seen as a positive, although quite accidental, merit. The fact that the feeble and ignorant chicks converse about their great experiences and ideals in a manner which is hyper-correct, stilted and more pompous than the everyday conversation of people, adds to the irony of their situation and the immoderate sense of their own wisdom which is fundamental to the story. Had Svevo's knowledge of the language he chose to write in, been greater 'The Mother' might well have been a less successful story.

GIOVANNI COMISSO

Giovanni Comisso was born in 1895 in Treviso, near Venice. He served in the First World War and then followed d'Annunzio in his semi-aesthetic, semi-political Fiume venture in 1919–20. An interesting view of d'Annunzio, his followers and the frenetic atmosphere in Fiume, and Comisso's own attitude to it, can be seen in his autobiographical *Le Mie Stagioni*. This meeting with d'Annunzio was influential not only on his way of life but also on his writing. In both he is a hedonist, a writer of the instincts, who writes, nevertheless, not only with opulence but also considerable discipline. In later years he followed a number of occupations including art dealing, selling books and travelling as a journalist in Europe, Africa and Asia. Much of his best writing is travel-writing, describing in vivid detail his keenly felt and equally keenly sought-after sensual impressions. *Gente di mare*, from which 'Pesca Miracolosa' is

taken, and *Amori d'Oriente* are perhaps the two sides of this hedonism; the former seems attractive and innocent in its descriptions of the sea and its people, the latter in its restless and rather mournful pursuit of sexual, gastronomic and touristic satisfaction, and because of its sensitive yet indifferent description of the sordid poverty of the East, seems rather arid. The chief beauty of his writing lies in his descriptive powers which stem from his strong *joie de vivre.* He died in 1969 in his home town of Treviso.

Comisso's writings are numerous and include poetry, descriptions of travel, autobiography and novels, among which are *Poesie*, 1916, *Il Porto dell'amore*, 1925, *Gente di mare,* 1929, for which he received the Premio Bagutta and which was praised by d'Annunzio, *Giorni di guerra*, 1930. *Storia di un patrimonio*, 1933, *L'Italiano errante per l'Italia,* 1937, *Amori d'Oriente*, 1947, *Le Mie Stagioni*, 1951, an autobiographical account of the years between the end of the First World War and the end of the Second, and *Donne gentili*, 1959.

ELIO VITTORINI

Vittorini was born in 1908 in Syracuse, the son of a stationmaster, amateur Shakespearean actor and poet and playwright. He left Sicily and worked in the north of Italy in the building industry and later as a proof-reader. He had had little formal education and was largely self-taught. His knowledge of English (acquired in the unorthodox way described in the passage quoted in this book) enabled him to earn a living by translating and introduced him to English and American literature. His translations include works by Poe, D. H. Lawrence, Faulkner, Powys, Steinbeck, Saroyan, Defoe, Caldwell and Fante. His early writings led to clashes with the Fascist authorities. His liberal rather than Marxist anti-Fascism led him to fight in the Italian Resistance from 1943–5 and after the war he edited *Il Politecnico,* 1945–7, a left-wing journal dealing with literature and politics, which led to a clash with Togliatti, the leader of the Italian

Communist Party. He stood for election as a radical in 1958. He died in Milan in 1966.

Vittorini believed that a writer should be involved in the politics and culture of his time. His opposition to Fascism led him also to a revolt against the traditional novel and against such influences as d'Annunzio. His novels are experimental but not obscure. The new novel that he creates has been described in various cases as lyrical, epic, melodramatic. The American novel appears to have strongly influenced his narrative, which is stylized, using little physical description, making great use of dialogue. His language is simple. In some passages – frequently in *Conversazione in Sicilia* – he writes in rhythmical cadences emphasized by the repetitions of leitmotives of words or phrases. A recurrent theme in his novels is sympathy with suffering mankind – the *mondo offeso*; this sympathy he expresses in the idea that perhaps some men have forfeited their humanity.

Non ogni uomo è uomo, allora. Uno perseguita e uno è perseguitato; e genere umano non è tutto il genere umano ma quello soltanto del perseguitato. Uccidere un uomo; egli sarà più uomo. E cosí è più uomo un malato, un affamato; è più genere umano il genere umano dei morti di fame. *(Conversazione in Sicilia)*

The most famous of his novels are *Conversazione in Sicilia*, 1939, a poetic visit to Sicily which reveals in conversation his view of the *mondo offeso*, and *Uomini e no*, 1945, a semi-autobiographical study of the Milanese resistance. His other novels are *Il Garofano rosso*, 1933–5, *Il Sempione strizza l'occhio al Fréjus*, 1947, and *Le Donne di Messina*, 1949. *Piccola Borghesia*, 1931, is a collection of short stories. *Diario in pubblico*, 1957, is his own account of his development as a writer and relation to the literary and cultural questions of his time.

BIOGRAPHICAL NOTES ON AUTHORS

MARIO RIGONI-STERN

Italian soldiers were on Russian soil on two equally disastrous occasions. The first time with Napoleon, as the cavalry of the *grande armée*, the second time when a jealous Mussolini hastened some units to the Don lest Hitler should secure for himself alone all the glory of crushing Bolshevism.

Five days before the German surrender at Stalingrad (31 January 1943) what remained of the Italian Expeditionary Corps fought its way out of the Russian encirclement at Nikolayevka. The Russian tactics were exactly the same as during the Napoleonic wars: 'inflict heavy losses on the enemy, but eventually do not bother too much and let them go. *General Winter* will take care of them.'

Mario Rigoni-Stern, then a sergeant major, was one of the few who managed to come home. He recorded his experiences in a very unpretentious, unrhetorical and moving book, *Il Sergente nella neve* (The Sergeant in the Snow) published by Einaudi, Turin, 1952, awarded the Viareggio literary prize, August 1952, and from which the extract is taken.

In spite of popular success and literary fame this modern Xenophon still lives in his home town of Asiago, in the Italian Alps and earns his bread and butter as a civil servant.

BEPPE FENOGLIO

Fenoglio was born at Alba, in Piedmont, in 1922 and died in 1963. Most of his work is centred on his experiences of the partisan resistance and the preceding Fascist period. His first volume of short stories, *I Ventitre Giorni della città di Alba*, appeared in 1952, his first novel, *La Malora*, in 1954 and *Primavera di bellezza* in 1959. The story printed and translated here is from *Il Partigiano Johnny*, a kind of 'overflow' novel from *Primavera di bellezza*, which Fenoglio obviously felt was becoming too long: this extra material was

published posthumously in 1968. It clearly has a very strong core of autobiography. Also published after Fenoglio's death were *Una Questione privata* and a translation into Italian of Coleridge's *Ancient Mariner.*

Fenoglio was a close, even fanatical admirer of Anglo-Saxon culture, and among his many linguistic experiments was a tendency to mix into his Italian prose words and phrases in English, and to invent unusual locutions based on English phraseology. He also used local dialect vocabulary, like several other Italian writers, many of whom have felt, not without reason, that standard Italian often seems to be lacking in saltiness and variety of expression as compared with English or French. His anglicisms in particular pose problems for the translator, since they are not always as accurately idiomatic as he would perhaps have liked to believe. At his worst his language can seem muddled and tortured (perhaps especially in *Il Partigiano Johnny*, which may have been left in an unrevised state); but equally often the reader can be arrested by passages where it has measured up to his striking powers of observation. His treatment of the scenes of violence which played such a prominent part in his youth is dispassionate, accurate and yet comprehensive.

PIER PAOLO PASOLINI

Pasolini was born in Bologna in 1922. He is a man of very varied literary and artistic activities, being a poet, novelist, critic, scholar of dialect and popular language, literary editor of the literary magazine *Officina* and recently writer and director of several films.

It is probably too early to characterize his writings, although many have tried to do so. Some of his own pronouncements on his literary position may be found in *Passione e ideologia*, 1960, a collection of his critical writings. A few general remarks, however, may be made about him. His 'realistic' or possibly 'mimetic' approach is shown

in his visual descriptions and linguistic reproduction. His two Roman novels, *Ragazzi di vita*, 1955, and *Una vita violenta*, 1959, show a Neo-Realist interest in studying the social conditions of the *sottoproletario* of Rome. His ideological position appears to lie between the two poles of a sort of Gramscian (Antonio Gramsci, founder of the Italian Communist party) Marxism and a strong religious interest in the Catholic Church.

His poetry includes *La Meglio Gioventù*, 1954, *Le Ceneri di Gramsci*, 1957, *L'Usignolo della Chiesa Cattolica*, 1958, *La Religione del mio tempo*, 1961, *Poesia in forma di rosa*, 1964. And his narrative includes the Roman novels *Ragazzi di vita*, 1955, and *Una Vita violenta*, 1959, *Il Sogno di una Cosa*, 1962 (written 1949–52), the general collection of writings *Ali dagli occhi azzurri*, 1965, and *Teorema*, 1968, which was written in conjunction with the film of the same name. His criticism includes *Sulla poesia dialettale*, 1947, *Passione e ideologia*, 1960, and *La Poesia popolare italiana*, 1960. His first film, *Accattone*, he made in 1961; in 1962 he made *Mamma Roma*. There followed *La Ricotta*, *La Rabbia*, *Comizi d'amore* in 1963, *Il Vangelo secondo Matteo*, 1964, and *Uccellacci e uccellini* in 1965; in 1966 *La Terra vista dalla luna*; *Edipo Re*, 1967 and *Teorema*, 1968.

ALBERTO MORAVIA

Alberto Moravia (a pseudonym for Alberto Pincherle) was born in Rome in 1907, the son of an architect. As a child he suffered ill-health and so received much of his education privately. He learnt French, English and German and read widely, not only in Italian literature, but also in European literature generally. His first novel, *Gli indifferenti* (*The Time of Indifference*), 1929, published by Penguin, was well received by the critics, although it caused a stir in official circles because of its criticism of bourgeois society. Until the war he was foreign correspondent for one or two Italian newspapers and then during the German occupation of Italy he had to go into

hiding. His novel, *La Ciociara*, 1957 (*The Two Women*, published by Penguin in 1961), was obviously inspired by his experiences with the peasants during this period. He now lives in Rome; he is the film critic for the weekly *L'Espresso* and contributes regularly to the *Corriere della sera* of Milan. He has travelled widely and has recently returned from China; he has written about his experiences there in *La Rivoluzione culturale in Cina*, 1967.

Moravia's novels include: *Le Ambizioni Sbagliate*, 1935 (*Wheel of Fortune*, 1938); *La Romana*, 1947 (*The Woman of Rome*, 1949, Penguin 1952); *Il Disprezzo*, 1954 (*A Ghost at Noon*, 1955); *La Noia*, 1960 (*The Empty Canvas*, 1961); his shorter novels include *Agostino*, 1944 (*Agostino*, 1947) and *La Disubbidienza*, 1948 (*Disobedience*, 1950), published together under the title of *Two Adolescents*, 1952, Penguin 1960. His short stories have been published under the titles *Racconti romani*, 1954 (*Roman Tales*, 1956); *Nuovi racconti romani*, 1959 (*More Roman Tales*, 1963), from which *Il Sorpasso* is taken; *L'Automa*, 1964 (*The Fetish*, 1964). A collection of essays, *L'Uomo come fine e altri saggi* was published in 1964 (*Man as an End*, 1965).

Although he has written many novels, Moravia is at his best in the short story, where he can express himself with more intense concentration. In most of the novels the hero is an intellectual because, Moravia says, 'I am convinced that the only possible hero interested in the middle class is the intellectual – the kind who does not compromise with reality. Industrialists, doctors or tradesmen have to compromise with reality because their outside interests are more important to them than their own ideas.' In the short stories he tends to deal more with the working class, but there are constant themes throughout all his works – sex, alienation, money and moral vice.

BIOGRAPHICAL NOTES ON AUTHORS

ITALO CALVINO

Calvino was born in Cuba in 1923 and brought up in San Remo on the Riviera. He spent the years 1943–5 in the mountains with the partisan Resistance, and has since worked for the Einaudi publishing company in Turin and edited the literary magazine *Il Menabò* along with Elio Vittorini. His main works have been *Il Sentiero dei nidi di ragno*, 1946 (translated 1956), and *I Nostri Antenati*, a trilogy comprising *Il Visconte dimezzato*, 1952, *Il Barone rampante*, 1957, and *Il Cavaliere inesistente*, 1959. These three short novels have been published in English in two volumes: *The Baron in the Trees*, 1959, and *The Non-Existent Knight*, 1962. He tried to counter the strong element of fantasy which characterizes these works in some of his short stories, and in *La Giornata di uno scrutatore*, 1963, but essays such as *Il Mare dell'oggettività* show him to be worried about the merely imitative realism which seemed to be the only alternative. In his latest pair of books, *Le cosmicomiche*, 1965 (translated 1969), and *Ti con Zero*, 1967, he has found a new use for his individual brand of fantasy in throwing up parallels between the most fundamental facts of biology and theoretical physics and the inner experience of the individual. The story in this volume is taken from *Ti con Zero*.

Calvino has always been a first-class entertainer, craftsman and comedian, and his work is extremely popular with English readers of Italian. His style, both verbal and mental, is unique and quite unmistakeable – in his latest work he has broken completely new ground in fiction-writing and tackled material which could easily have become discouragingly abstruse, but he retains his hold on the reader by the elements of commonsense and self-mockery in his lively, idiomatic style. He has always been able to create a singular fusion of colloquial zest and academic precision in his language, and gives the impression of enjoying the act of writing for its own sake. Indeed throughout his work runs the preoccupation with writing as an act in itself, as the

deliberate, even arbitrary creation of an objective world which exists independently of real life, however much it may have been inspired by real life to begin with. This preoccupation is itself externalized in some of his stories, of which the one reproduced here is one of the clearest and simplest examples.

NOTES ON ITALIAN TEXTS

THE MOTHER *(Svevo)*

1 *Ve ne le dico*: this phrase, which produces an effect of grammatical hyper-correctness unexpected in a conversational context where a more natural idiom would be, for example *ne parlo*, is a good example of Svevo's somewhat stilted written Italian, the literary aspects of which have already been mentioned in the Biographical Note above.

2 *Curra, curra*: this represents a sound rather than a word, used for calling chickens, and could have been rendered in the text by any one of a number of regional British variants, e.g. 'coop, coop, coop, coop'. However, since this particular Italian word has phonetic associations with the verb 'correre', which fit in with the implications and sound associations of the phrase which follows (*egli era il primo ad accorrere*), and which make a definite link between Curra's name and his character as it is afterwards described, the Italian name has been retained in the translation.

3 *Albeggiava*: this is a consciously 'poetic' word, formed on *l'alba*, the dawn. In other contexts this might have been translated directly into English, which uses the identical idiom of 'dawn' or 'dawning'; this is not the case here, but an understanding of the word's literal meaning is obviously helpful in conveying the full evocative meaning of the text.

4 *Nel cui animo generoso albeggiava la combattività*: this close link between warm-heartedness and aggression may seem strange to the English reader who looks on competitive sports as a healthy release of real aggressiveness, and not as an only apparently aggressive game between friends. In context the phrase involves a cultural difference in attitude towards violent feelings, and violent actions, which has to be accepted before it can become meaningful. It is, however, possible to see in the text not only the unity of feeling which would be assumed by an Italian reader, but equally the contradiction of feelings embodied in the character of Curra, who meets aggression inimical to his passionate and loving feelings and never recovers from it.

NOTES ON ITALIAN TEXTS

THE MIRACULOUS DRAUGHT OF FISHES *(Comisso)*

1 *Pesca miracolosa*: a direct quotation from the story of Christ's fishing with the disciples in the Lake of Gennesaret. The implications for this story are obvious.

2 *Novaglia*: in Italian, Novalja, in Serbo Croat, is not an island but the name of a town on the island of Pag off the Dalmatian coast of the Adriatic. The island is famous for its cheese, the 'paški sir', red wine and ham.

3 *Veliero*: a sailing boat and in this case a small trading coaster.

4 The expression *preziose iniziative di lavoro* is elliptical and impossible to render literally into English.

5 *Grappa*: an Italian spirit made from the second pressing of the grapes, skins and pips, after the wine has been taken off. In Yugoslavia it is known as 'rakija'.

6 *Carnoso*: difficult to translate; it does not have the pejorative sense of the English 'fleshy'.

7 *Pasta*: originally anything which could be moulded and can have the sense of clay or stucco.

8 *Sodisfatti* is no mistake. Comisso prefers it to the normal modern Italian *soddisfatto* and is perhaps influenced by the lack of double consonants in his own Venetian dialect.

9 Comisso frequently quotes snatches of foreign language as local colour in his descriptions of travel. There are many examples of this in *Amori d'Oriente.* 'Ti' is 'you' in Croatian. Vieco obviously means 'Your turn now, Giovanni.'

10 *Inebbriava*: literally, made drunk.

11 *Slavo* is the popular Italian term for any Slavonic dialect spoken on the other side of the Adriatic. Slovene, Croatian, Serbian, Macedonian and even Bulgarian, all come to be described as 'slavo'. More accurate terms, like for instance 'Serbo-croato', are only used by academics.

12 A large number of people from the coast and islands of Yugoslavia emigrated to California in the early twenties. They established flourishing communities there.

NOTES ON ITALIAN TEXTS

WARTIME AUTOBIOGRAPHY *(Vittorini)*

The first extract is taken from *Uomini e no*, 1945, which was suppressed after the first edition. It is an example of Vittorini's narrative style and shows his simplicity and use of repetitions. The theme of his father and his literary leanings is frequent in Vittorini's writings, e.g. in *Conversazione in Sicilia*, where the father meets the same lack of sympathy from his wife. Father and son wandering in the countryside is one of Vittorini's recurring themes, see for instance: *Le città del mondo*, Einaudi, Turin 1969.

The second passage is taken from *Diario in pubblico*, 1957, and quotes, with many omissions, an article from *Pesci rossi*.

1 The father in *Conversazione in Sicilia* is recalled reciting various Shakespearean parts.

2 Curzio Malaparte (1898–1957): novelist, satirist, pamphleteer playwright, film-producer and journalist. He was editor of *Fiera letteraria*, a literary review, and of the newspaper *La Stampa*.

3 *Solaria*: a Florentine literary journal, published 1926–36, which was European in outlook and published amongst others the works of Ungaretti, Montale, Gadda and Pavese.

4 Giovanni Papini (1881–1956) was a literary, religious and philosophical essayist and founder of several reviews. He was for a time a futurist, before the First World War and interventionist and he became a Catholic in 1921.

5 Roberto Farinacci (1892–1945) is taken as an example of a leading Fascist. He was secretary of the Fascist Party from 1925–6 and founded and edited two Fascist newspapers.

6 *Confino*: an Italian legal term which implies enforced residence in some locality away from one's normal domicile.

7 *Letteratura*: a Florentine review founded in 1937 and intended to be the cultural heir of *Solaria*.

8 The term *fascio* (literally a bundle) came to be used during the nineteenth century for some workers' organizations, particularly the groups of peasants and workers involved in the Sicilian uprising of 1894 (*i fasci siciliani*). The term acquired its present connotations in 1919 with the foundation of the anti-socialist *Fasci di Combattimento* of Benito Mussolini.

NOTES ON ITALIAN TEXTS

NIKOLAYEVKA 26 JANUARY 1943 *(Rigoni-Stern)*

1 *Isbe, isba*: more frequently transcribed as *izba*, is a typical Russian peasant log hut, decorated outside with wood carving and bright colours.

2 The reader with a knowledge of Russian must not look for a scientific transcription of the Cyrillic alphabet here. Rigoni had no formal training in Russian, he merely picked up some phrases and later recorded what he could remember they sounded like, using Italian spelling conventions. Besides, no standard Russian is spoken in the area which had been occupied by Italian troops, but Ukrainian.

3 *Vestiti di bianco*: for camouflage in the snow.

4 *alpini*: light infantrymen, trained to action in the Alps. They proved extremely useful in the First World War, but what use their skill could be in the Russian steppes, only Mussolini knew. Rigoni served in this corps.

5 *Quattro gatti*: four cats, the Italian idiom for a handful.

6 *Facciamo baccano per tre volte tanto*: literally, we raise noise for three times as much (as such a handful could raise).

7 *Muso*: colloquial for faccia, viso.

8 The last phrase of the *Ave Maria*: 'pray for us sinners, now and in the hour of our death'.

9 This was done whenever possible in order to send the dead man's last possessions to his family.

10 *Vestone*: the name of the battalion.

THE AMBUSH *(Fenoglio)*

As is explained in the note on the author, this story is a chapter from a longer novel. It deals with the period of the Resistance in a small area of Piedmont, near the towns of Alba and Asti. In 1943 Mussolini was deposed in Rome and a new government under Marshal Badoglio made peace with the invading Allies. Mussolini was rescued from captivity by German paratroopers, and set up a new Fascist republic (Italy was still technically a monarchy) in the northern half of the country which was still occupied by German troops. Anti-Fascist partisan groups started guerrilla resistance in the mountains in collaboration with the slowly advancing Allies:

the normal situation, as in this story, was for the partisans to stick to the mountains while the plains, cities and main communication routes were still controlled by the Germans and Italian Fascists.

In this story the autobiographical hero Johnny is second-in-command of partisans in the village of Mango. The commanding officer is an airman known as Pierre, the sergeant a regular soldier called Michele.

1 *Badogliano*: partisan groups were set up under varying political auspices. Johnny has had a spell with a Communist group, but has now passed over to the *badogliani* who support the legitimate government in Southern Italy.

2 *Presidio*: a word redolent of the regular army, from which many of the *badogliani* have come. In a previous chapter it is pointed out that the Communist groups use the word *distaccamento* for a unit of the same size.

3 *U.N.P.A.*: a kind of part-time youth militia, of which boys of sixth-form age would automatically have been members in the Fascist period before 1943.

4 *Smasire*: not found in dictionaries, and probably a dialect word.

5 *Mammellone*: literally 'large breast'. This is one of the many Italian and dialect words which designate different kinds of hills. Another one found in this story is *poggio*.

6 *Breda*: an Italian weapon. During this period Italians showed a distinct and justified cynicism about the efficiency of their own weapons, and were continually trying to get hold of foreign ones, the favourite being the American tommy-gun.

7 *Platonicamente*: one assumes that Fenoglio is using this word in an attempt to express the absolute and unalterable nature of the physical and mathematical laws which govern the consumption of ammunition.

8 *Exertion*: for Fenoglio's use of English vocabulary, see the Note on the Author.

9 *Desertità*: this coinage from *deserto*, although perfectly comprehensible, is not a normal part of Italian vocabulary. The same applies to *lampantezza*, from *lampante*, in this paragraph.

10 *Cassetta*: the coachman's box or seat on a horse-drawn vehicle.

11 *Cozzonare*: 'to urge on with blows'.

12 *Sopralluogo*: an 'on the spot' inspection or inquiry.

13 *forte . . . beduino*: a repetition of a phrase used to describe Michele in a previous chapter, when he was first introduced to the reader.

14 *Biolca*: a dialect word for an old-fashioned measurement of area.
15 *Ritano*: another local word not found in a standard dictionary.
16 *Lemuri*: *lemures,* in ancient Rome, were returning spirits of the dead.
17 *Graziani*: an army chief who remained loyal to Mussolini, and commanded the Fascist republican troops in the north.
18 *Nord*: in the novel this is the *nom de guerre* of the commander of all the partisan groups in the region.

THE TART *(Pasolini)*

This story was written in 1954 and has been collected together with other writings in *Ali dagli occhi azzurri,* 1965. It illustrates the author's realistic narrative and in particular his interest in popular language. The whole story is strongly influenced by Pasolini's study of *romanesco* (Roman dialect) and contains many dialect and slang words or phrases, which are given in the translation or explained in the notes. Perplexed and interested readers may find some help in the short glossaries at the end of the Garzanti editions of *Ragazzi di vita* and *Una Vita violenta.*

1 The vividness of the visual descriptions show Pasolini's cinematic leanings.
2 Not from the town of Naples but from the territory of the old kingdom of Naples.
3 cf. Henry IV Part 2, Act I, scene 2. Falstaff: 'I can get no remedy against the consumption of the purse.' Probably fortuitous.
4 The word is not so forceful as in current English usage.
5 A football team.
6 Two very characteristic Roman utterances.
7 To establish squatters' rights.
8 A suburb to the east of Rome.
9 The botanical road names are reminiscent of some English estates; they suggest uniformity and an ironic contrast between the names and reality.
10 Cigarettes produced by the state from Italian tobacco.
11 Literally, 'daisies at Christmas'.
12 Literally in Roman, 'sons of prostitutes'.

13 In spite of the name, this is a slow train. Italian train gradings are a system of graduated hyperboles.

14 A town north-east of Naples and north of Salerno.

15 Also Tor Pignattara. A suburb east of Rome adjacent to Centocelle.

16 *Capire* is not 'to understand' here, but it is used meaning 'to be in', 'to fit in', 'to get in', 'to be contained'. It is commonly used in this sense, not solely in Rome, but generally in the South of Italy.

17 Colloquially *dritto* means roughly the same as *furbo*. It implies astuteness, decisiveness and unscrupulousness, and has no one equivalent in English. It occurs frequently in this story, and also the forms *dritteria* and *drittarella*.

18 The fashionable, expensive part of Rome.

19 Literally 'shepherdess'.

20 Shop assistant or errand-boy.

21 The value of the lira against the pound sterling is approximately that of today. This would therefore imply a more expensive flat.

22 An old town thirty-nine kilometres from Rome.

23 The collective word is formed by analogy with Roman *pippa* – to masturbate.

24 *Pappone* is formed from the verb pappare, to eat greedily, cf. *magnaccia* (see later) from *magnare* or *mangiare*, to eat.

25 *Disperato* in this context implies a number of things – her frustration in trying to make herself understood, the desperation of the southern immigrant, hopelessness, etc.

26 A technical term in chemistry, the same in English as in Italian, meaning that there was no intervening period of transition between the two stages of Nannina's development.

27 A mountainous region in the south of Tuscany.

28 A name applied to several plants with arrow-shaped leaves. Possibly *Sagittaria sagittifolia*.

29 *Grana*: a slang term for money.

30 From *ciavatta*, Roman form of *ciabatta*, a slipper.

31 The phrase makes more sense if applied ungrammatically to *saletta*.

32 See note 17.

33 A comic-strip magazine.

34 Roman daily founded in 1878.

35 Slang term for 100-lire note or coin.

36 Film studios to the south-east of Rome. Nannina was going there to be an extra in films. But to earn 'easy money' in that milieu is considered dishonourable for a woman among southern Italians. Hence Mario's violent reaction.

37 Literally, 'crooks' etc., from the adjective *scellerato*, wicked.

38 *Gli*: used here in the plural in accordance with modern Italian usage. Most grammars still consider it incorrect.

39 *Sacco* and *saccata*: slang for 1,000-lira note.

40 'lansquenet', a card-game of German origin.

41 'Carosello' can have the sense of a tournament, a roundabout or manoeuvres of vehicles. Pasolini here uses the popular form *carosiello*.

42 A popular corruption of *pantomina*, a pantomime.

43 A cinema, see below.

44 cf. note 24.

45 Literally 'pretend to be absent-minded'.

46 From *moretto*, diminutive of 'moro', a moor. Here 'black-haired'.

47 A gesture which indicates cunning or *dritteria*.

48 Suburb to the north-east of Rome.

49 The main cemetery of Rome.

50 Term for head, cf. *capoccia*.

51 Presumably a policeman with a moustache, known to Alfio.

52 A famous Roman prison. Its full name is Regina Coeli, 'Queen of Heaven': a religious dedication to the Mother of God, but also an extremely sarcastic name for a prison.

OVERTAKING (*Moravia*)

1 *Va' a capire certe cose*: an idiomatic expression meaning 'to understand certain things you will have to go a long way (further than possible)'.

2 *Era fatta al tornio*: literally 'she was made on a lathe', meaning that she had a very good figure.

3 *La mia bella bicolore grigia e blu: macchina* understood.

4 *Via Candia, viale Giulio Cesare, piazza della Libertà* are all situated in west Rome, just north of the Vatican, near the river Tiber.

5 *Ce lo sapevo*: the pleonastic *ce* is a common feature of colloquial Roman speech, used several times by Moravia in this short story to get across the Roman flavour of the story; other examples are *ce lo sapevamo, ce la facevo.*

6 *Uso mare*: literally 'for use at the seaside'.
7 *Bullo*: another Roman expression: self-confident, cocky, almost arrogant.
8 *Sull'Aurelia*: the Via Aurelia leads out of Rome, north-west to the coast, and then follows the coastline as far as Genoa and beyond.
9 *Santa Marinella*: a small town on the Tyrrhenian coast, about seven miles south of Civitavecchia.
10 *Fregene, Ladispoli*: small towns between Rome and Santa Marinella.
11 *Mo'*: commonly used in southern Italy, colloquially, for *ora*, *adesso*.

THE ORIGIN OF THE BIRDS *(Calvino)*

This story is one of the series narrated by the unpronounceable Qfwfq, imagined by Calvino as a kind of universal bore who can always give you the inside story on every physical, geological and biological phase in the history of the cosmos. Qfwfq appears in many forms, and it is important for the reader not to visualize him too specifically as a human being.

1 Each of the stories in *Le cosmicomiche* and *Ti con Zero* uses as its starting point some scientific fact or theory such as this one. (Occasionally Calvino produces two stories based on two mutually contradictory theories.) Qfwfq then takes up his own eye-witness account.
2 *Sarebbero andate*, etc.: to designate the future in the past in Italian one uses the conditional perfect tense, not the straight conditional as in French.
3 *Sento*: Calvino's style often involves a great deal of switching between historic present and orthodox past tenses.
4 *Fregacci*: *frego* is a hastily sketched line, and *accio* a derogatory suffix, in this case giving the impression of the old man's harsh emphasis.
5 *Pianta*: generically the word means 'plant', but it is frequently used in conversation in place of *albero*.
6 *Man mano*: basically this means 'progressively, by degrees'; for a more active use of the phrase compare note 8.
7 *Alla deriva*: conveys the idea of floating downstream on a river.
8 *Man mano che*: conveys one movement responding progressively to another. Compare note 6.

9 *Fa capolino*: *capo* with a diminutive suffix; the phrase has a slightly childish ring.

10 *I nostri*: this term is the equivalent of 'the goodies', the hero's 'side' in Saturday morning cinema serials. The parallels with a stereotyped chase scene are obvious and deliberate.

11 *Sfigurare*: 'to cut a poor figure'.

12 *Li*: these totally redundant object pronouns, referring to a noun already mentioned, are common in Italian speech.

13 Purely for fun, Calvino has invented in passing a new explanation of a well-known primitive method of telling the future.

14 *Spiumio*: a word coined by Calvino meaning a flock of feathers from 'piuma', a feather.